THE LITTLE BLACK BOOK

Patrick Laughy

ISBN:9780987962812

DEDICATION

This book is dedicated to the memory of Police Service Dog Duke III, the best partner a cop could wish for

ACKNOWLEDGMENTS

Many people helped in the creation of this novel. My special thanks to:
Suzy for editing and infinite patience.
Linette for expertise and eternal encouragement.
Laurrie for her support and input.
David for an awesome cover.

CHAPTER ONE

Detective Sergeant Doug Campbell raised his right hand to adjust the headphones that were becoming increasingly uncomfortable against his ears. In that split second, the tape recorder beside him whirred into action and the wail of the dial tone filled his head.

After hours of inactivity, she was finally making a call.

Campbell shifted position, endeavoring without much success to make himself more comfortable in the cramped cement box located in the basement area of the building. The confined space served as B.C. Tel's phone room in the expensive Vancouver West End high-rise apartment block.

All the building's telephone lines fed from the street into this room and he was tapped directly into the pair that led upward to the penthouse suite.

Years of wire-tapping experience had attuned his mind to the reading of the digits as they were dialed. As the number was clicking away in his ears, he scratched it down into the daily 'Hot' log and then settled back onto his heels and prepared to listen to the conversation.

The sound of the shot was hollow but unmistakable to a man as experienced with firearms as Campbell was. Despite his recognition of it for what it was, it had been completely unexpected. As a result, he froze momentarily; disbelieving his own ears, then threw his headphones off and lurched to his feet.

His soccer-honed reactions helped him to respond quickly. He kicked the steel door of the small room open and raced across the dimly lit basement hallway toward the twin bank of elevators. He reached them before the B.C. Tel room door had rebounded off the wall and slammed closed behind him.

*****

Vancouver Police Inspector David Walker raised his eyes and noted the heavily overcast February sky as he unlocked the door to his unmarked Police car and climbed in behind the wheel. Settling into the seat, his nostrils filled with the new-car smell of the factory fresh 1987 Chevy.

He laid his briefcase on the passenger seat and then pushed the key into the ignition.

The car had been issued to him only three days previously. It was one of the perks that had come with his promotion to Inspector and his transfer to his new position as head of the Vancouver Police Department's Major Crime Unit.

With the intention of letting the vehicle warm up for a few minutes, he got out to pick up the cardboard box that he had earlier carried up from the dock. He placed it on the ground near the rear of the car.

The box contained the items he had packed up from his old office at the joint-forces Coordinated Law Enforcement Unit and which would now grace his new office at VPF Headquarters. He had enjoyed his stint in the elite special unit formed to fight Organized Crime, and better known as CLEU, but was definitely looking forward to his new position within his own force.

He placed the box into the trunk of the car, closed the lid and then walked back to the driver's door and got inside, buckling up as he slipped the vehicle into drive and began his morning commute to work.

* * * * *

Carol Anne Jenkins's mind hadn't managed to process any information after she had dialed the last number of her call. It couldn't; she was dead.

The call hadn't been one she had considered especially important. It had been something that she could do to fill in the time while she waited for her guest to finish with the routine checking of the ledgers and counting the cash.

Carol had no reason to expect that her visitor was intending anything untoward when she had answered the penthouse door. The accountant was a regular caller. The ritual taking place in the dining room was a regular occurrence, something that happened every two or three days.

After answering the door Carol had exchanged pleasantries and led the accountant down the hall and into the dining room as usual. She had then left the accountant to check her figures and gone into the privacy of her bedroom to make the call.

It had been a perfect opportunity to call and touch base with her sister while the routine review of the contents of her previously couriered packages and their accompanying ledgers was being concluded.

The dum-dum .22 caliber bullet had entered her head at the base of her skull. She had been dead before the dialer had finished returning to its fixed position after the completion of the last number she'd entered.

Carol had immediately slumped against the side of her bed. As her head dropped to meet the surface of the shimmering black silk bedspread, the accountant caught the falling handset of the phone and in a smooth, fluid motion, replaced it into its antique cradle, and then looked down at the body briefly. The words were spoken softly but with a vehemence that was saturated with unadulterated vengeance.

"Well Bitch, now we both know exactly who's the one ending our relationship, don't we? Permanently; just like you wanted it baby; but not exactly what you had in mind I'm afraid."

* * * * *

The enforced immobility of the ride in the elevator up to the penthouse had given Campbell a chance to re-evaluate his situation. He found himself regretting that he hadn't taken the time to call for backup before heading for Jenkins's apartment.

It wasn't that he was afraid of what would greet him when he had reached the penthouse door. The tough little Scot didn't know the meaning of fear in the same sense as the average police officer tends to consider it. It was just that he was too damn good a cop to blunder in and risk losing an arrest because he was alone, and couldn't hope to cover all the possible exits on his own.

In addition, and not for the first time during the seemingly endless elevator ride, he cursed himself for not signing out one of the portable radios when he had started the shift the night before. Recriminations aside however, by this point he was committed to the action he had taken, and he had no intention of stopping his upward progress to take the time to locate a phone to call for backup.

He was absolutely convinced that there had been a shooting in the apartment and he had every intention of checking it out immediately.

It wasn't the best scenario for a take down, but before the elevator reached the penthouse level he was comfortable with the decision to act on his own.

He unholstered his regulation Smith and Wesson .38 cal. snub-nosed Police Special and was moving into a combat crouch as the elevator doors began to part.

Unfortunately the accountant had anticipated Campbell's response to the gunshot, and when the doors of the elevator slid open, the Detective Sergeant didn't have a snowball's chance in hell.

*****

Robyn Jenkins shifted restlessly at her desk and glanced at the clock on the wall across from her.

Experience had taught her to be wary of nights like this when the majority of the shift was uneventful and went unusually slowly. It inevitably meant that all hell was going to break loose during the last couple of hours.

She had been out on only one case so far that night, returning a drunk fifteen year old runaway to her foster home and smoothing things over as best she could.

Disliking inactivity, which she found inevitably led to an insistent desire to have a cigarette, she began to tidy the top of her desk in an attempt to keep her hands busy. It irritated her no end to have to admit that despite having quit over a year ago, she still felt the urge at times like these.

Forcing the craving into the recesses of her mind, she reached for the novel sitting on the corner of her desk, flipped it open and tried to get into it yet again.

* * * * *

Campbell became conscious briefly as the medical crew in the Emergency Room of Saint Paul's Hospital began to work on him.

All he could feel was intense pain.

A benevolent God, and an inserted drip laced with painkillers, let him lapse back into unconsciousness as the frantically working medical team began the long, painful process of digging four .22 caliber dum-dums out of him in the process of saving his life.

* * * * *

Robyn lifted her hands from the typewriter and carefully flexed her fingers, gently working out the kinks and stiffness that threatened to cut off the flow of her final memo of the shift.

As she had anticipated, and true to form, it had turned into an absolute bastard of a night.

The investigation of two sexual abuse cases and the accompanying apprehensions of an eight year old boy and a fourteen year old girl had left her emotionally drained.

She closed her eyes and sucked in a deep breath. The

sound of her voice echoed in her small office as she verbally expressed her general opinion of whole situation.

"Damn the full moon and everything it brings with it!"

Over the past few minutes the subdued atmosphere of the night shift had given way to the noise of moving bodies and snippets of conversation. Dayshift was beginning to arrive in the outer office area.

As the sounds began to register, Robyn let out a soft sigh of relief in the knowledge that they would shortly take up the strain of the steady flow of cases handled by the Emergency Services section of the Ministry of Social Services and Housing.

Day shift duty was much less stressful than afternoons and nights. All that was required of day shift staff was the follow up on overnight reports and the referral of clients to the regular District Offices.

On night and afternoon shifts there was no referring of cases done, only immediate responses to emergencies and these had to be dealt with without the assistance and resources of the District offices, which were closed to the public during those hours.

Robyn placed her fingers back onto the keys and with an ultimate, determined effort she attacked what was to be her final report of that miserable February night.

* * * * *

The windshield wipers beat an increasingly louder tattoo as David Walker drove the blue unmarked Chevy Impala out of the rain and into the underground parking lot of 312 Main Street, the recently renovated and expanded building that housed the heart of the Vancouver Police Force.

Walker allowed himself a brief smile as he parked the car in the slot directly under the six inch black letters centered on the otherwise barren cement wall in front of him. The bold

'RESERVED - INSP - I/C MAJOR CRIME' brought home for the first time, in a concrete way, the fact that his transfer was indeed fact. Today was the official beginning of a new, and what he expected to be an extremely interesting phase of his career.

He locked the car and pulled the cardboard box out of the trunk before heading for the elevator that led upward to where his office was situated in the newly-constructed addition over the secure parking area. Only months ago the entire area had been a paved outdoor parking lot.

Walker considered himself lucky that the Major Crime section had offices in the new area of the Headquarters building. Big windows and modern air conditioning and heating were simple comforts that he'd managed to get used to during his previous three year tour of duty, seconded to CLEU. The Co-coordinated Law Enforcement Unit; a joint VPF and R.C.M.P organized crime task force had just been formed at the time and the Federal Government had built a new building to house it.

During the recent construction of the new section of the Vancouver police headquarters, the builders had also completely renovated and updated the old part of the Headquarters building. However, many of the new heating and air-conditioning systems just didn't seem to work properly once they had been installed in the refurbished areas.

As far as working conditions were concerned, the ultra modern CLEU building had definitely spoiled him. He had grown very comfortable in modern surroundings and he was pleased to find out that he would not have to revert to antique offices with his promotion and the accompanying return to VPF Headquarters.

Thinking of the CLEU building made him realize that as much as he was looking forward to his new spot as officer in charge of Major Crime, he was also going to miss the comradeship between the two forces that had resulted in his having been lucky enough to be selected to become an integral part of the joint force Vancouver Police and R.C.M.P. intellitg-gence unit.

It had been good working with the Mounties. They always had the best of everything, from equipment to experts, and there were never any jurisdictional problems when you were working with Horsemen. If a crime occurred in Canada, there were no provincial borders to worry about; it was their baby as the national police force, and any concern over Municipal or Provincial boundaries didn't even enter a CLEU officer's mind if they happened to pop up during an investigation.

R.C.M.P. involvement also guaranteed that, when an investigation called for it, there were very accessible channels already in place to ensure the immediate querying of international police forces and Intelligence Agencies on a worldwide basis.

The project that he had been working on at the time of his recent transfer was a case in point. They had been close to cracking a Canadian headquartered, international drug smuggling ring. It was possibly the largest ever in Canadian history.

He felt a small jab of regret at the realization that due to his promotion he would not be in for the kill on that one. It had been a very interesting and satisfying investigation to be part of.

CHAPTER TWO

David exchanged a few greetings with other officers as he made his way to his office. He had come in early to get things organized. His secretary, Cindy, had not yet arrived and he found that he had to put the box down and pull out his keys in order to unlock the main office door. This gave him access to the Major Crime outer office and, by way of that, the doorway that led to his own. He repeated the procedure with the keys when he reached that and was finally able to cart the box inside and set it down in the center of the large desk that dominated the room.

Moments later he had the contents of the box nearly emptied and was sitting at his desk studying the pictures of his two kids. The photographs now held prominence on one corner of the large surface. He had just placed them where he could easily see them while working, when he heard Cindy enter the outer office and begin to move about.

The photographs of his children were fairly recent and he found himself smiling as he looked at them. They lived with their mother and he didn't get to see them as often as he would have liked.

Kevin had just turned nineteen and had finally begun to take life seriously. He was now supposedly toiling diligently through his first year of law. Diane, younger, but by far the more mature of the two, was seventeen and completing her grade twelve this year, after having skipped grade eleven.

David was a little concerned that she might get herself into trouble with the leap into the social structure of older peers, but he had a good deal of faith in her common sense and that was helping him to deal with his anxiety for the time being.

Time would tell.

After a brief knock his door opened up enough for Cindy

to stick her head inside. There was a flash of shimmering red hair as she shook her head, letting the remaining raindrops fly and then gave him a broad smile.

His gaze had shifted from the kids' pictures to respond with a grin as she spoke.

"Good morning Inspector. It's great to have you back and congratulations on the promotion; coffee in ten minutes."

"Thanks Cindy, it's good to be back, and I could use the coffee."

She nodded and pulled her head back out and shut his door.

Walker had known Cindy for a good ten years. She had started as a clerk in the police property room when she was twenty years old and worked her way up through the civilian ranks to the point that she was now considered one of the key secretaries in the force.

Unlike many of her contemporaries, Cindy had not married a policeman and at age thirty she was the mother of three and happily married to an easy going and, from all accounts, loving high school teacher.

Walker knew Cindy well enough to realize that her family came first with her, but that her work was a close second. He liked her and had always gotten on well with her when their paths had crossed over the years. He considered himself very lucky to have taken over a section that provided him with such an experienced and efficient secretary.

David was not what the department referred to as a paper man.

He did his required reports well enough of course, but at heart he was a street policeman. At his new rank, however, he knew that he would be afforded little time for direct investigation. His main responsibility now would lay in administration and supervision. At least that was how his superiors would see it.

Having a pro like Cindy around was going to make the paperwork much easier for him to handle. It was his intention to do his best to convince the powers that be that the officer in charge of Major Crime should lend his experience in street level investigation whenever possible. He was hoping that they just might buy into the fact that he should be given the opportunity to use his experience and talent in a more direct form. He wanted to be able to insert himself into the actual nuts and bolts areas of serious crime investigations and give hands-on direction to his subordinates whenever possible.

He wasn't kidding himself. Getting that particular concept accepted was going to be an up-hill battle, but he felt that he had a couple of things going for him.

The first one was Cindy. She was very competent when it came to moving paper around in an expeditious and effective manner.

The second was a result of standard Vancouver Police departmental procedure.

It was policy to take care, when transferring replacement personnel of 'in charge' or 'second in charge' rank into a section, to ensure that one of the two current officers holding those positions would be remaining in his position, had at least three years of experience in his job and would be remaining here for at least one more year.

Both of the top men were never moved out of a section at the same time.

As a result of this policy, Walker's Staff Sergeant was not only a five-year veteran of Major Crime, but he was also very well known throughout the Department as a paper man.

It was David's intention to do his level best to strengthen that reputation.

He planned to leave as much of the administration of the section, as he could safely manage, to his Staff Sergeant.

At this point in his career, he very much wanted to do his best to regain a hands-on feel for the street again. He intended to take every opportunity offered to thrust his energies directly into the investigation and apprehension activities of his new section, and leave as much of the administration and supervision as possible to his immediate subordinate.

David's silent evaluation of his chances of accomplishing this goal was interrupted by the buzzing of his intercom.

He searched for, found, and punched the correct button, which luckily for him was flashing brightly. He was instantly rewarded with the sound of Cindy's voice.

"Deputy Chief Foster would like to see you in his office as soon as possible."

David glanced at the clock above his desk, somewhat surprised to be getting a request for an audience with one of the three top men in the Department at 08:00 hours on a Monday morning.

"Thanks Cindy, let his secretary know that I'll be right over."

There was an audible click as the intercom connection was severed. David got up from his desk and moved across the room to check himself out in the full length mirror that covered the back of his office door.

He was a tall man, six foot two inches in his socks and he carried his one hundred and eighty-five pounds well. He had the general build of a professional swimmer, without the acute slimness normally associated with the sport. His black hair still grew thickly, but was just beginning to turn gray at the temples in a manner that others seemed to consider flattering to his ruggedly handsome features.

He ran his hand over his cheek, not for the first time regretting his heavy beard. He had shaved just over two hours ago and already he could feel stubble. He shrugged at his reflection as he straightened the knot of his tie, then grabbed his jacket off the hook and opened his office door. He headed through the outer office and then crossed the hallway to the elevators. He punched the button for the top floor. His thoughts went to Foster as he rode upward.

Deputy Chief Foster, one of the two current Deputies on the Vancouver Police Force, had been in Walker's Academy class and although David did not consider him a close friend, there was a history and a mutual professional respect between them.

David knew Foster to be an ambitious man; his rise to the rank of Deputy at the age of forty-one was proof of that. Foster had a reputation of backing his men and commanding their respect. He was also known for his ability to hatchet unmercifully those under his command who did not live up to the level of competency that he expected of them. Throughout his career men under his supervision had often quit, been suddenly transferred or been fired if they happened to come to Foster's notice as having in some fashion let him down, caused him embarrassment or in any way tarnished his image as an administrator.

David exited the elevator and walked to the end of the hall then entered the Deputy's outer office. He was greeted with the infamous frosty smile of Foster's secretary. He took a seat to await the invitation into the inner office.

To say that he was dreading working under his ex-classmate would be wrong. His respect for Foster as both a street policeman and an administrator was high, but as a veteran of departmental politics and in-fighting, he'd always had the sense to watch himself carefully whenever he found himself working under the powerful Deputy.

David was, however, and always had been, confident enough in his own abilities to feel sure that he could live up to Foster's expectations.

It went without saying that any member of the force instantly recognized that the power wielded by a man in Foster's position could be very helpful, if it was used to support the position of a subordinate. Find yourself in the good books of Deputy Foster and you were guaranteed to move up the rank structure. Conversely, fall out of favor and you could kiss your chances for promotion goodbye.

The intercom on the secretary's desk buzzed and she picked up the phone, spoke briefly then nodded at David.

"He'll see you now"

As Walker entered the Deputy's inner office, Foster looked up from his desk and flashed a polished smile in his direction.

"Ah...David, good to have you back on board...CLEU's loss is our gain!"

He pushed himself back from the big desk and rose to shake David's hand as he waved him into the chair on the other side of the desk.

"Coffee's coming, sit down. I had hoped to welcome you to the section properly later in the morning, but I'm afraid that something has come up and we'll have to save the pleasantries for some other time."

Foster returned to sit behind his desk as David seated himself across from him. There was a file folder situated directly in front of the Deputy, centered on his large blotter and Foster flipped it open as he adjusted himself more comfortably in the big chair.

He busied himself reading the top sheet of the file as his secretary came into the office with fresh coffee for them and it wasn't until she had left the room and David had taken his first sip of the steaming brew that the other man spoke.

"I understand that while you were at CLEU, you coordinated the investigation into the..."

His eyes dropped down to the second page of the open file.

"...Carol Anne Jenkins case. Originated as a vice investigation within our Department and was passed over to CLEU when it suddenly developed into a large drug operation with an international flavor, as I understand it?"

He lifted his eyes to meet Walker's for confirmation, registered David's nod and continued.

"It grew into something pretty damn big, by the looks of it. Were you still running the show when your promotion and transfer came through?"

David nodded again and Foster closed the file and pushed it into the centre of his otherwise uncluttered desk.

His eyes fixed David's for a second as he raised his mug to

his lips for a taste of the steaming coffee.

David knew the man well enough to recognize that Foster was, at that moment, making a decision on something that he had been considering for some time. He waited, without comment, for the Deputy to continue.

Finally the mug was returned to the coaster on the side of the desk and Foster leaned back slightly in his chair.

"The whole damn thing blew up this morning, and I'm afraid it has landed in my…or should I say our, lap."

He let his words hang in the air for a second, then continued.

"Someone snuffed out Miss Jenkins this morning and in the process also managed to pump four slugs into Detective Sergeant Doug Campbell."

His brow creased in an obvious frown of displeasure as he continued.

"Who, for some strange reason, didn't bother letting the rest of the team know what was going on at the time of the incident. It seems that he didn't trouble to take a portable with him when he started his shift, and found himself having to deal with the incident on his own."

David interjected as he registered the meaning of the other man's words and his stomach immediately knotted.

"Doug Campbell? Christ, how bad was he hit?"

Almost as an afterthought, Foster allowed a trace of concern to fill his expression.

"It's fifty-fifty at the moment. We're waiting for the emergency staff at the hospital to finish up. Pretty bad, I'm afraid."

Having noted David's reaction to the news and taken the time to add his own touch of concern to the tragedy, the Deputy continued.

"David, I want you to take this on for us. In a way it's the only reasonable course of action; after all it is a Vancouver murder investigation now, and jurisdictionally speaking, that's ours without question. In addition, you're up on the investigation that led to the current situation and in the best position to get to the bottom of this in a hurry. I've spoken to CLEU as well as to the Chief about this and am happy to report that I have their agreement that you're the man for the job. Although I realize that it's unusual for the Inspector of Major Crime to take on an investigation personally, especially since it's your first day in the position, it's been very obvious to all concerned that you're the best person we've got to look into this shooting. This one's a bloody mess. It needs to be straightened out and brought to the proper conclusion as quickly as possible."

He paused to look directly at David and smiled briefly.

"It's also come to my attention that you tend to prefer street work to riding a desk. This would certainly provide you with that opportunity."

David returned the Deputy's gaze and their eyes locked.

"It's true that I like to get away from my desk whenever possible, but I wouldn't have expected, nor been too eager, to be asked to personally investigate under these circumstances. Just coming from CLEU, who will also have a vested interest in the incident I'm sure, I know that the separate interests of the two investigations are going to overlap invariably. That'll bring with it the usual friction between the two participating agencies. It can't help but lead to jurisdictional infighting."

Foster's smile faded and he cut David off.

"It is a difficult situation to be sure, but be that as it may, the decision has been made. I want you to leave the section in your Staff Sergeant's hands for the time being and turn your entire energy toward solving this as quickly as you can."

He looked directly at David as he spoke, assessing briefly how his words were being received before going on.

"Naturally you can have whatever support staff you need. Please get started at once and have a brief outline of what you intend and the current status of the investigation prepared for me within two hours.

David recognized the statement for the dismissal that it

was. Foster didn't bother to look up from the neat stack of reports on his desk as David got up and left the room to make his way back to his own office.

CHAPTER THREE

Robyn gave a long, relaxed sigh as she lowered herself into the steaming tub and let herself sink down into the enveloping, lightly scented water.

It felt so good, almost sensual in its intensity.

She was exhausted, but the combination of cold white wine and steaming hot bathwater was quickly dulling the aches and pains of both mind and body.

Her fingers gently twirled the stem of the wine glass, and then she drained it in one gulp before refilling it to the brim, emptying the bottle and dropping it gently to the floor in the process.

Bed was going to feel good. She was going to sleep like a log.

Three days off, thank God.

*****

It had taken nearly three hours for the medical staff to get the four bullets out, but Campbell had made it out of the hectic surgery alive.

Two detectives were stationed in Campbell's recovery room sharing the cramped space with the various hospital staff members who were hovering around the injured policeman's bed, adjusting the battery of tubes and monitors that had been attached to his unconscious body.

If either of the detectives had noticed the frown on the doctor's face as he approached them, they chose to ignore it.

"Look, this is really quite unnecessary. He's going to be out for several hours and he needs to be left alone to rest. My God, we damn near lost him at least once on the table and we still don't know if he's going to make it!"

The older of the two detectives responded with a practiced nod of his head.

"We know that Doc, but we've got a job to do too. We want the bastard that did this and we've got to be here just in case he comes round. There were only two witnesses to this and the other participant isn't likely to drop into our office to offer up a confession."

The doctor shook his head in exasperation and angrily spun on his heels before leaving the room.

The two detectives exchanged glances, shrugged and then turned their eyes solemnly back toward the bed that held their fallen comrade.

They had no difficulty in understanding and sympathizing with the doctor's perspective, but they had their own anger and frustration to deal with. As far as they were concerned, the doctor was on his own.

*****

Deputy Chief Foster pushed his chair back from his desk as David entered his office.

It was exactly one hour and forty-five minutes since their last meeting and Foster was pleased to note that David had easily met the two hour deadline that he had been given.

"Okay David, how are you going to proceed?"

David dropped into the chair across the desk from the Deputy and faced him squarely before speaking.

"As I see it, we have a couple of problems to sort out as fast as we can. Firstly, although the murder investigation is obviously ours from a jurisdictional point of view, as is the shooting of Campbell, we have to consider the ongoing investigation being conducted by CLEU. We need to take care that we don't step on their toes. We have no option but to liaise very closely with them on this. At the same time, we have to accept the fact that they have a different goal in mind than we do. Oh, they'll be concerned about the murder and the fact that one of our members has been shot; but what they're really going to be after is the successful conclusion of the drug investigation. This drug case is going to be big, perhaps the biggest to hit Canada to date."

He paused for a second, looking directly at Foster to see if his boss was following, then he continued.

"Secondly, there is going to be one hell of a lot of outside pressure on this, both from the Horsemen and the public. The press is going to have a field day, leading to a public hue and cry for the perpetrator to be arrested and brought to justice in record time. The Mounties will want us to clean up our jurisdictional mess as rapidly as we can so that they can get on with their drug conspiracy. In the interim, they aren't going to look kindly on us muddying up the waters with our murder investigation. To date, this has been an undercover operation for them and now for all intents and purposes, it's blown. They're going to want us to keep out of their hair while they try to salvage as much as they can, based on their investigation to date. They aren't going to want us to tip their hand; in fact they're going to be hesitant to give us access to the information that they've gleaned so far, something that we're going to need in order to bring the murder investigation to a successful conclusion. It is pretty obvious that the murder was a professional hit and that the reason for the hit is very likely tied directly to the drug conspiracy."

Foster nodded his head in agreement and motioned for David to continue.

"Dealing with the public over the murder and shooting of a cop, without tying our investigation in with the overall drug investigation being handled by CLEU won't be easy, but it will have to be done if we want to keep them onside. The longer the murder goes unsolved, the more digging reporters are going to do and it won't take long for them to pick up a thread that will lead back to the drug investigation and blow CLEU's chances of trying to keep it undercover right out of the water. The only way to deal with that one is to come up with a suspect very quickly and bring the murder investigation and the public outrage to an abrupt close. Dealing with the Horsemen will be a far more serious dilemma. For fear of having it get out to the general public, they will not want to provide us with any detailed information relating to the drug conspiracy. We require that information if we are to be successful in finding our killer. Their justifiable concern will be that doing so might destroy any chance of keeping the whole thing under wraps until they have everything they need to lay charges and proceed against those involved in the drug side of it.

Foster leaned back into his chair and frowned.

"How are you going to deal with that?"

David smiled.

"Well, luckily, we don't have to request information from them in relation to their progress to date, since I was the primary investigator on the undercover operation from the start. I know as much about that particular investigation as they do. But I will need to know what's happened since I left and on an ongoing basis, if I can reasonably expect to affect an early arrest on the murder. Let's not forget that although CLEU is a joint force operation, the man in charge is a Mountie. As a result, CLEU will likely be hesitant to keep us up to speed on their investigation and will, if they deem it necessary, attempt to put pressure on us by way of the big guns in Ottawa. It's not difficult to put ourselves in their shoes. Their first impulse will be to back off on any information requests by us. I'm going to be counting on you
to deal with any of that kind of interference."

David paused and Foster nodded to indicate that he understood and was prepared to play his part.

"Since you've given me carte blanche for support, I may be able to draw ongoing information from the actual detectives who have been working on the case at CLEU; at least from our VPF members. That will provide me with up to the minute info on the case. CLEU might just decide to close our guys out of it in a move to ensure that we don't get what we need and possibly jeopardize their case. I propose to deal with CLEU openly and lay my cards on the table with them. I don't think I'll have a problem with Inspector Wright; we've worked together for the past three years and have built up a good rapport, but I'm afraid that Ottawa is going to come in at some stage of the game and Wright may well be ordered not to co-operate, or more realistically, to appear to co-operate while providing little, if any, real information. This is going to be a hot one, and if I'm to get to the bottom of it in a hurry you're going to have to run interference for me up top in our own department to resist any pressure from Ottawa."

Foster leaned forward, placed his elbows on the desk and removed his glasses. He rubbed the area at the bridge of his nose where the nose-pieces of the glasses rested and inevitably irritated his skin. That accomplished he replaced the glasses and looked up toward David.

"I agree with your assessment, and you have my word that I'll keep both the R.C.M.P. hierarchy and the press off your back to the best of my ability. I'll bring the Chief up to date on this shortly, so that he can be prepared for the onslaught. Now, don't let me keep you any longer. You've got a job to do. Whenever practicable, I'll expect an update on your progress each morning at 10:00 hours."

David nodded his understanding and stood up. As he was turning toward the door the Deputy spoke.

"David, I'm sure that I don't have to impress upon you the urgency of this case. The pressure you mentioned earlier is already beginning to build. I'm counting on you to bring this to a conclusion, one way or the other, in a very short period of time."

Once again the eyes returned to the desk and David knew he had been dismissed.

As unnecessary as it had been, the hint of a warning cloaked in the Deputy's final words was not lost on Walker.

*****

The precise movements of the accountant's fingertips removed the last screw from the .22 and placed the remaining pieces of the gun into the small box to join the rest.

That job finished, all that remained was the dumping of each piece in different areas throughout the city. No ballistics test would ever be carried out on this murder weapon.

The gun had served its purpose and had, in fact, already been replaced.

The phone rang and the accountant quickly wiped the gun oil off both hands before picking it up.

After the initial confirmation of contact the disembodied voice on the other end of the line simply delivered the message.

"The cop isn't dead; he made it through the operation."

The accountant didn't offer a reply; it wasn't necessary.

*****

At the sound of the gate latch, Cato became instantly alert.

The massive Rottweiler moved with surprising agility, bolting upright from the carpeting, abandoning his preferred sleeping spot in front of the glass doors that led to the large outside deck and the ocean beyond. They provided the dog with a perfect spot to rest while offering an excellent vantage point for him to keep an eye on the front of the property.

Any thought of a nap was forgotten as he shifted smoothly into an aggressive, stiff-legged stance and cocked his head to listen.

He then strode purposefully across the living room, hackles up, moving toward the front door of the house which was on the far side of the room.

As was his habit when presented with an intruder into his territory, his low pitched, throaty growl served to fortify his determination to allow no stranger access to his master's domain.

Walker had trained the dog well; relying on experience gleaned during his years of duty as a member of the Vancouver Police Dog Squad. Cato had never bitten anyone, but he had turned away numerous strangers whose intentions, for whatever purpose, had been to trespass on his master's property.

The dog moved directly to the window beside the door and stared out though it. From that position he was unable to see either the gate at the top of the stairs leading up from the dock, nor the one that fronted the stairway that led to the cabin above the house. His ears did tell him though that it was the gate leading up to the cabin that had caused the sound that had awakened him.

He also knew from experience that any person responsible for opening either of the gates would have to come within his line of sight if they wished to climb the stairs to reach the front door.

He stood there motionless, waiting patiently for that to happen.

A person reaching those stairs and looking through the window would be instantly aware of his presence. Previous occurrences of this nature had left no doubt as to Cato's ability to back up the growls that he was currently emitting with more direct action if it became necessary. Without exception, the individuals involved had made a hasty retreat and had considered themselves lucky that their response had satisfied the big dog, who looked quite capable of coming straight through that window if he decided to.

When his actions had caused previous transgressors to rapidly back off the property, Cato had watched them carefully until they were out of what he considered his area of responsibility. The big dog had then returned to his original position in the room, and had done so with an obvious air of satisfaction for a job well done.

There was no viciousness in the massive animal, only conditioned response to stimulus as specified by his training.

Normally the deep, frightening growls emitted by Cato were sufficient to deter anyone and the dog was momentarily surprised when the sound of the footsteps on the grass of the front yard continued on toward the doorway.

The deep growls issuing forth from his throat had become continuous by this point and his big frame moved into a low station in anticipation of the necessity to attack if the door was opened.

All the while his ears had been rapidly processing the sounds made by the shuffling feet. As they came nearer, he cocked his big head slightly to one side and began to listen with rapt attention to the specific nature of the tread, his eyes straining to catch the first glimpse of the intruder.

The big dog's brain was busily analyzing, searching for any sign that he should recognize the unique pattern of the footsteps that had, surprisingly, so far shown no intention of retreating.

CHAPTER FOUR

Robyn came out of her alcohol and exhaustion induced fog slowly. The persistent buzzing eventually pulled her back into the land of the living.

In her dazed state she knocked the hand unit of the phone off the cradle in her first attempt to stop the noise. She then had to roll halfway out of bed to pick it up off the floor.

"Hello, Hello, Damn it! Hello!"

The droning of the dial tone greeted her and she swore under her breath as the reality of the situation struck her. It wasn't the phone that had awakened her; it was the bloody apartment intercom buzzer.

She dragged herself the rest of the way out of bed and stumbled out of the room into the hallway. By the time she reached to press the button of the intercom unit, she was almost fully awake and at least functioning mentally.

"Yes?"

"Robyn Colleen Jenkins?"

Robyn was in no mood to play question and answer. She snapped back.

"Who wants to know?"

There was a slight pause before she got a response.

"Detective Boyd, Vancouver Police…I wonder if I could come up and speak with you?"

Robyn let out an audible sigh.

It was unusual, but not unheard of for the police to contact her at home. It went with the territory. She also realized that the cop was only doing his job. Most of the venom had left her voice by the time she replied.

"Ya, sure, c'mon up."

She buzzed him in.

*****

The door to David's waterfront house swung open surprisingly forcefully.

Anyone seeing Mrs. Jenny Ferguson for the first time wouldn't have expected the diminutive sixty-two year old widow capable of moving quite so quickly or with such determination.

Cato however, was no stranger to Jenny Ferguson. By the time the door had begun to open he had recognized her footsteps. He was now welcoming her eagerly as she entered.

He dropped his front end down and left his backside up in a playful bow as his entire hindquarters began to seesaw vigorously back and forth in what appeared to Jenny as a valiant attempt to make up for the short stub of his tail.

He greeted her as a long lost friend, which of course she was, in a manner of speaking.

Mrs. Ferguson was David's part-time housekeeper and one of her duties was to check on Cato when David was at work and give the dog a chance for a run in the yard while she tidied the place up.

David was very good at picking up after himself and rarely left the house in anything but a clean and neat state. As a result Jenny seldom had very much to attend to when she arrived to let Cato out. Nevertheless, it was an arrangement that both of them found rewarding. David got a woman's touch around the place and Jenny got one more reason for getting up each day.

The stocky little woman smiled and paused as soon as she spied Cato and gave the big dog the expected, and by now obligatory, scratch behind the ears and a vigorous, if brief, body rub.

She then she sent him outside and began to move about the house checking to see what needed to be done.

As happy as she was with the arrangement that she and David had come to, Jenny would have liked to see it end.

As far as she was concerned, it wasn't right that David hadn't remarried by now. She was of the firm opinion that he was still a handsome and virile man and that it naturally followed that he needed a woman of his own.

*****

In the hospital room, the older of the two detectives shifted uncomfortably in his chair as he reached out to accept the coffee proffered by his partner. The younger man dropped into the seat beside him and glanced over at the still inert form on the bed. He asked halfheartedly.

"Anything?"

They had been in the room for four straight hours now and with the exception of the sounds of the monitoring machines and Campbell's labored breathing, the room had been as still as a tomb.

"Nope…just the same, he's still in never-never land."

*****

Detective Boyd took Robyn gently be the shoulders, and she turned her dazed eyes up to him as he spoke.

"Look, I know that being told that your sister is dead is a hell of a shock for you, and that what I'm asking of you isn't going to be easy. If we had someone else to make the positive identification of the body, we wouldn't be requesting that you to do it, but with both your parents dead…"

Robyn nodded slowly and lowered her brimming eyes.

"I'll be alright, just give me a few moments."

Boyd released her and Robyn sat down as she struggled to regain her composure.

*****

Getting the floor number had been easy.

The news broadcasts were filled with information on the shooting and gave Campbell's name hourly.

A check with the hospital had provided what limited information that was available. They said he was still unconscious and in critical condition.

There was no sense in taking any action until the hospital indicated that he was definitely going to pull through. There was every possibility that he would yet die.

If he pulled through, if he regained consciousness, then it would have to be done.

The accountant walked across to the big glass doors which opened onto the apartment balcony. The view of the sea was restful, the cargo ships floating at anchor in English Bay, and the small whitecaps glinting in the gentle breeze.

For the time being, a regular check of the detective's condition was all that was necessary, and in the meantime a recon of the hospital and a few preliminary preparations seemed reasonable...just in case it became necessary to ensure that Detective Sergeant Douglas Campbell didn't ever speak again.

*****

Mrs. Ferguson turned slowly, surveying the spotless living room with satisfaction before she set Cato's newly filled water dish down and gave the big dog a final scratch behind the ear.

Pleased with her work, she left the house and crossed to the gate. She opened it and began to make her way up over the rocky narrow path and cement stairway that lead to her small cottage. The ancient cabin was a fair distance above, close to two hundred feet. It was perched on the cliff overlooking David's property and the waters of Indian Arm beyond.

She shook her head slowly and muttered to herself as she made the climb.

It wasn't right, him living there alone. It had been three years now since the unfortunate death of his second wife from cancer. A real shame that. Jackie had been a beautiful girl. It had been such a shock to everyone, they only having been married the four years and so much in love. David had taken it hard and Lord knows she understood why. The man had worshipped the ground Jackie walked on.

Divorced from his first wife, distrustful of the entire female portion of the human race, it had been hard for him to accept and give his love to Jackie in the first place. Then to have found so much love with her only to have it ripped away in its prime.

Mrs. Ferguson shrugged her shoulders and sighed.

It wasn't going to be easy, but she was determined to redouble her efforts in doing what she could to help him to forget, and to reach out for someone new.

There were those who told her that it was not her place to interfere. Well, it might not be her place. But someone had to help the poor man.

* * * * *

Robyn was floating in a dream world as Boyd guided her gently into a worn leather chair that formed half of the available seating in the waiting room adjacent to the offices of Major Crime.

She was only half listening as he spoke to her. Her entire thought process had been short-circuited by the experience of identifying her sister at the morgue and attempting to accept the fact that Carol was actually dead.

Boyd made sure that she was aware of her surroundings before he spoke.

"It'll only be a moment."

The detective left her in the room and crossed over to the door leading into Walker's outer office. He nodded curtly to Cindy, then entered Walker's door without knocking, something that he wouldn't, under normal circumstances, have done.

David looked up from the notes he had been reviewing. Before he could speak Boyd beat him to the punch.

"Look Boss, this girl just isn't up to giving a statement now. Christ she's hardly more than a kid, and she's just identified her sister's body."

Walker was surprised. Boyd had worked for him as a Patrolman when David had spent his last stint in that division as a Sergeant. It wasn't like the man to enter the office of a senior office unannounced, nor to question a direct order.

There was an edge to his voice as he cut Boyd off.

"What the hell's gotten into you?"

Boyd seemed to collapse into himself, his solid frame slumping. He raised his hand slowly.

"Sorry sir, it's just that it's been a long shift; Campbell getting shot and all, and she's a really nice kid. Not what I'd expected at all considering her sister's background and record. She's just finished working a night shift and I got her out of bed to come down here. She's really shook"

David's initial anger dissipated instantly. He knew and respected Boyd and all things considered, was prepared to let the affront pass without further comment.

He took a deep breath and looked over at the obviously tired and somewhat disheveled detective before he spoke.

"Time is of the essence I'm afraid. We can't put this off; remember that Doug Campbell took four slugs this morning. We've got a possible cop killer out there."

Boyd took a second to respond, but before he did, he nodded slowly and with some effort, stood squarely again.

"Sorry Boss…it's been a rough few hours, and she really is a nice girl. She's in the waiting room, I'll ask Cindy to give her a coffee and keep an eye on her until you're ready for her, if that's okay with you? I have to head back to the apartment and give the guys a hand with the door to door interviewing of the people in the building."

David smiled.

"Of course. I won't keep her long, I just need an initial statement from her."

He glanced up at the clock.

"I'll want a team meeting as soon as you have the first stage of the investigation under your belt. We've got to cap this one fast. Pressure is already beginning to cause problems upstairs. Get in touch with me as soon as you've finish up at the crime scene. Let the others know that I expect everyone to stay until I have a basic understanding of what transpired there. I've authorized unlimited overtime on this."

CHAPTER FIVE

Walker was placing a fresh pad and pencil on the desk in front of him as Cindy brought Robyn Jenkins into his office and got her seated in the chair across the desk from his own.

It was immediately apparent to him that Boyd's assessment of her condition hadn't been far off the mark. She appeared to be taking it very hard, and looked utterly exhausted.

The sisters must have been closer than he would have expected and he, like Boyd, found that surprising. Knowing what he did of the sister's history, and her involvement in the CLEU investigation, and having Robyn's basic facts in front of him had not prepared him for the obvious depth of Robyn's loss.

They just didn't seem to be poured from the same mold at all.

"I'm Inspector Walker. I'm very sorry to have to speak to you so soon after your sister's death, but I'm sure you understand that we must begin our investigation as quickly as possible. I'll start by confirming the basics. Just interrupt me if I have anything wrong, or you have anything to add."

He looked up from his notes long enough to ensure that she had understood what he'd said. Satisfied that she had, he began.

"Robyn Colleen Jenkins, date of birth, January 18, 1961, twenty-six years of age, apartment 607 at 1422 Bidwell, here in Vancouver. Telephone number 873-1020. Employed as a Social Worker with the Ministry of Social Services and Housing, having been with them for the past three years."

He glanced up and she nodded slowly in confirmation. David then drew a line under his notes and did his best to give her a reassuring smile.

"Now, if you would just tell me as much as you can about your relationship with your sister, her lifestyle and anything in particular that might give us any inkling as to why she was killed."

Within the recesses of Robyn's mind the shock of the loss was slowly giving way to the first strains of anger at her sister's death.

She valiantly fought back the threat of new tears as she turned the brunt of that anger on David, simply because he was close at hand.

She lashed out at him.

"You might have the common decency to be honest with me. You know as much about Carol's lifestyle as I do, perhaps more. Don't tell me that you haven't run her name through your computers and read the printout of her record."

Walker was initially taken aback at the sharpness of her attack.

He said nothing for a second, putting the pencil down on the pad in front of him and pushing his chair back from the desk slightly before meeting her eyes directly.

"Look Miss Jenkins, I was simply trying to save you any unnecessary pain. I have no way of knowing how much you know about your sister's way of life and I wouldn't have brought up her criminal past if you hadn't. If you want me to be candid with you, that's fine with me. It will certainly make this interview both shorter and more effective."

Robyn was instantly ashamed of her outburst. It wasn't like her. She had enough training in psychology to understand why she had done it, but that in no way justified it and she knew it.

She tried to hold the tears back, but the dam burst and she let them flood out.

David said nothing as he picked up the box of tissue from the top of the credenza behind his desk and walked around to her. He offered her the box which she took without looking up at him and immediately selected one and began dabbing and blowing.

David turned to pick up a chair from its position against the wall and moved it to face her, then sat down beside her.

"It's okay, go ahead and cry. I'd say that you're definitely entitled. I'll get us some coffee and as soon as you are feeling a little better, and if you are up for it, I'll buy you lunch and we can finish our talk after you've gotten some food into you and had a bit of a breather."

*****

His first realization of consciousness was pain - intense, burning pain.

Campbell had no more than managed his first moans when the door to the room opened and a nurse appeared at the side of his bed. He was aware of her adjusting the tubes attached to him and then, almost immediately he felt consciousness slipping away again, and with it the excruciating pain.

The older of the two detectives waited until the nurse had finished working on the intravenous drip then turned to his partner.

"You'd better go and phone the old man, he said that he wanted to know if there was any change."

The nurse was moving back toward the door now.

"Excuse me, the Doc said that if he came around it would be a good sign and that you'd put him out again for a while. How long, approximately, will he be out?"

The nurse paused at the open door and glanced back at the bed before she spoke.

"Two to three hours I should think. His signs are good. I think he'll more than likely make it now, but it's still touch and go"

The detective nodded and motioned for his partner to make the call.

The younger detective followed the nurse out of the door

and had to fight his way through the throng of reporters in the waiting room next to the nursing station. He pulled open the half-door located in the center of the counter fronting the station and went inside to find a free phone. He punched the button for an outside line before dialing.

It didn't occur to him that the information he was passing on to the Staff Sergeant who answered Walker's line needed to be considered confidential. He made no attempt to keep the conversation private.

Several of the reporters heard enough of the one-sided call to ensure that the next news broadcasts were carrying the report of the improvement in Campbell's condition.

*****

It had been simple to make all the necessary purchases after visiting the hospital. Back at home and standing in front of the mirror the accountant turned slightly to view the result, and smiled at the reflection.

The white smock was slightly wrinkled now and a stethoscope dangled from one pocket. The white shoes were somewhat scuffed and looked comfortably worn. Coupled with the blond hairpiece and heavy horn-rimmed glasses they gave the outfit a professional, worked-in look. It definitely afforded a disguise that would make a later positive identification of the wearer unlikely.

The twenty-two fit snugly in the pocket opposite the stethoscope. It was compact enough to make additional camouflage unnecessary.

The small badge, reading Dr. G. Thompson, and pinned in place over the top left pocket of the smock completed the effect nicely.

*****

David had been somewhat surprised when she had accepted his suggestion that they walk after their lunch. It was something he tried to do after his mid-day meal whenever possible.

She was more composed now - quiet, yet alert and aware of her surroundings as they strolled at an easy pace along the Stanley Park seawall.

The overcast February day had brought out few joggers and they found themselves almost alone by the sea.

Robyn had been sharing her thoughts on the case with him, prompted occasionally for more detail when he felt it was needed. As they neared the Lions Gate Bridge at the harbor entrance he was satisfied that he had drawn as much information from her as was available.

He then began to lay the facts before her as he saw them, combining her input with the information that he had gleaned from other sources.

"Your sister left home when she was seventeen. She held some clerk type positions in various offices for about a year, and then gave that up to work the street. Her first arrest for solicitation came at eighteen. There were two more arrests for the same thing and then shortly after she turned nineteen she left the streets. She met someone who had the money to keep her and he set her up in the penthouse. Shortly after that she began working as a high class call girl. She moved on from there to set up an exclusive cathouse. In the process she made some pretty heavy connections within the underworld. We have some idea of who her customers were because we've had the apartment block under surveillance at night off and on, but we don't have a definite suspect in mind for the crime."

David was aware that he was covering territory that would not be pleasant for her to relive. He used the time it took to fill and light his pipe to give her a chance to absorb the facts of her sister's early life before he continued.

"In all honesty, there are too damn many to choose from at the moment. So what we're looking for at this point, is motive. Being able to isolate anyone who had a reason to kill her will help us to narrow the field. It can't have been robbery. Our people are still going over the apartment, but there was eighteen hundred dollars in cash in the top drawer of one of her bedside tables and a good pile of very expensive jewelry in the jewelry box in her bedroom. We know that she didn't usually see johns at that time of the morning. When killed she was wearing only a dressing gown and no makeup. That makes the suggestion that it was a customer that killed her even more remote. There was no sign of forced entry or of a struggle. That indicates that she knew her murderer and willingly let him enter the apartment. That's further supported by the fact that she was shot from behind while she was sitting on her bed making a phone call."

Robyn nodded and turned her head to look out at the water as she silently listened to him.

"The killing itself looks professional. The weapon used. The position of the bullet's entry. No obvious evidence and no indication that the suspect was in any hurry, all support that conclusion. Is there anything more that you can tell me that will give us an insight into who may have had a reason to kill her and possibly give us a starting point for the direction the investigation should be taking?"

She stopped walking and turned to face him. Her hair was caught by the strengthening breeze off the waster and he could see her swollen red eyes narrow in thought.

"There was so much more to her than you know. She wasn't just the person that your statistics paint her."

She shook her head slowly.

"Did your computer tell you that our parents were killed in a house fire when Carol was twenty? I was eighteen at the time and in my first year at university. I was completely devastated by their deaths, in more ways than one. I was flat broke and suddenly homeless. Carol picked me up the afternoon after the funeral. She spend two full days with me, getting me set up in an apartment, getting me a car, giving me a bank account with a balance of ten thousand dollars. She continued to provide for me until I graduated with my Masters Degree. She called me daily right up to the day that she was killed. She was always there when I needed her."

Walker was unable to keep the look of surprise from his face. He flushed slightly, embarrassed without quite knowing why.

"No, the computer didn't tell us that. I'm sorry. I really am."

Robyn smiled for the first time that day.

"You know, I think you really are. You're a surprising man, Inspector David Walker."

She turned from him and began to walk back the way they had come. David briefly glanced out at the container ship gliding in under the bridge and then he turned to follow her.

They walked side by side in silence, back toward the car. A light rain began to fall.

When they reached his car, Walker opened the passenger door for her and then moved around to the driver's door and slipped in behind the wheel. After starting the car, he adjusted the heat and defrost controls, and then pulled out his pipe and pouch and began to prepare the bowl.

Robyn leaned back, molding herself into the passenger bucket seat and closing her eyes. David struck a match and as it flared she shifted slightly to look directly at him. She didn't speak until he had finished igniting the tobacco and had adjusted his window to allow the exhaled smoke from his first few puffs to slip outside into the slowly building rain.

"It will be rough on me, but I think that we should go to her apartment. I've been there often and I might be able to tell you if something is missing. That might give us a possible motive. I don't know what else to suggest."

Walker puffed on his pipe a few times as he considered her suggestion, then nodded and put the car into reverse to back out of the parking spot.

"Okay, it'll only take us a few minutes to get there. How about work? Have you contacted them?"

Robyn nodded.

"Yes, I've got five days compassionate leave in addition to my regular three days off. I also have quite a bit of banked time that I can take off as well if I need to."

Her eyes began to brim with tears again and David looked back to the road to afford her what privacy he could. Her voice drifted across to him a few seconds later, hollow and filled with the grief that swelled within her and would not be ignored.

"I'm a little frightened David. She was all I had. I'm feeling so very much alone."

He nodded.

"Yes I know. Do you have a steady man or a close friend that you could call for support to help you get over the initial period? I think it would help if you had some one to talk it out with."

Robyn shook her head slowly.

"No. No one I would consider that close".

David raised his eyebrows then slumped back into his seat before turning his head slightly to get a better look at her.

She was a beautiful woman, striking features, shimmering light brown shoulder length hair; tall, and with an unquestionably gorgeous figure.

In evaluating her attractiveness and knowing that siblings often shared attractive physical traits, he could easily understand why her sister had been able to successfully move into the high priced call girl league.

No doubt about it, if the sister had looked anything like Robyn, she had been a stunner.

He found himself more than a little surprised to learn that someone with Robyn's looks didn't have a steady man in her life. There were several things about her that reminded him of his late wife Jackie, and it was hard for him to accept that she wasn't in some kind of long term relationship.

In addition to her good looks and outgoing personality, she was obviously a warm and caring person.

Tears had begun to well up in Robyn's eyes again and he

was pulled out of his thoughts as he watched them form. His heart went out to her and he was frustrated by his inability to comfort her as much as he wanted to.

"I could tell you that I know how you feel, but you probably wouldn't believe me."

She turned her head to face him, sniffing softly.

"I'm not sure that I understand."

David let his shoulders drop and glanced briefly from the road to look at her.

"I lost my wife to cancer a few years ago. We'd only been married for a short period. At the time, she seemed very much all I had too."

Robyn studied him closely and dabbed her eyes to remove the last traces of her tears. She then found herself consciously re-evaluating her earlier assessment of him.

Initially she had found him professional, but somehow cold and seemingly detached from the reality of the horror of her sister's murder. Perhaps she had been unfair, finding coldness in the professional necessity for him to treat it simply as a serious crime rather than the tremendous personal loss that she felt it to be.

Had she misjudged him? Was he, beneath that outward, cold professional exterior; actually able to recognize and empathize with the huge emptiness that filled her?

Could it be that this, however brief, removal of that stern outer shell of armor that had been carefully built up over years of investigating hellish and, at times, unfathomable crimes had offered her just a hint of a look at the man that was hidden within.

That little glimpse intrigued her enough to help her see beyond her own sorrow and self pity.

She found herself wondering about what else made up this man, what other interesting discoveries lay below any chinks that she might be able to open in his armor?

CHAPTER SIX

The younger detective entered the hospital room carrying two coffees. His partner looked up from the form on the bed briefly; acknowledging his presence, then turned his attention back to Campbell.

He took the proffered Styrofoam cup without looking at it and raised it to his lips. Instantly, he grimaced and came close to spitting the mouthful out.

"Christ, no sugar! You know I take sugar. Normal coffee is bad enough, but this hospital crap is undrinkable at the best of times, and without sugar."

The younger cop shrugged.

"The damn machine was out of sugar."

The scowl on his partner's face deepened appreciably.

"Well try at one of the bloody nurse's stations; they're bound to have some sugar for Christ sake."

It had been a long day and their shift was almost over. The junior detective wasn't about to get into an argument now. He said nothing in reply. He shrugged again, took an audible slurp from his own cup then turned on his heel and left the room.

Once outside, he was relieved to note that the crowd had thinned out considerably. The majority of the reporters had left shortly after the news of Campbell's improved condition had been relayed and the bulk of the cleaning and maintenance staff seemed to have called it quits for the day as well.

The hallway was nearly deserted.

He walked directly to the nursing station which was around the corner and part way down the next hallway.

Before he spoke, he couldn't resist leaning over slightly to peer down into the promising cleavage offered by the undone top three buttons of the starched white uniform being worn by the well endowed young nurse sitting alone at the desk.

"Haven't got any sugar in there by any chance have you?"

The nurse glanced up from the schedule she was working on and followed the direction of his gaze. The cop flushed slightly and grinned as his eyes moved back up to meet hers.

There wasn't even a hint of a smile on her face.

"Not in there, and not in here either. Try the cafeteria."

She waved a hand in the general direction of the elevator and returned to her work.

He took one more brief look. They really were a magnificent set of tits. He momentarily considered the possibility of chatting her up, with a view to perhaps creating an opportunity to glean a better look at those luscious mounds after his shift.

Then, realizing that the chance of a successful conquest was probably fruitless in view of her earlier curt dismissal, he shrugged and headed for the elevator.

* * * * *

The light rain had turned into a downpour by four in the afternoon when Campbell regained consciousness again. A strong wind was battering the pelting raindrops against the pane of the single window in the hospital room.

Campbell couldn't place the sound. For a few moments he stared blankly at the ceiling above him, and then he tried to move and found that he couldn't.

The effort had brought the pain back and as the first wave coursed through him, he rolled his head from side to side restlessly.

"Where am I?"

The older detective who had been half-dozing rose with surprising speed, notebook and pen in hand.

He moved across the few steps to the bed and leaned over slightly.

"Easy Doug, just relax…you're in hospital. You took a few slugs, but you're gonna be okay."

Campbell heard the words through the haze of pain and pain killers, but he didn't actually register their meaning. His mind was clearing now, slowly, but steadily, and with the clarity came a stronger surge of pain and he began to moan softly, pitifully.

* * * * *

Parking was not to be found within three blocks of the hospital.

The accountant had noted that fact on the recon conducted earlier in the day and had decided then that it would be necessary to leave the red Chrysler LaBaron convertible four blocks west of the intended goal.

A short walk was probably just as well, as it would serve to provide time to rethink the approach and escape routes.

* * * * *

David had just parked the car and shut off the motor when the police radio crackled into life.

"Car six?"

He glanced briefly at Robyn and then reached under the dash for the mike.

"Six, go ahead."

"Car six, request that you switch to TAC two."

David acknowledged receipt of the message, reached down under the dash again, this time finding the switching unit by feel and shifting the channel selector of the Motorola from channel one to the second tactical channel.

"Car six."

The Chief Dispatcher had been waiting for him and the response was immediate.

"Six, Detective Scott advises that Detective Sergeant Campbell is now conscious."

David acknowledged and switched the radio back to channel one. He replaced the mike in his holder below the dash and turned to face Robyn.

"I've go to go to the hospital. The policeman who was shot this morning by your sister's killer has regained consciousness."

Robyn nodded slowly and Walker noted the color draining out of her face.

She had been steeling herself to enter her sister's apartment and now it wasn't going to happen. While she was relieved at not having to do it immediately, she was also fully aware that not doing so would mean that she would be left on her own and that was definitely not an appealing idea for her at the moment.

David sensed what was going through her mind.

He considered the situation for a second before speaking.

"Look, this shouldn't take too long. You can come with me if you want and have a coffee in the hospital cafeteria while I'm upstairs. Then we can go back and check out your sister's place when I'm finished."

When she didn't respond immediately he though that he might have read her wrong.

"Or if you prefer, I'll drop you off at your place before I head for the hospital."

Robyn, who was very much dreading being left on her own, sat bolt upright in her seat.

"No, I don't think I want to go home. If it's all right with you I'd rather have people around me, a coffee in the cafeteria sounds fine."

*****

The accountant stepped out of the elevator and, as the young clean-cut man passed, immediately recognized the detective with the Styrofoam cup in his hand for what he was.

The man's mind was obviously somewhere else and he didn't give the accountant a second look as they briefly crossed paths.

The accountant had anticipated that there would be police watching the wounded cop. The question was, how many, and where would they be?

That remained to be seen and this chance meeting indicated that there was obviously going to be one less cop present in or around Campbell's room now. That was encouraging.

Plainclothes officers rarely worked alone, so there would still be at least one man keeping an eye on the wounded officer, probably stationed in the room with him, or just outside the room.

The coffee cup in the young cop's hand was a good sign for another reason. It was a fair indication that the police were not expecting any trouble; probably not guarding Campbell as such, but just there to be available when he came round.

There were four doors leading off the hallway the accountant had entered after rounding the corner. Carrying a clipboard, and looking preoccupied with the information it contained, the accountant checked the individual room numbers as they passed.

There were three more doors to go.

The old detective was bent over the bed with his back to the doorway and his ear near Campbell's mouth.

Concentrating as he was, he didn't hear the door to the room open. Nor did he hear the soft crepe-soled shoes as they crossed the room or the muffled retort propelling the first silenced .22 cal. slug just before it struck the back of his head.

The detective took two more head shots and Campbell's limp form promptly took three in rapid succession.

The sound given off by the silenced weapon as it discharged was minimal. The walls and doors were thick. If someone had been just outside the door, they might have heard something. There was no one outside the door.

The only other person, other than patients, presently in that section of the hospital wing was the young nurse with the big boobs, sitting in the nursing station near the monitors, still working diligently on the schedule on the desk in front of her.

She didn't hear a sound from the room itself, but a split second later, the warning buzzer and accompanying flashing red emergency light on the monitor nearest to her suddenly came to life.

She got to her feet and moved quickly, around the counter and through the half door at the end. She transversed the hallway in front of her and entered the second hallway, at the end of which Campbell's now lifeless body awaited.

Her entire mind set was elsewhere when she passed the accountant. As a result, she paid little attention to the doctor standing in front of the bank of elevators situated halfway down that hallway.

All her concentration was on what the monitor had told her. On wondering what could have gone wrong with the patient in the room at the end of the hallway to initiate the alarm.

Several additional nurses and a doctor appeared from around the far corner and hurried to join her as she opened the door to Campbell's room.

*****

Using the enclosed staircase and not the elevator, the accountant moved down to the next floor of the building and opened the door a crack. After a quick glance around to ensure that no one was observing, a few steps down the hallway led straight into the safe confines of the linen storage room. It had been unlocked on the previous recon of the hospital, and it was unlocked now.

Once inside, the disguise came off quickly.

Smock down the laundry chute. Glasses, hairpiece, stethoscope, identity pin and white tape peeled off the black shoes into the bottom of the garbage under a good five inch layer of other refuse.

Gun wiped clean as a precaution, despite the surgical

gloves that had been worn, and then concealed in the centre of a stack of sheets and finally the gloves themselves removed and added to the other articles in the garbage receptacle.

With any luck, it would be days before the gun was located, and it was very probable that the rest would never be found.

The accountant took one last quick look around the room to ensure that it appeared normal, and then opened the door, confirmed that the coast was clear and was down the hall and into the stairway to the ground floor and out a convenient exit door at the back of the building.

It had taken less than three minutes for the accountant to get from Campbell's room to the street and it would be another four minutes before anyone in the blood-spattered hospital room thought to inform either the police or hospital security of what had transpired in that room.

*****

David had taken a few minutes to get Robyn settled in the cafeteria before he started up to Campbell's room. When he reached it he found complete bedlam.

The door was wide open and a group of medical staff was grouped around it immobilized by the scene inside. David had to force his way through them to gain entry. It took him only a few seconds to register what had happened and he immediately took charge.

He raised his voice above the din, addressing a doctor who was just standing up from where he had been kneeling over the inert form of the old detective.

When he spoke, David's voice was loud and it carried enough authority to be heard over the several verbal exchanges that were filling the room.

"Are they both dead, doctor?"

When the man nodded affirmatively, David addressed everyone.

"Listen up everyone. I'm Inspector Walker, Vancouver Police. I want all of you to leave the room and wait outside in the hallway until I can speak to you. You will do it now please."

He herded them out as they began to chatter among themselves again, and was just closing the door to the room behind him when the young detective carrying a coffee in one hand and a packet of sugar in the other, rounded the corner of the hallway and started toward him. A look of surprise and astonishment filled the man's face.

David's first impulse was to vent his anger and frustration on the young man, but he held himself in check, simply taking the coffee and sugar out of the man's hands and setting them unceremoniously on the floor, before physically stationing the speechless man in front of the closed door to what had been Campbell's room.

"Don't move… no one goes in until I say so…got it?"

The color drained out of the detective's face and the best he could do was nod his head to demonstrate his understanding.

David had not identified himself. There had been no need. The young detective had once worked for him for a year when he was in patrol.

Luckily for him, there had been a flicker of recognition on the man's face when David addressed him. If David had been forced to identify himself or say any more than he had, he doubted that he would have been able to hold his displeasure in check.

His eyes held the detectives for a split second, and then he turned his back on him and moved quickly down the hall and around the corner to the nurse's station. He opened the half door and reached for the nearest phone.

It took him less than a minute to make the necessary calls. He then walked rapidly back to the milling group of medical staff. They were talking excitedly between themselves, and he interrupted the exchanges forcefully.

"Give me your attention please. I'm afraid I'm going to

have to ask all of you to remain here until the investigating officers arrive and have an opportunity to speak to you individually."

CHAPTER SEVEN

It looked more like a police station than a hospital floor.

They were everywhere, uniformed and plainclothes.

Twenty minutes had passed since the shooting and the initial stages of the investigation; the sealing off of the crime scene, and the securing of escape routes out of the hospital were complete. The pressure of meeting the need for rapid organization was over and the pace of David's mind began to ease a little.

It was then that he realized that he had completely forgotten about Robyn.

His eyes rapidly searched among the wave of milling policemen until he spotted Detective Boyd.

"Ted."

He waited until the detective had crossed to him before continuing.

"I've left Miss Jenkins downstairs in the cafeteria. Would you please go down there and give her my apologies. No need to tell her what's happened here. She's got enough on her mind. Just tell her I got tied up and see that she gets home safely. Let her know that I'd still like to take her up on her offer to assist with a search of her sister's apartment and tell her I'll call her in a couple of hours to set it up."

Boyd nodded and was turning to leave when Walker added.

"In consideration of what's just happened you'd better stay with her until I call, if she'll agree. I shouldn't be too long here. I don't imagine that she's in any real danger, but it's becoming more and more obvious that we're dealing with a contract killer here who doesn't like loose ends. I don't want to take any chances that Miss Jenkins may be included in his list of people who need to be removed. I'll be getting a team briefing before I join the two of you later today, and I may have a better idea of what level of risk she's facing by then. See that she's stays safe until then"

Boyd had no more than left when the reports began to come in.

The hospital wing had been locked down within four minutes of Walker's call. No one had gotten out after that time without being checked. So far he had heard nothing from the containment teams. The hospital staff members who had been present at the scene upon his arrival were all receiving initial interviews. So far nobody remembered seeing anyone who seemed out of place, or any unusual activity. All the rooms on this floor and on the floors above and below were currently being checked room by room, with emphasis on unoccupied rooms near either the elevator or the stairs. There had been no reports back on those results as yet.

Walker had begun to release men who were no longer needed, sending the uniforms back to work and his own men back to the station to work on their reports and prepare for the briefing that he would be expecting in less than an hour.

In another fifteen minuets he was down to the four man squad that was necessary to protect the crime scene itself. They were all on the floor where the crime had taken place. There was enough manpower to keep the area secure until the Ident Squad had attended for prints and forensics.

The hospital staff that had been on the actual scene had been told their prints would also have to be taken and arrangements had been made to ensure they would still be on shift and able to fulfill that requirement when IDENT got to the scene for a forensics sweep.

He was about to leave himself when he was approached by a serious young uniformed Constable.

"Sir, I've found the gun, or at least I think I have…"

Walker didn't give him a chance to finish.

"Show me son, let's see what you've got."

He followed the Constable down the stairs one floor and into the linen supply room. Once inside and with obvious pride, the man raised his hand to indicate the pile of sheets stacked on the shelf.

"I noticed that these sheets weren't stacked as uniformly as the others, so I lifted them off one at a time and there it was."

Walker moved over to the stack that had been indicated.

"Did you handle it?"

The young patrolman registered a shocked expression at the very suggestion.

"Oh no sir! They taught us not to. I didn't even touch the sheets themselves with my hand; I used my pen to lift them off."

Walker stifled a grin and reached over to clasp the Constable firmly on the shoulder.

"Well done son. Okay, you park yourself in front of this door, and see that no one gets in here until I say otherwise and lend me your portable."

The now beaming patrolman eagerly offered his radio and Walker switched the channel selector to TAC two.

"CD, this is car six. Is that Dogmaster I requested still in the area of the hospital?"

The Chief Dispatchers' response was immediate.

"181, are you still at the hospital?"

"181, yes, I'm in the parking lot."

The Chief Dispatcher interjected.

"Car six, where do you want him?"

*****

The rising flames issuing forth from the barbecue were momentarily fanned by one of the powerful bursts of wind coming directly in from the sea and gusting briskly across the high-rise apartment patio.

At this time of the year, the flames were large enough to attract unwanted attention. The accountant looked around slowly, ensuring that no one was watching and might do something stupid, like notifying the fire department.

In a rush to complete the task, too many pages had been selected and placed on the fire at one time. It had been a stupid and unnecessary risk.

There was no need to hurry, just one page at a time, make sure that each page of Carol's damned appointment book burned completely, until not even a single line of the document remained for later scrutiny.

As the accountant stirred the last fragment of paper into the now dying flames, all thought of Carol disappeared.

Despite the many pleasant hours that they had spent together, it was as though she had never existed

* * * * *

David waited until the Dogmaster had downed and stayed his partner, then he motioned the handler over.

"We've got the murder weapon in there. It's between the sheets in the middle stack. I want you to let the dog get the scent from the gun and then do a room-search for articles. I'm sure there is more evidence in there, but if there is, it's probably regular hospital stuff; none of the witnesses saw anyone who didn't appear to belong in the crime area. If it is, we won't know it's the suspect's when we find it and it won't be any good in court unless we can tie it directly to the suspect. If your partner can pick up the suspect's individual scent from the gun, I want you to apply him to the rest of the room. Anything he comes up with will then be directly tied to the gun by scent and in that way to the suspect, and thereby useable in court as evidence.

David paused to allow his words to sink in and then continued.

"I don't expect to get any prints from the gun. This guy is a pro, so if the dog mouths it we can live with that. At least it's a risk I'm prepared to take. If you can see to it that he doesn't mouth it, that's all the better. I'm not expecting you to pick up a track of the suspect. I realize that it would be impossible under the circumstances. I also know that this isn't going to be an easy room to search for evidence. It's obviously fairly well-used and will be contaminated with the scents of many people. But we've got a few things going for us. The room is small and the scent of the suspect is relatively fresh…"

Walker checked his watch.

"…approximately thirty minutes old. If the dog is able to isolate the suspect's scent from the gun, anything that he homes in on from that point will be tied directly to that specific scent. It's very possible there are only two recent human scents in there that are fresher than the suspect's - mine and the P.C.'s."

He indicated the police constable standing firmly in front of the door.

"You can let the dog have a whiff of us before you take him inside and that should make it possible for him to discriminate between us and what he finds on the gun. One last thing - there is going to be an 'odor of guilt' on that gun and anything else in there that the suspect has handled. That's going to give the dog a fair chance at discriminating between the overlaying scents and zeroing in on whatever the suspect has handled or worn."

Ordinarily the Dogmaster would have been insulted to have his chances of success or method and reasoning behind the purpose of deploying his dog outlined for him by another policeman. He was, after all, an expert in his application of his K-9 partner, and recognized as such by the courts.

Taking detailed direction or suggestions from an ex-Dogmaster however, was more than acceptable; and Walker had a very good reputation as a former Dogmaster. His expertise in that area of police work was well known and respected by the other members of the force.

It was because Walker and his police dog Tiger had been a very productive K-9 team when they worked the road together, that the Dogmaster who now stood in front of him hung on his every word, took no offence, and simply nodded his understanding of what he was being explained in such detail to him.

"If anyone can do the job, Rex can."

Walker couldn't resist a grin. He appreciated the confidence the Dogmaster had in his partner.

David knew only too well that that type of mutual trust was implicit in the formation of a successful K-9 team. He had also noted the Dogmaster's 'humanization' of the dog, in that he'd related to his partner as 'anyone', not 'any dog'.

David found himself silently agreeing with the Dogmaster.

If anyone could do the job, Rex more than likely could.

He motioned for the Constable, who had been listening intently to the conversation, to move away from the door and both he and the young uniformed cop received a good sniff from Rex before he was taken inside the room by the Dogmaster and given the scent from the gun and the command.

"Rex, seek, find it out boy."

The Dogmaster closed the door to the room behind him and Walker waited impatiently outside with the young patrolman as the team began to work.

David knew that he should release the policeman back out onto the street to take some of the regular patrol calls that would have built up by now due to the recent manpower pull into the hospital crime scene. But he also recognized that the lad was very excited about the possibility that his finding of the gun had made all this possible, and that he was just as anxious as David to see the dog complete the task that had been set for him successfully and come up with any additional items of evidence.

Inwardly acknowledging these facts, Walker didn't have the heart to order the rookie uniform back onto the road and thereby destroy his chance to see just how important the finding of the gun might be. He knew that it wouldn't take the dog long to either fail or be successful at the task his master had presented him and he felt that the young patrolman had earned the right to see it through to the end before he sent him back out to the mundane duties of routine patrol.

In just under eight minutes, the door to the room opened and the Dogmaster and his big German Shepherd partner came out.

Walker didn't need to hear the words of praise passing between man and dog to realize they had been successful. One look at the dog and he could read the answer to that question in the high stationed tail and perked ears of the excited Shepherd.

The obvious pride in the Dogmaster's face served to fortify David's reading of the dog, and he laughed.

"What have you got?"

The Dogmaster downed the dog and left him on stay to one side of the door, then looked over at the two men and motioned them inside. They followed him, and as David passed the still alert dog, he took the time to add his praise to that of the Dogmaster.

"Good boy Rex."

On the floor inside and arranged in a neat row were the following: one pair of horn rimmed glasses, one blond hairpiece, one stethoscope, one identity pin reading Dr. G. Thompson, a rolled up ball of white tape, and a pair of surgical gloves. The gun itself was exposed on top of a small pile of sheets, those above it having been pushed to one side.

The Dogmaster looked Walker in the eye and beamed.

"He didn't touch the gun and I think we'd better take the dog downstairs and check whatever's at the end of that chute over there. He indicated like a bastard around the entry flap."

Walker nodded in satisfaction.

It felt good to finally have some concrete, direct evidence in the case. Forensics would finally have some material to work with, and he felt more positive than he had all day.

He looked over at the young patrolman.

"Well, we wouldn't have any of this without you. I think you'd better go along with the Dogmaster and find out what's at the other end of the chute. Just do as he tells you. Whatever you may find down there, I want it sealed in evidence bags and initialed by both of you. The two of you wait here until I send someone down to take these exhibits off your hands. You can initial them while I'm gone, but please handle them carefully and bag them before you give them to the IDENT exhibit man Once you've handed them over head on down and see if you get lucky at the other end of the chute."

Before he left, Walker paused long enough to comment to both men.

"My thanks to both of you and to Rex. I'll be putting in for a commendation for you and my special thanks to you, Constable, for having the diligence to locate the gun in the first place. Most would have missed it. By the way, I'll expect you to present at the team briefing at the Major Crime boardroom. Please see that you both attend."

The young policeman beamed. For him, the day had started out as fairly dull.

Now he found himself being ordered to attend a bloody Major Crime debriefing. From his perspective things were definitely looking up.

CHAPTER EIGHT

It was after seven-thirty by the time David finished speaking with Boyd and released the detective from duty.

It had already been a long day for him and he was beginning to feel a little tired as he closed the door behind the detective and turned to rejoin Robyn in the living room of her small but functional west-end apartment.

Now that he had effectively put the rest of the case to bed for the night, he felt he could allow himself to slow the pace and unwind a little.

When he entered the room it took him a second to locate Robyn's stationary form in the darkness. His eyes became attuned to the minimal light and he spotted her sitting in a big comfortable looking chair by the window.

She was staring blankly out between the open curtains and seemed unaware of his presence in the room. He cleared his throat to announce himself. Robyn glanced over at him and then stood.

"I'm sorry. I was just sitting here in the dark thinking. I'll close these drapes and put some lights on."

She applied herself to that task and David could see the puffy circles around her eyes revealed in the brightness of the first light she turned on. It was apparent to him that she had, in reality, been sitting there in the dark crying.

His first thought was that he ought to leave her in peace, but he relented when she managed a little smile, and made an obvious attempt to pull herself together.

Perhaps it wasn't isolation that she needed now. Keeping her busy doing something over the next few hours, was probably more on the mark. At least it might help her to get through the initial anger and disbelief over her sister's death.

He was also pretty sure that going with him to her sister's apartment would help Robyn accept the finality of the woman's death. It would be a first step toward eventual closure, and it could also serve as a method of keeping her mind focused on putting the pieces of her own life back on track.

In addition, and despite the tiredness that he had acknowledged to himself only moments ago, he had to admit that her initial offer to go through the apartment with him might well lead to new leads in the case with regard to possible motive.

The more he considered it the more he was convinced that checking out the apartment together could well accomplish the killing of two birds with one stone. It might just help her draw herself up out of the dark little hole of grief that she had quite naturally sunk into, and it could very well offer insight into the murder investigation itself.

He drew on his reserve energy and met the challenge head on.

"I hope that you didn't mind me having detective Boyd stay with you?"

Robyn replied with a shrug.

"No, not at all, he was very nice."

David sensed that she was being less than truthful, but that wasn't particularly important to him. Boyd had been asked to stay with her to ensure that she was kept safe and that had been accomplished.

"If you feel up to it, we can check out your sister's apartment now."

Robyn brightened noticeably, lifting her shoulders and running her fingers through her hair. David knew in that instant that he had been right to draw her out and involve her in some form of positive activity.

She confirmed his impression by managing a believable smile as she headed toward the hallway and bathroom beyond.

"Yes I need to get out of here. Just give me a minute to fix myself up a little. I must be a mess."

His eyes followed her as she left the room. He brought out

his pipe and used his forefinger to tamp down the cold embers before bringing them back to life with a match.

The fact that she was worried about her looks was a good sign that she was coming out of the initial shock. He was glad, for somewhat surprising to him, he could empathize with her hurt as it brought back memories of his own pain at the loss of Jackie.

He sincerely hoped that doing something positive together would take her mind off her immediate sorrow and, in so doing, would give her a lift. It might also help him to redirect his mind to the needs of the current investigation. If so, all the better.

Checking out the apartment would do them both good.

He heard her come out of the bathroom and start down the hall to her bedroom and he called after her.

"May I use your phone? I have to call my housekeeper and let her know that I'm going to be late getting home so that she can go over and let my dog out for a run."

Robyn appeared in the doorway long enough to give her assent and David picked up the phone and dialed.

By the time he had finished speaking with Mrs. Ferguson Robyn had rejoined him in the living room. She had changed her clothes, and although she wore little makeup, she looked considerably refreshed. David found himself subconsciously assessing again, just how beautiful she was.

It had been long time since he'd actually taken the time to bother to notice what a woman looked like. It hadn't seemed to be important after Jackie had died, but in Robyn's case it was somehow different.

He found himself trying to analyze why that was.

Was it because he empathized with her loss and recognized her pain? Was it because she reminded him quite a bit of Jackie? Or, was it because his hidden, but deepening loneliness over the past few years was finally forcing him to come out of his shell and take note of what the world around him had to offer again?

He found himself admitting that he was both confused and

surprised about the way he was reacting to being around her. He, for whatever reason, perhaps a combination of reasons, had to admit that he was not only seeing Robyn as a beautiful woman, but he was, at least subconsciously considering her in terms of a potential lover.

Without doubt, speaking as a professional, it was certainly an improper thing to be doing from the point of view that he was an investigating officer and she was part of a murder investigation, albeit, certainly not a suspect.

To top it off, she was fourteen years his junior and desperately vulnerable and alone. No doubt the thought of a new relationship would be the last thing on her mind.

Despite all this, his eyes stayed on her as she readied herself to leave, and his train of thought continued as she moved about the room, adjusting lights and grabbing her keys and purse.

He was definitely finding himself warming to the sensations that she had stirred up in him. While they had admittedly lain dormant for some time, he had certainly experienced them previously. And they were telling him she just might be a little interested in him as well.

Few things in his personal life made David feel uneasy, but he felt uneasy now.

He had learned to live without Jackie.

He had made an admittedly imperfect existence for himself in the world around him. It hadn't been without its drawbacks by any means, but it had been bearable and it had been safe. No more hurt, no more risks.

He had been very close to seriously considering his life as over when he'd lost Jackie, closer than anyone around him at the time would have dreamed. He had managed to deal with that devastating realization once but he was certainly not confident he could do it again. Why was he finding himself attracted to this woman?

He pushed the thought aside as they left her apartment and headed for his car which he'd left parked in front of her building.

A ten minute drive and they were at her sister's building.

As Robyn had her own key to the penthouse, there was no need for Walker to roust the apartment manger to gain entry. He and Robyn went directly up in the elevator. Once inside the suite, David took time to gauge her reaction to facing the task before them prior to commencing their exploration.

She seemed to be okay with it, intent upon conducting the search, and not on the memories the room held for her, and the sister it would obviously remind her of.

Robyn was aware of his hesitancy to begin and the reasons for it.

Being in the penthouse was rougher than she had anticipated. She felt a little shiver of unease move through her as she let her eyes drift over the familiar surroundings, but she was determined to hold her grief in check.

With a halfhearted smile delivered in David's general direction, she took a deep breath and set her purse down on the table in the entrance hall.

She then removed her coat, which David took from her, and after adding his own, placed both on the table beside her purse.

Robyn turned slightly to look down the short hallway.

"Where do we start?"

He found the light switch and flicked it on then moved down the hallway, and she trailed along behind him, a little hesitantly, but even more determined to see it through.

David flipped another light switch on and began to survey the large living room that led off the hall, before answering her.

"Well my people have searched thoroughly, I'm sure. I haven't read the report on the final results yet, but I have a general idea of what they found and there would be no sense in us repeating what they've done. To begin with, let's just go through each room and see if you can tell if anything is missing or has been moved."

Robyn nodded and her eyes began to shift around the

large room, then she moved across to the large coffee table that sat directly in front of the couch.

She scrutinized the top of the table, moving an assortment of books and magazines aside then glanced up at him.

"She normally kept her appointment book right here; I suppose your people have taken it."

Without waiting for him to reply, she moved over to a matching glass end table at the end of the couch where the phone was located.

David ran his mind back over the earlier briefing he had received from the initial investigating team and shook his head.

"No, there was nothing like that. We were wondering if she had one and where it would normally be kept. It was probably taken by her killer, and may well have been the reason for the killing. The company that she was keeping was pretty heavy. An appointment book would have given us somewhere to start. Is there any other place where she may have put it and we might have missed it?"

The revelation that the appointment book had not been found took Robyn by surprise and she was only half listening to him. She moved a few magazines near the phone then turned to face him.

"Did you find her diary?"

David shook his head again.

"We didn't find any personal papers. We figured she must have kept that kind of thing hidden somewhere. We didn't come up with as much as a bank statement, which is very unusual, and leads me to believe that the murderer was able to remove pretty well everything that could have given us any clue as to why she was killed."

Robyn turned abruptly away from him and started toward the bedroom. Sensing her urgency, David followed her. He stood in the doorway watching her as she turned the light on and moved across to the large antique roll top desk that was centered on the far wall of the room.

She rolled the top up and he watched in fascination as she

pulled out the centre of several small drawers that were situated above the writing surface, and then bent down so that she could see into the dark interior, before reaching deep into the recess.

He heard a faint, metallic click and, his curiosity aroused, he crossed to join her. He reached the desk in time to observe the inlaid leather top of the writing surface pop up slightly to reveal a hidden compartment below.

"It was my father's desk. We used to play with it as kids."

David lifted the hinged cover and leaned it back. Nestled inside of the shallow, but relatively wide area below the hinged cover were a neat stack of envelopes and a little black book.

He and Robyn exchanged a look of satisfaction as Robyn lifted the contents out and took them over to the bed.

She didn't appear to notice the dark stain of dried blood on the upper edge of the cover as she spread the articles that she had removed from the compartment out on the surface. When she had finished, she stepped back and pointed toward the untitled black leather covered book.

"That's her diary. She showed it to me once. She said it was her insurance for a comfortable old age."

David reached for the book eagerly and Robyn turned away as he lifted and opened it. He was immediately immersed in the thorough examination of each of the articles.

Robyn, who was standing behind him, felt her resolve to keep control of herself slipping. The sight of Carol's diary had brought the reality of the situation back to her in a rush.

She moved across to the big sliding glass door that opened off the bedroom onto the large deck beyond, slid it open and stepped outside into the immediately chilling breeze. She welcomed the cold; it seemed fitting and it helped her thwart the threatening tears, and for that she was thankful.

She moved to the railing and turned to face directly into the wind turning her attention to the vista beyond. Her gaze swept the horizon to take in the choppy waters of English Bay with its gently rolling freighters at anchor and the mountains, still visible behind them, rising like ghosts in the overcast sky.

CHAPTER NINE

Robyn had lost all track of time and it wasn't until she heard David calling to her from the open patio doorway that she realized where she was. She suddenly felt very cold.

As she came back inside he gave her a concerned look and quickly closed the door behind her. Once he had locked it he turned and grasped her arms just below the shoulders and began to rub them briskly but gently.

Robyn sighed, enjoying the warmth he was generating and strangely pleased that he was concerned about her wellbeing.

Once David felt the warmth returning to her arms, He led her out of the bedroom and back to the couch in the living room. He sat her down and pointed to indicate the articles that he had spread out on the coffee table before her.

"You many not know it but you've just dropped a real bombshell. CLEU has been investigating a massive drug importing ring that was using your sister as a cutout. Despite surveillance and a phone tap, they had been unable to nail down the identities of the people at the top of the organization. This diary of you sister's contains everything they need: names, dates, places".

The color drained out of Robyn's face as David continued.

"By itself, it isn't sufficient evidence to nail them, but the information it provides will justify surveillance on everyone involved. Once that's in place, it won't take long to gather the necessary evidence to put these gentlemen away for a very long time. The most incredible part about the whole thing is the names themselves. It's hard to believe that the people named in Carol's diary could be part of a thing like this. With one exception, these guys are upstanding citizens, public figures. When this investigation is completed and hits the press, it'll cause one hell of a stink. A strange mix, politicians and political appointees scrambled together with an obvious link to organized crime. In consideration of some of the names in this diary, when the ring is exposed it might even bring the Government down. Your sister seems to have been riding pretty high in the food chain in this group."

His excitement at the find was catching, and Robyn found herself reaching out for the book. David's hand caught her wrist gently.

"No, you know too much about this already. I have a pretty good idea now why your sister was killed. She knew too much and they probably found out we had her under surveillance. Considering how well positioned in the justice system these guys are, they probably knew exactly how far along CLEU was in the investigation. They probably figured that if we scooped her she could lead us directly to them. Unless I miss my guess they had her hit professionally and that's why her appointment book is missing. They were determined to cut Carol out of the picture cleanly and leave us with a dead end and no evidence leading to them."

Robyn found herself getting angry again, and not just over the fact that her sister was dead, but at specifically what was behind her death. Cold shudders passed through her as she listened to him speak.

What kind of people considered life so cheap that they would do something like this to another human being, simply to protect their own skins?

"Are you saying she was killed because someone was afraid that the police would make her tell them who was behind this drug thing?"

David nodded.

"Yes, or that she would accidently lead us to them. This diary gives me a pretty good idea of where to start looking for the people who hired the hit man."

He opened his notebook and turned it toward her.

"I've listed everything we found, where and when. Will you please make sure that it's correct and then initial the page to confirm it? I'd like you to put your initial on each of the articles themselves as well, just beside mine if you would. It's very important to ensure the continuity of this evidence for court purposes."

Robyn did as she was asked and as she finished he picked up a small green plastic bank book from the pile.

"By the way, there's a will in there that says you are Carol's sole beneficiary and this bank book indicates deposits in excess of four hundred thousand dollars. She also had a safety deposit box; the keys and a list of its contents are in one of the envelopes addressed to you."

It was too much. Robyn felt herself beginning to collapse again. The tears welled up in a tidal wave and she couldn't stop them. David silently cursed himself for being so insensitive and took the pen from her limp hand before he moved over to her and put his arms around her and sat down beside her.

She welcomed his encompassing warmth and gave herself to it, letting the pain and sorrow flow from her, taking the opportunity to draw on his strength without compunction.

He held her silently, providing what comfort he could, and for the first time since she had learned of Carol's death, Robyn made no attempt to check the flood.

She wanted it to come; she wanted to cry it all out and be rid of it.

They sat like that for a good ten minutes, her soft, ragged sobs filling the room as he cradled her in his arms.

Finally the rush eased and he released his hold on her a little to give her room to catch her breath and wipe away the last trickle of tears with a tissue.

When she had finished, she looked up at him and managed a teary smile.

"Thanks, I needed that."

David returned her smile and she slowly disengaged herself from his arms. His eyes met hers.

"Anytime."

Robyn, drained, but feeling much better, got to her feet.

"Well, what now?"

David scooped up the contents of the table top and placed them carefully into a large envelope. The diary he kept apart, placing it on top of the envelope in a separate plastic bag.

He then placed both packages in his briefcase before he spoke.

"You feel up to spending a little more time with me or are you getting fed up? I can take you home now if you like, before I go down town and lock these exhibits up. I also want to make a couple of copies of that diary before I tag it for evidence. If you want, you can come along and when I'm through we could go out for a bite to eat before we call it a night."

Robyn felt physically exhausted, but she knew that even as tired as she was, sleep was going to be impossible for her. She also didn't particularly want to be alone, at least not yet and his mention of eating brought the realization that she was ravenous.

By this point she felt that David was sincerely sympathetic to her feelings and she managed a small smile for him.

"I couldn't sleep if I tried. I'd like to go along it you don't mind."

David nodded and they crossed the living room, entered the hall and moved down to the bedroom door. She followed him somewhat listlessly and as he reached to turn the light switch off, his eyes rested on the extra large television set against the far wall of the room and he hesitated.

"A lot of money tied up in there, I wouldn't have expected that she'd have the time to watch it a lot."

Robyn managed a small laugh and moved across to the set and built in cabinet that surrounded it. She opened the light oak doors to the right of the screen and stood aside, revealing an expensive VCR and at least thirty tapes.

"Tools of the trade she called them."

David crossed to her, a mystified look clouding his handsome features as he moved to join her. They had mentioned a collection of pornographic videos at the earlier meeting, but he hadn't considered them as being unusual under the circumstances.

Robyn continued.

"Porn David, some of her clients requested it. I've never seen any of it, but, Carol said that it covered the gamut."

He grunted and closed the cabinet, and then led the way out of the apartment, closing the lights off as they went from room to room and locking the door behind them.

Once down and back outside the building he opened the passenger door of the unmarked cruiser and held it for her before moving around to the driver's side and sliding in behind the wheel.

Twelve minutes later he pulled into the underground parking area at headquarters.

Robyn had chosen to stay in the car in the secure police underground parking garage and wait for him there while he copied the diary, then tagged the envelopes and diary in the property room and watched them being locked up.

Robyn used her solitary break to let her mind drift back over and relive some of the good times that she had shared with Carol, the warmth and closeness that they had enjoyed together.

She was beginning to take the steps necessary to accept the finality of her sister's death, not willingly, but accepting them nonetheless.

A dull sensation of loss centered in the pit of her stomach and chest was slowly replacing the anger and sorrow that had been dwelling there since she had been told of her sister's death. She felt so alone. Her plaintive plea filled the car.

"Why Carol? Oh God, why you?"

* * * * *

David laid the two copies of the diary on his desk and sat down. He hadn't turned his office light on and the room was only softly lit by the glow given off by the big mercury-vapor street light which filtered through his office window from its outside location on the sidewalk twenty feet away.

Being physically away from Robyn provided him with an opportunity to do some thinking while he ran off the copies. His feelings for her were developing faster than he was comfortable with. He was beginning to be concerned that it could very easily get out of hand and he felt a need to sort things out before he even considered allowing it to proceed to the next stage.

He had accepted his earlier conclusion that he was interested in developing a relationship with her. But he found himself beginning to seriously question whether or not he might now be using the fact that there was a possibility she might be in danger from the hit man as an excuse to keep her with him. Perhaps he was taking advantage of it to advance the whole relationship scenario.

He wasn't particularly comfortable with that idea.

Was he using the possible danger as an excuse for his staying with her? If so, he was out of line and he knew it.

For several years he had taken steps to prevent any serious relationship possibility like this from developing. He had kept clear of any commitment, a casual sex thing when it became necessary or presented itself, but never anything more.

His interest in Robyn was already deeper than he could have anticipated a few short hours ago.

Experience and common sense told him he definitely needed some time to think it out before it went any further, especially in view of the fact that she was part of an active investigation into murder.

* * * * *

Robyn was hurt and confused.

Once back in the car, David had, for some unknown reason, become cold and abrupt with her. In the short time he had been away from her, his general attitude toward her had changed noticeably and she was at a loss to understand why.

Upon rejoining her, he had almost immediately, and in her view, feebly backed out of the dinner suggestion and once he had done that, he'd said very little to her as he drove her back to her apartment and dropped her off in front.

It would have been easy for her to tell herself that he was wrapped up in the case and determined to marshal all his efforts in that direction and considered her to be a distraction, but she sensed that there was something more to it than that.

She was beginning to realize just how complex a man David was.

CHAPTER TEN

David's alarm went off at four-thirty in the morning.

He was the type of person who, given a minimum of six hours sleep, was immediately functional upon waking, and he had showered, dressed and made a pot of tea before five.

Sitting at his desk in one corner of the living room, he poured himself a cup and opened a photo-copy of the diary. He read quickly, skipping the facts he considered irrelevant to the case and made notes of any important names and information as he plowed his way through the document.

The diary covered a period of approximately two years and it was the last year that gave him the material he was primarily interested in. He found himself wearing two hats as he made his notes, looking at the case from the point of view of picking up information that could lead to identifying the murderer, which was his main goal; but also looking for material that might be pertinent to the overall drug investigation.

By six-fifteen, he'd composed two lists of facts and was satisfied that he'd gleaned the main points of interest the diary had to offer.

He got up and stretched, which in turn was Cato's signal to get up from his favored position whenever David was working at his desk.

The big dog shifted out from under the desk and moved over to David, pushing his head against David's thigh and demanding to be noticed and stroked. David drained the remnants of his cup with his right hand and absently stroked the dog with his left.

With the diary out of the way for the moment, David's thoughts shifted back to Robyn.

He had behaved badly last night and he knew it. His

conduct had been completely out of character. He could only halfheartedly justify it by admitting to himself that the strong emotions he was beginning to feel for her had scared the hell out of him.

Their depth and strength had not only been completely unexpected, but were very unnerving for him.

In many ways he felt as if his entire world had been turned upside down. His carefully engineered life of solitude since Jackie's death had become, if not perfect, at least comfortable and in its own way had been a safe and secure haven for him.

Robyn entering the picture had put that at risk and replaced it all with all the pros and cons that a new relationship could bring.

At they same time, he recognized that the current situation was not something that she had engineered. The problem was his, not hers. His treatment of her the night before was extremely difficult for him to justify in the light of day.

He had not only treated her badly, but completely unfairly and his conscience was bothering the hell out of him. He should have been up front with her. He should have met the damn thing square on, as he did with any other problem. Running away from a situation was never a good way to deal with it and he knew it.

He was determined that, despite the busy day ahead, he would find time to see her and do what he should have done in the first place. If his feelings were this strong, he owed it to her to tell her so. He would explain his interest in her and why that fact had made him screw up so badly the night before.

She'd understand or she wouldn't. Either way he would know where he stood with her and they could take it from there.

He went into the small kitchen and set the mug in the sink then went back out into the living room, and called Cato.

He let the dog out the front door into the small yard that fronted on the gangway leading down to his dock. Leaving the door open, he went back inside and got his suit jacket and overcoat on before plucking the ring containing his boat and car keys off the hook by the door.

Cato came rumbling back inside as he returned to the doorway and he gave the dog a final pat and spoke affectionately to him.

"You watch the house, boy."

David left, closing and locking the door behind him. He then went down the three steps that led to the floating gangway, noting that it was high tide. The gangway itself was almost level as he walked down toward the wharf and boat below.

David watched his footing carefully, experience telling him the walk could be a treacherous one when the temperature was below freezing and the water had been at all rough the night before.

When he reached the boat, he placed his briefcase inside the small cabin then untied fore and aft and climbed back aboard. Inside the cabin again, he started the boat up and left it idling while he went back outside and moved around to the front to apply the scraper to the ice that had formed on the windshield overnight.

He cleared away a patch big enough for him to see through, then returned inside and threw the powerful inboard of the Glasscraft cruiser into gear and backed it smoothly away from the dock.

It was a short five minute run to the government wharf and the parked police car. He docked and properly secured the boat, then moved up the dock to the stairs leading to the street above and started the car.

He left it to idle with the defroster cranked to high as he got out and scraped the thin layer of ice off the front, side and back windows.

*****

It was just after seven in the morning when David strolled down a hall on the third floor of the CLEU building and dropped into the chair across from Inspector Bob Wright.

"Thanks for coming in early Bob, I've got a fixed morning meeting with my Deputy and I wanted to give you this before I reported it to him on the off chance it might be delayed in reaching you if I didn't."

He set a photocopy of the diary down in front of Wright and continued.

"This is a copy of Carol Jenkins diary. With the help of her sister I was able to find it last night. I think you'll find it holds all the information necessary to ensure you can break the drug investigation wide open. Based on its contents, I'm confident the murder was a contract hit aimed at getting the girl out of the way so that she couldn't lead us to them. One thing had been bothering me about that scenario at first. I couldn't figure out exactly how they knew we were working on her. The diary goes a long way to explaining that however, as I'm sure you'll agree, once you've had a chance to read it."

A look of eager interest flooded Wright's features and he reached for the copy and flipped to the first page.

David leaned back in his chair and let the other man read for a few seconds, then passed over a copy of one of the pages of notes that he had made earlier in the morning as he scanned the document.

"I went over it earlier and made these notes on what I considered information important to your case. After reading the whole thing, I'm no longer mystified as to how the group knew that we were working on Carol. The answer lies in the names of the people behind the ring, Bob, I'm sure of it. Because of the positions they hold, they've had a direct line into your investigation from the start. The minute they twigged to the fact that we were watching and tapping her, they moved to eliminate her. It's obvious to me the CLEU investigation was enough to sign her death warrant, and it's clear to me now that information was, and still is, being leaked to the group operating the drug ring. That information is coming from the CLEU investigation itself; by way of a person or persons in positions of power in the Justice system in Ottawa."

Wright made no attempt to hide his surprise as he dropped the copy onto his desk and faced David squarely.

"Let me get this straight. Based on this document, you are suggesting that someone in the R.C.M.P. in Ottawa is passing on our information to the suspects in this case?"

David nodded.

"Easy Bob, don't go getting scarlet fever on me now. No, I don't think that any member is passing on info to help protect these bastards, but I do think that some of the principals in the ring are themselves in a position to have a look into this or any other investigation the R.C.M.P is conducting any time they want to. That's why it's been so hard for us to get to them; they've always known what we were going to do before we did it. Have a look at some of those names in that diary and you'll see what I mean. What I'm suggesting to you is that we put a lid on this investigation at this end and keep any progress we're making to ourselves for awhile."

The pained expression on Wright's face eased a little and he looked down at the photocopy on his desk with renewed interest as he spoke.

"Christ, if what you're saying is true, this thing is likely going to turn into a very high profile hot potato."

He thought for a second, silently flipping through the pages of the diary, and then glancing at the names listed on David's notes, before speaking again.

"David, you're asking me to fail to provide my superiors with information I'm required by law to give them. If your suspicions are correct, this will shake Ottawa to the core when it becomes public knowledge. It's too big for me to sit on. If I don't report through proper channels on this, they'll have my ass when it comes out. It's alright for you; you're going to keep your Deputy informed. You've got to realize that I can't just sit on this. It's not a decision I can make on my level. You know that."

David let his eyes lock with Wright's.

He nodded and then shrugged.

"Okay Bob, I understand the position I'm putting you in. I've given this a lot of thought. I could have simply held this back from you, but I didn't do that because, whether you like it or not, you are directly in charge of the CLEU investigation. With the location of this diary, we now each have an interest in criminal investigations that will require the information included in this book if they are going to reach the proper conclusions.

Wright raised his hand to interrupt.

"You've got no argument from me there, but…"

David cut him off.

"Good, now before you say anything let me finish. What I'm asking of you is that you read it, and then, if you accept my evaluation of the material it includes, do your level best to see to it that the fact we have this information doesn't go through the same channels as it has up to now and to do everything in your power to ensure that whatever headway we achieve doesn't get back to these bastards this time. I know you or your superiors are going to feel obligated to report the contents of that diary to some political people. After all, when this thing breaks it is going to more than slightly embarrass the Federal Government. It could well bring them down. So, I'm asking you to tread very carefully when you pass along the information contained in this diary. I'm expecting you to do your level best to isolate its contents from those who are directly involved in the drug ring. Let's not give these guys the chance to cover their tracks any more than we already have. Be damned careful to put the information in hands that won't turn it over to those responsible for this mess and thereby warn them off. They feel confident that they have an inside line to the CLEU investigation into their crimes at the moment. Let's let them think they still do. Keep the info from this diary in as few trusted hands as you can."

Wright leaned back in his chair and sighed.

"I'll do my best to keep a lid on the diary's contents...but Christ, the influence and power of some of these names, my God, how many favors are they owed and from whom? You know bloody well this is going to have to go to the Commissioner of the R.C.M.P. You also know he will consider it a gift from the gods and will use it to apply pressure to the government in whatever way he can. The brass in Ottawa lives for the day when something like this falls into their hands. You can be damned sure they will use it to their best advantage. Direct control of the CLEU investigation under these circumstances is going to be pulled out of my hands almost immediately. And it will be immediately removed from any Joint-Forces overview. Headquarters will pull this in-house as soon as they get wind of it. "

David stood up and fixed his friend's eyes with his own.

"I didn't have to bring this to you Bob, and if I didn't trust your judgment implicitly, I wouldn't have. I'm asking you to do your best to keep it under wraps for as long as you can comfortably manage, and hopefully with the information we now have, we can bring this thing to a successful conclusion quickly and you won't have to keep the lid on it for very long."

* * * * *

The clock on the wall of the Crime Lab read just after nine when David entered the IDENT office at VPF headquarters. He noted the grizzled features of Carl Higgins nestled over a microscope on the bench across from the counter that acted as a barrier to everyone but staff members.

David reached down and let himself in through the half door and crossed over to the veteran who had headed the crime lab for as long as David had been on the job. He said nothing for a few seconds, fully aware of just how much Higgins disliked being interrupted when he was working on some piece of evidence.

Carl, who had been immediately aware of David's presence, made no attempt to rush what he was involved in. He had been functioning successfully under tremendous pressure for years, and one of the ways he maintained his sanity was by brooking absolutely no inference into his work from anyone, regardless of rank.

He and David had always gotten along and when Carl did finally look up from what he was doing he smiled in recognition as he spoke.

"I'll have something for you by one o'clock this afternoon David."

Without another word, he turned his attention back to the microscope and went back to work.

*****

Robyn found that she was walking aimlessly.

She had called David's office, wanting to speak with him, curious to know if he still gave a damn about her or not.

He hadn't been in and she had left a message, and then suddenly found herself afraid that he would call back and that she would hear something that she didn't want to. She immediately left her apartment in a panic to give herself a chance to reevaluate her confused feelings and make some sort of a plan as to how she would respond to whatever he did have to say to her when they next spoke.

She knew that she was behaving irrationally.

She hadn't slept, she hadn't eaten and she was already feeling the chill of the bitter, wind driven rain. She kept telling herself she was being silly, that she had no right to expect understanding, warmth and support from a veritable stranger, no right to expect him to understand her need even if it was crying out for attention.

How had she misread him so badly? Had she seen things in what she had been sure was mutual attraction that in fact didn't exist?

Christ, what a mess she was making of things!
She felt so stupid and so very, very lost and alone.

CHAPTER ELEVEN

David waited for Deputy Chief Foster's secretary to provide them with coffee, and then he leaned forward and opened his briefcase. He pulled out the second set of notes he'd made after reading the diary. Using them as a guide, he gave Foster a rundown of what had transpired since their last meeting.

The only additional hard evidence he had garnered since the hospital shooting related to the diary. David outlined what it contained and offered his assessment of the situation to Foster. He then detailed his visit to Inspector Wright at CLEU and emphasized his concern over the obvious leak of information that was making its way from the investigating team, via Ottawa, back to the principles of the drug importing and distribution ring.

Foster listened without comment. When David had finished with the diary outline and had placed the notes back into his briefcase, he looked squarely at this superior.

"More important, from our point of view, are the investigations into the murders. I've got some solid leads to follow up on those, thanks to the diary, and I'll be starting on them as soon as I finish here. Carl promises me a report on the physical evidence from the two crime scenes by one o'clock this afternoon. Once I've followed up the leads from the diary and seen what Carl has come up with, I think we'll find ourselves with a pretty good idea of exactly why she was killed, who ordered it and probably a line on the person who actually carried those orders out. I'm going over to see the coroner now. Perhaps the postmortems will offer something as well. All things considered, by tomorrow morning's meeting I expect to have something fairly concrete for you."

Toying with a pencil, Foster considered David's words for

a few seconds, and then he got up and crossed over to the window and turned his back to David as he stared outside at nothing in particular.

"These names in the diary, is it possible that she just made them all up?"

He turned back to face Walker and David, a little surprised at the suggestion, shook his head.

"No, I hardly think that's likely. They all know each other, and when you think about it, it explains a lot of things. How come CLEU was getting nowhere fast with their investigation? How did these guys seem to be able to plug every hole just after we found a trail that might lead to them? Luck and coincidence simply can't explain away all the things that have been going wrong with the investigation. In fact, it's damn funny that we didn't realize it before now. They're good, they're powerful, and they're ruthless. No, she didn't make them up."

Foster let out a deep breath and crossed back to his desk and sat down. He picked up the pencil again and began to twirl it listlessly.

"Well all I can say is that I'm damn glad this is a CLEU investigation and not solely ours. When this thing reaches a conclusion the reverberations will be felt all across the country. Damn, I wish that diary had never shown up!"

He looked from the pencil to David.

"Please don't get me wrong. I want these men caught and brought to justice as much as you do. It's just that this is going to get damn messy. The shit is going to hit the fan in Ottawa and, as is inevitable, some of that shit is going to end up landing on us. Were not just talking a few big time crooks here, these people are pillars of society and the leaders of our country. You call them powerful. Jesus, David, you have no idea just how powerful, and they have a lot of friends - friends whose names are not listed here and who will do everything in their power to ensure that the CLEU investigation is buried and if necessary everyone who is associated with it is buried as well. I wouldn't want to be in Wright's shoes right now."

David closed his briefcase and stood up.

"Bob Wright is a good man. At least now he's warned and knows what he's up against. His bosses are going to take personal control of this first chance they get, we all know that, but I'm hoping he can find a way to minimize just how much external pressure that will put on our murder investigations."

The Deputy stood to walk him to the office door.

"I strongly doubt he will have much say on how that will be handled David. I have a feeling the backlash from this investigation is going to be far stronger than any of us can imagine. These people aren't just anybody. There are those who would tell you that they are a law unto themselves and they wouldn't be too far off the mark. Christ David, the Solicitor General of Canada's name is on that list of yours…do you really think that a prosecution, warranted or not, will ever result from CLEU's current investigation?"

David stopped just inside the now open doorway. He glanced down at his feet, and then looked back up at Foster.

"Well sir, let's just say that I've got a full plate at the moment with three murders on it. It's my job to bring the murderer or murderers to justice, and I'll direct all my energies toward that end. I have, however, no intention of forgetting what was in the diary; after all none of our victims would have been killed if the people named on that list I just gave you hadn't ordered their deaths. I'm not about to let anyone hinder this particular CLEU investigation if I can prevent it, and that includes the R.C.M.P. Commissioner. These people may be in positions of power, and they may, quite literally, make the laws of the land, but they are in no way above them."

Foster Frowned.

"Admirable sentiments David, I'm sure; but I have my doubts as to just how successful you will be in that particular endeavor, in consideration of what you are about to find yourself up against."

The frown changed to a polished smile.

"Of course, it goes without saying, that once the murders

have been looked after, you will have my complete backing in your quest to support the continuation of the drug investigation."

** * * *

Robyn had given up. There was nowhere else that she had even the slightest desire to go and she simply couldn't physically stay out in the cold walking around any longer.

She had no more than returned to her apartment and taken off her coat when the phone rang.

She stared at it, letting it ring four times before she picked it up.

"Hello"

"Hello Robyn. It's David Walker returning your call."

Mixed emotions filled her. The sound of his voice immediately warmed and strengthened her and that feeling now conflicted with everything that had occurred over the past few hours. Try as she might, she could not dismiss the feeling of coldness that had surrounded his words at the end of the previous evening.

There was a strained silence before he spoke again.

"Look, I just called to tell you that I'm sorry about last night. I'm afraid that I behaved like an ass. It's not something I want to try to explain to you over the phone. Would you consider having a quick lunch with me? I've got a couple of hours clear between about eleven and one; I could pick you up about eleven-fifteen or eleven-thirty."

Robyn did her best to keep any form of emotion out of her voice as she spoke.

Last night had hurt and she wasn't about to set herself up for a repeat performance. On the other hand, she did get a sense that he was being sincere, and honestly regretful of the way he had acted in the final few minutes of the previous night.

Silence filled the line for some time as she wavered between acceptance and refusal. Finally she felt the pressure for an answer increase and she spoke.

"That would be fine. I'll see you then."

* * * * *

The Coroner opened one of the three files on his desk as he continued.

"Not much I can offer you that will help you find your killer, Inspector Walker. No indication of the height of the suspect based on trajectory. The victims were all low stationed at the time of the shootings. Appears to be a professional hit, knew where to put the slugs, but then you'd already guessed that, I'm sure."

David was only half listening to the man speak.

He hadn't expected to get anything surprising from the coroner and the telephone conversation he'd just had with Robyn was still bothering him.

It was obvious she had been hurt by his sudden and unexplained rejection of her the previous evening. For that he was sorry, but that type of reaction would seem to support his supposition that she felt at least some level of attraction for him. If not, she wouldn't have given his rejection the night before a second thought.

He was experiencing conflicting emotions about the upcoming meal. While eagerly anticipating spending time with her again, the very level of the intensity of that anticipation was enough to concern him.

The coroner had noted his preoccupation and cleared his throat.

"Are you still with me Inspector?"

David pulled himself back to the present.

This damn thing with Robyn needed to be sorted out one way or the other very quickly, so that he could get himself back on track.

* * * * *

They agreed on hamburgers from a drive-through and another walk around the seawall.

David was pensive, but had definitely shed the coldness of the night before, and despite her aimless trek earlier in the day, Robyn found herself looking forward to the walk.

They found a bench that was somewhat protected from the brisk wind coming off the sea and settled down onto it.

David filled and lit his pipe.

In spite of his earlier concern over how he was going to explain his feelings to her, he found himself feeling strangely relaxed and at ease.

He had been marshalling his thoughts as they had walked silently and he finally drew in a deep drag from the pipe and was about to speak but Robyn beat him to the punch.

"Before you start David, I'd like to ask a favor of you. It may sound silly to you, but it's important to me."

He placed the stem of the pipe between his teeth and, leaning into the back of the bench, gave her his full attention.

"In view of everything that's happened, I need someone to talk to, someone to bounce things off. I used to have Carol, but now… well, I need a friend. Although we've only known each other for a short time, I feel that I can trust you. I realize that it is a little presumptuous of me, but would you mind my asking you to be that for me?"

Her request gave him pause.

He had carefully worked out in his mind how he would deal with explaining his concern over the growing attraction he felt for her. The direction of the conversation wasn't going the way he had had envisioned it at all.

His intention had been to rationally explain to her that while he found himself strongly attracted to her, he was uneasy about getting into any new relationship with any woman. Her request was not something he had anticipated and it threw him off track.

What she was asking of him now didn't really hold any

threat to him. The kind of relationship she was asking him to consider wasn't what he had been expecting, and that made it much easier for him to entertain.

He was surprised by it and somewhat disappointed. He had been so certain that the spark he had felt for her had been a mutual thing. What he'd had in mind went further than the friendship she was now suggesting. He was relieved in a sense, but also felt strangely deflated and a little unsure of how to approach this new reality.

His own feelings aside, he sensed that the question she had proffered was an important one to her, and that it required an honest answer. It was not an unreasonable request and it certainly took the pressure off, in that it required no long term commitment from him.

"No. Of course not."

Robyn smiled and nodded her head slowly.

"If we hadn't met under the circumstances we did, if we had met somewhere by chance, would you still be willing to spend time with me? It isn't just because I'm down and need some support is it; because if that's the case, it wouldn't work for me. I may be wrong, but I think you have some feelings for me and that's very important to me right now. I need someone I can trust as a friend, someone who understands how I feel and can help me sort things out and move on."

He thought for a moment, weighing her words carefully, and then replied.

"If you are asking me if, irrespective of the investigation, I would like to have you for a friend, the answer is an unqualified yes."

Satisfied with his response, she continued, the words coming out in a rush, as if she were afraid that he would interrupt and not let her finish.

"David, I've never had a great deal of success with men. Oh, don't get me wrong, I've had my fair share of relationships, but they never seemed to work out as I expected. I was always a little overweight as a kid and in fact I didn't really blossom and take charge of myself until after I left university. I've never had a great deal of self confidence when it came to relationships. Even now, I don't really have any, what I would consider, really good friends, just a lot of acquaintances. In every relationship I've had with a man, I've always given everything and expected that I would be loved in return. Needless to say, it didn't work out that way and I got hurt several times, sometimes very badly. I finally managed to be absolutely honest with myself about the whole thing about two years ago. I realized that men were simply using me until something better came along. Since that time I've pretty well revamped my outlook and become far more particular about whom I get involved with. I have a pretty good idea now of what I'm looking for and how to choose my friends with that in mind."

Her eyes were riveted to his, trying to analyze his reactions to what she was saying as the words spilled out.

David removed his pipe from his mouth and was about to speak, but she raised her hand to silence him.

"No, please let me finish. As I said, I only got it straightened out in my own mind about two years ago and I decided then that I wasn't going to get into another relationship with a man until the feelings were mutual. I also decided to get myself into shape and lost thirty pounds, changed my hairstyle and started buying decent clothes. As I was doing that, I gave a great deal of thought to what I wanted in a man, something I'd never done before. I then laid down some very strict guidelines for myself and the result has been that I haven't had a relationship for the past year. At first, I found it hard, I'd always thought I needed a man in my bed; it made me feel secure and wanted. At least that's what I thought at the time. It took me a while to be able to handle life on my own. I'm not quite all the way there yet but I'm doing alright and I know now I only got what I asked for when men used me. It won't happen again. For awhile I gave up on the idea of having a steady relationship, period. Then I came to realize I was just over-reacting and feeling sorry for myself. What I really wanted was a man of my own who cared as much about me as I did him. I then realized that when I met the right guy, I'd know it and I immediately stopped looking so hard. I also learned over time that I didn't want a man my own age. I've never really felt comfortable with guys in my own age group. I feel more at ease when I am with more mature men."

She gave a short nervous laugh. David's mind had been racing to edit and register all the material that had poured forth from her.

He flushed slightly and sat forward on the bench.

"I don't know what to say. It seems to me you've thought things out pretty carefully, at least you understand what you're looking for now. I can certainly sympathize with what you've been through. It's not easy to find the right partner in life."

He stood up and reached down to take her hand. They began to walk slowly along the seawall again. He didn't talk for a few minutes, letting his thoughts gel, looking for the right words.

CHAPTER TWELVE

They had walked along slowly, side by side, in silence for several minutes.

Robyn had bared her heart to him and she was anxious to know how he was going to react, but she made no attempt to rush his response, and in due time it came.

"I married young, nineteen. It was never particularity good, but I didn't know that at the time. We had two kids, a boy and a girl. It lasted twelve years and it had a messy ending. It hit me hard. Suddenly I was thirty-one years old and single and figured that life for me was basically over. I met Jackie three months after my wife and I separated. She was only nineteen at the time, but in many ways more mature than I was. She'd been experimenting with men for a couple of years, and had had several experiences not unlike you've described. She was fed up with the singles bars and the one night stands. She knew that I was hurting and she simply adopted me. Under the circumstances, even if I had wanted to, I didn't have the strength to fight her off. After a few days, I simply accepted it. What man in his right mind wouldn't? She was young, beautiful and she appeared to love me more than anything else in the world. The way I looked at it, the worst that could happen was that she would grow tired, or worse, bored of me. I was in for the surprise of my life, because that didn't happen. She was wonderful, she did love me and she unselfishly gave me everything she could of herself. It was hard for me to accept at first, I simply couldn't believe my luck. Once I realized what a prize I had, I panicked and found it hard to believe it was true. Within a very short period of time I realized I was in love and for the first time in my life, I knew what real love was. We had four unbelievably good years and then she died quite suddenly from cancer."

Even after all this time, and consciously suppressed as they had been, the memories were strong enough to fill his voice with emotion and he stopped speaking for a few seconds until the worst of it had passed.

"I think that's why I was attracted to you in the first place. I see in you many of the qualities Jackie had, but to be honest, I just don't believe I could be that lucky twice in my life. I've managed to create an existence for myself I can live with. I have my work, and that and the renovations to the house keeps me busy."

Robyn nodded.

"You're afraid of commitment because you're afraid you'll be hurt again. I felt the same way, but I finally realized that idea was just a cop-out and decided I would simply have to be very careful of whom I trusted in the future. You don't think you can find another Jackie, and you are absolutely right. There will only ever be one of her. But that doesn't mean that you can't find happiness again with someone else."

David nodded, not totally convinced by her argument, but sensing the truth of it. Robyn said nothing for awhile, and then continued.

"I'd like to get to know you better David. I'd like us to become good friends."

He turned to face her squarely. They stood looking at each other briefly and then he pulled her gently into his arms and hugged her tightly.

"Okay, let's try being friends. I can live with that."

She gave a little sigh and snuggled closer, slipping her arms around him.

* * * * *

Carl Higgins waved David into a chair and continued reading the report that was laid out on the desk in front of him.

It was a three page report and, ignoring David, he finished it before 'grumping' to himself and pushing it aside to look up at Walker.

"We got a few hairs from the inside of the hairpiece. They'll need testing and that will take some time. We've run ballistics on the gun and the slugs. It's the right gun. We were able to bring up the serial number which had been filed and managed to match the gun to a case number..."

He looked down at his desk and pushed some papers around until he found the report that he was looking for.

"...this is the report; gun was taken in a B&E seven months ago."

He passed the report to David and turned his eyes back to his original report.

"We pulled one partial hair from the hinge of the glasses. Appears to be the same as the others we got from the wig. We'll run it too. Smock is a little hard to size; you can wear them big or small. It's really a matter of choice. However as a guess I'd say our killer stands about five foot eight or nine and has a medium to slight build. The only prints of value came from the stethoscope, probably don't belong to the suspect though; no prints on the inside of the gloves, too much powder."

He leaned back in his chair, lifted off his glasses and rubbed his eyes.

Still holding the copy of the original B&E report, David stood up.

"Thanks Carl, I know you put a rush on this and I appreciate it."

Higgins shrugged.

"I liked Doug Campbell."

He looked pointedly at David when he continued.

"And you know I don't like a hell of a lot of people."

David smiled and nodded.

"You'll give me a call on the hair?"

Higgins raised his hand, impatiently waving David out of the office.

"Yes, yes, now get the hell out of here and let me get back to work."

* * * * *

David didn't offer Boyd a seat. He simply passed him the photocopy of the B&E report covering the theft of the gun.

"This is the gun that was used at the hospital. Check with the detectives in District Three and find out where the initial investigation took them, if anywhere. Get everything you can on it. Go back to the original complainant if you need to; and have a report on my desk before nine tomorrow morning."

Boyd nodded and left. He was immediately replaced in David's office by two other detectives. David didn't invite them to sit either.

"Find out when Simpson and Edwards are working today at CLEU. I want you to liaise with them and take this list with you."

He handed them each a copy of the list of names that he had made from the diary.

"Find out how many people mentioned here have previously shown up during the CLEU investigation, in however small a manner, and get the CLUE team to bring you up to speed on the investigation itself and any ties to these names. Get warrants for taps on the lines of every name that resides in our jurisdiction and structure surveillance on them. The Staff-Sergeant will allocate manpower. CLEU will be expecting you and they will take care of the taps and surveillance on any of these people who are out of our jurisdiction. Have a report on my desk by nine tomorrow outlining your progress to date."

There were six names on the list and both detectives were now reading them. The older of the two shook his head slowly.

"Holy shit! One of these guys is an appeal court judge. Who the hell will have the balls to issue a warrant for a tap on his line?"

David had anticipated the question. He handed the detective a small slip of paper.

"Just call the number on there and tell them who you are and that I have asked you to call. They've already been briefed on this and you won't have any trouble getting the warrants you require. One thing…keep this to yourselves. I don't want any of this getting out."

David glanced up at the clock as they left. It read four-sixteen. No wonder he was feeling a little tired. He'd put in a long day.

He got up, pulled his coat off the rack and left the office, locking the door behind him.

*****

The phone rang while David was in the process of making himself a drink at the bar in the corner of his living room. He cursed under his breath, put his as yet, empty glass down and crossed over to his desk to answer it.

"Hello."

"David, it's Bob Wright, I have some interesting news for you…"

"Shoot."

"I thought very carefully about what we talked about this morning. At nine o'clock I called the man who I considered could handle it. I briefed him on what we had. He was very interested, and seemed sincerely concerned that it would be handled above-board. He thanked me for bringing it to his attention and told me he'd get back to me. At ten o'clock I got a call from no less than the Assistant Commissioner. He congratulated me profusely on the material and told me that I could expect to have a visitor before the day was out. At shortly after three the Regional Director of CSIS, Matt Birch, sashayed into my office and sat down. He too, congratulated me on the investigation and calmly informed me that the case would now be transferred from CLEU and would become the responsibility of CSIS. When I pointed out to him that the investigation was a criminal matter and as such not into the normal area of concern for our illustrious newly formed national spy agency, he simply smiled and replied 'That in consideration of the people who were the alleged perpetrators of the crime'... Those were his words David, so help me God, 'it was very obvious that the security of the country was threatened and could be compromised and that the Canadian Security and Intelligence Service was therefore obliged to enter the case and see it through to a satisfactory conclusion.' I was dumbfounded. This guy was good David, one thousand dollar three-piece suit, manicured hands, Rolex watch, just as polished as they come. He then told me he would need the complete file on the investigation by tomorrow morning and advised me to expect orders from Ottawa confirming that we would no longer be responsible for the case."

Wright paused for a few seconds to let these facts settle in and then continued.

"Look David, I've been effectively stopped. There is nothing I can do now. I'm quite sure that the orders will be here when I come into the office in the morning. You know this goes against my grain, but I've been damn effectively completely cut out of the loop, and you can believe me when I say that I'm here if you need any help...just give me a call, preferably at home...I have a feeling CSIS will be watching me pretty closely for awhile."

David cut him off.

"I don't think that would be a good idea Bob; this is CSIS we are dealing with. I'd be willing to bet your home phone will be tapped by morning. I do appreciate the offer though. They may be able to put you out of the picture, but I'm no Mountie, and they can't gag me with an order from Ottawa. Look, I'm definitely going to need your help with this, but I'll contact you some other way. If you're open for some advice from a friend, I'd suggest you play it cool for a while and make it look like you've dropped this thing just as any reasonable man would. I'll be in touch, and thanks again for the heads up, don't think that I don't know how much of a chance you took by calling me on this."

"Horseshit David, just don't hesitate to call; I'm here if you need me."

*****

The accountant replaced the hand unit into the cradle and sat back. The message had been brief and to the point. 'It is time to take a long vacation, not to worry, it's all looked after, simply pick up the tickets at Canadian Airlines in the morning. Sunny Mexico, relax, soak up the sun'.

What a load of bullshit.

Something had gone very wrong and they weren't saying what. It wasn't a good sign, definitely not a good sign at all.

These people were not the kind to consider a vacation to be the best way to deal with a crisis. At first glance it would appear that there was more to this than met the eye, and yet one had to be careful not to read too much into it on the off chance that it could be something relatively minor.

A good deal of thought would be necessary to ensure that preparations were made to deal with any little surprises that might be on the horizon.

CHAPTER THIRTEEN

The man who had originated the call to the accountant had not left the room he was in and returned to the others immediately after hanging up the phone.

Instead he crossed over to stand in front of the French doors that afforded a sweeping view of the vast lawns of the estate, that even in winter bespoke the time and money spent on their care.

Always, in the back of his mind, he'd known that this time would come. It had been too good a thing to last forever.

Justice Richard London of the British Columbia Court of Appeal was neither a pessimist nor a quitter. The fact that he might actually face charges and be sent to prison had not even entered his mind. There was no earthly way that such a thing was going to happen to him.

What did bother him was that after ten years of astounding success, the exquisitely engineered and tremendously profitable organization appeared to be on the brink of necessary liquidation.

He gave a deep sigh of acceptance before turning to cross the room and then opened the door of his study and entered the adjoining Library.

His nostrils took in the comforting aroma of fine cigars, old leather and aged brandy.

There were five other men in the Library, sitting comfortably around the big solid oak table in the center of the large room. He sensed their controlled but none-the-less, obvious eagerness to have him report on how the call had gone.

Despite that fact, he made no comment until he had refreshed his brandy and sunk comfortably into the thickly padded leather armchair at the table's head.

His penetrating eyes met theirs individually in a swift

sweep and he took a swallow of his brandy before speaking.

"Arranged, the accountant will be in Mexico by tomorrow afternoon. The flight and accommodations are booked in the name provided by Jim."

He nodded in the general direction of James Kincaid, Head of Customs and Excise for the British Columbia Region.

"Money has been wired to an account in the same name, courtesy of Bill"

William Hampton, long time Liberal party hack and successful importer of antiques snorted and removed the big Cuban cigar from his mouth.

"I still don't like it, think we should have finished it here and now, and been done with it."

London was, as usual, restraining a desire to lash out at Hampton, a man who he considered weak and spineless. The building concern over the operation made the job that much harder and he was about to release his fury when the deep, polished voice of the Solicitor General for Canada cut through the heavy atmosphere of the room like a serrated knife.

"Now Bill, we've already discussed that at length. We don't want any more police attention leveled locally here in the lower mainland. There has been more than enough of that already, thanks to the botch-up the accountant made in the first place. My God, we've had three policemen killed in a hospital. We've voted and, as usual, the vote will stand. An accident in a foreign land under an assumed name is far cleaner and it provides no way to tie this back to us. A clean break, that's what we want."

A short, heavy, balding man with thick lenses sitting at the far end of the table from London cleared his throat. These men knew each other well and each turned his attention in the direction of the sound, realizing from long experience that it was an indication that the man was about to speak.

A basically insecure and simple individual, he really didn't fit easily into this company. His key to the organization lay in his brain. He was their comptroller and his proven abilities in that field held their respect.

The all waited patiently for him to speak.

"I believe we must turn our attention back to the main discussion now that we have dealt with this Mexico thing. Gentlemen, we have still not settled the main point of tonight's meeting. Do we sell off our business interests based on the facts before us or do we gamble and brazen it out?"

George Carstairs, the oldest in the room and the originator of the basic concept of the organization, stared at him for a few seconds and then smiled.

"As usual Craig, you have put the problem into its simplest terms"

He leaned back in his chair and swung his eyes to survey the group before continuing.

"Mr. Bellow's is, however, quite correct gentlemen. We must make a decision on this situation, and we must make it quickly. We've already had an open discussion on the question and I would suggest that we have Arnold recap the facts for us before we put it to a final vote."

Five sets of eyes now turned toward the Solicitor General, who rose and took his customary stance, right hand in his pants pocket and left resting comfortably on the highly polished table top.

"There is no need for me to restate the reasons for continuation. We have been able to make a substantial profit to date, somewhere in the neighborhood of the one billion dollar mark according to Craig. Gentlemen, we have a good thing going here and we all know it. That said, we must evaluate the danger that is inherent in a continuation and, as I see it, our ability to render that danger impotent if we apply ourselves collectively toward that end. Since we are in a position to know exactly what the police know on a day to day basis, we can accurately list our current problems. First, there is the CLEU investigation and its results to date. Dismissing the diary for the moment - I'll return to that later - we know that all that has been achieved by way of that investigation was the awareness that Carol was the front, cutout or contact person for an organization bringing drugs into the country. They are also vaguely aware of the size of the operation and of the identities of many of the street level suppliers and pushers involved in it. However, they know nothing of who makes up the top positions in the organization above Carol's level of involvement. That is why we had Ms. Jenkins removed. Without her, there is no serious imminent danger to us. With her out of the picture as well as a few lesser members of the organization, we should have had nothing to fear. Unfortunately, this diary has surfaced."

He paused for a second to reach down and pick up the thick photocopy which he then tossed into the middle of the table.

"As you know, it contains the name of each man at this table. It suggests that we are in fact a conspiracy and that we control the major drug flow into Vancouver and thereby into Canada and a large portion of the United States. It is in fact a naive, but fairly accurate account of how our organization is set up and operates. Although it is without doubt very damaging, it's hardly sufficient evidence to warrant a charge against any of us. It does however provide enough information to guarantee a substantial investigation, and the question remains as to whether or not we can in fact ensure that any such investigation will stagnate and eventually fizzle out long before it reaches a successful conclusion."

He surveyed their faces again and, satisfied that he still held their undivided attention, he continued.

"Secondly, due to the actions of the accountant, we now have a murder investigation being conducted by the Vancouver Police. It seems to me that the Mexican accident will ensure that an acceptable conclusion will be reached there - one that will in no way reflect on any of us. What we must do tonight is decide to cease our operations very soon, or satisfy ourselves that we have the resources necessary to absolutely guarantee that we can guide and thereby eventually destroy, any investigations that may be launched against us."

He sat down and reached for his brandy snifter; rolling it slowly in his palms before raising it to his lips.

London expelled a heavy cloud of cigar smoke and then turned his attention to Banks.

"We have to rely on you there Arnold. As Solicitor General you're in a far better position than the rest of us to know what can be done about the two investigations currently under way."

Arnold Banks nodded.

"Well, I have already taken some action, indirectly of course, in that I've not been officially advised of anything to date. As I said earlier, without the diary they have nothing that could seriously hurt us. With the diary, they have suspicion and enough to warrant a full fledged investigation. It did occur to me that without the diary itself, there would be little to back up the suspicions, thereby making it a far simpler task for us to make any investigation ineffectual."

He bent over and picked up his briefcase and placed it onto the table and opened it. There was a deathly silence in the room as he reached inside and extracted a black leather-bound book. He looked at it for a split second and then held it up for them to see clearly.

"This gentlemen, is the damaging document."

A sense of immediate relief filled the faces around him. He allowed them to savor the sensation briefly and then returned the book to his briefcase and closed it.

"There are, however, two copies, one of which we already have in our possession. Now, while a copy is not as damaging as the original, and certainly very unlikely to be accepted into court system for example, we must nevertheless make every attempt to see to it that all copies of this diary are destroyed as well as the diary itself"

George Carstairs interrupted.

"Wouldn't it be better if the diary and the copies were not to disappear, but simply be purged of any references to us and then returned?"

London smiled and stood up

"Good idea, can you imagine the confusion that would achieve among the investigators!"

Banks thought for a second and then laughed.

"You know, it might just work. It isn't going to be easy to get hold of both of the copies of course, but if it can be done and if we could remove everything relating to us from them, the law enforcement agencies involved would not only be confused, but would be immediately at each other's throats trying to affix blame"

He peered across at Kincaid.

"Could your people deal with this kind of thing Jim - the doctoring of the diary itself?"

Kincaid shrugged his shoulders and then nodded.

"Don't see why not, the book itself is relatively common. If my people can produce passports and other government documents that pass for the real thing, I don't suppose redoing this will be too much of a problem. It will take time, of course."

Banks stood up again and glanced toward London.

"I'll just use your phone Richard, if I may, and see what can be done. If I'm right, there is only one more copy of the diary that we don't currently have. We already have the original and the copy forwarded to CLEU. If we can get the other copy and then make the necessary changes in the original and make two copies of that before returning all three to where they were before we managed to secure them..."

*****

The limo deposited Banks at the Vancouver Bayshore Hotel shortly before ten. He paused at the desk long enough to pick up his messages and a paper, then he went directly to his room.

He had been running over the evening meeting in his mind during the ride from London's majestic home to the hotel and in retrospect was satisfied with the results.

In the end there had been no definitive decision as to whether to fold up or continue. That had been put on hold with a view to the recovery of the last copy of the diary. He had little doubt that it could be accomplished, and that the required changes could be made to the original document.

There had been agreement that the six would not meet again, as a group, until the diary had been dealt with one way or the other. Now that the police had their names by way of the diary, it was too risky for them to be seen together as a unit until that had been done. As was normally the case, London would be the contact man, informing the rest once the diary had been handled. They would then each vote on the question of continuing the operation or shutting it down.

As he entered his room, he found himself wondering if maybe they were being foolish to tempt fate. After all, they had all done very well over the past ten years. My God, each of them was a multi-millionaire!

He closed the door, put on the security lock and placed his briefcase on the dresser.

Subconsciously he recognized what the real motivation for continuing was. It was for the majority of them at least, the excitement of the challenge. They were all feeling it and wanted to take it on. Wanting to prove that they could continue to beat the system just as they always had.

The phone rang and he picked it up.

"Hello."

"Arnold, it's Jim. I've pushed my people to the wall. They say that they can get it done in three days. They'll destroy the photocopy and redo the original and then make two copies of it. It's already in their hands and I expect to have it and the copies ready for you on Friday night."

Banks considered for a second.

"I'm scheduled to leave on the Friday morning flight for Ottawa, but I can justify staying an extra day here. Let's have dinner at my hotel on Friday, say eight o'clock...and Jim; I think that it might be prudent from now on to stop using the phone for these kinds of messages. Face to face meetings only, and as few as possible."

*****

Impatiently sitting by the phone for over two hours, while halfheartedly attempting to read a book, the accountant got it on the first ring. In recognition of the voice, the frustration at waiting boiled out.

"It's about bloody time! What the hell have you been doing?"

The response was delivered without emotion, in cold, concise terms. It completely ignored the accountant's opening verbal assault.

"Pick me up at the steam clock in Gastown in forty-five minutes."

The line went dead. Despite the obvious rebuke contained in the delivery of the message, the accountant was pleased. Why not? One hundred thousand dollars would improve the bank account very nicely.

CHAPTER FOURTEEN

The passenger door of the La Baron convertible opened and the big man slid in beside the accountant. Closing the door and fastening his seat belt, he nodded toward the roadway.

"Let's drive; you can drop me off after we finish our business."

The accountant shrugged, started the car and pulled out into the light early evening traffic.

This was the first occasion on which the accountant had actually met with one of the principals of the drug cartel face to face. Recruited through a mutual friend, interviewed and hired over the phone, present at meetings via speaker-phone only, it gave a sense of power to be this near to one of them. It had taken a very long time and a definite shift in the positions of power to get this close to any of them.

The brief and to the point directions issuing forth from the passenger seat brought the accountant out of a private reverie. The sleek red convertible made a left, a right and then settled down into the traffic before the passenger spoke again.

"Pull over here and we can complete our transaction before you drop me off."

The accountant wheeled the car over to the curb and slipped it into park.

"You're sure you got them all, and there are no other copies?"

The accountant nodded and turned in the seat to pull a briefcase from the floor behind the passenger seat of the car.

"Yes, as agreed, for one hundred thousand dollars. With the right level of persuasion, dear little Carol was quite prepared to part with her nest egg. She assured me the tapes in here are what you asked for and that there are no other copies. Your check made out to her for that amount is also in the briefcase. By that point in our negotiations, she was no longer able to make any use of it."

The passenger nodded and pulled an envelope from his inside jacket pocket.

"A check in the same amount made out to the name you'll be using in Mexico. As you have no doubt confirmed, an account in that name has already been set up for you and you will have no difficulty in cashing this upon you arrival there. You will note that I have post-dated the check for three day's hence. That will give me an opportunity to review the tapes and ascertain their content is what I have agreed to pay for."

The accountant, who had been in the process of passing the briefcase toward the passenger seat froze in mid-move and clutched the case firmly.

"Why postdated?"

The passenger laughed.

"I told you, I want to make sure I'm getting what I paid for. You have nothing to worry about. The check is perfectly good; it's in the name of a fictitious individual I created six months back and there is just over one hundred thousand in the account. The check will clear with no problem. You don't really think I would cheat you after all these years? Especially when one considers just how effectively you've handled the group's little problems in the past. After all, you know who I am now. You can find me any time you wish."

The accountant was not totally convinced.

"You could stop payment."

"Why would I do that? I consider these tapes to be worth far more than the amount I'm paying for them. It's a business investment to me, nothing more. I also happen to respect your abilities and value my life rather highly. I'm sure that you didn't expect me to simply hand over one hundred thousand in cash without ensuring I'd received value for my money?"

The account wavered for a split second; eyes fixing on those of the man in the passenger seat, then passed the briefcase over without further comment and accepted the envelope in exchange.

It was a reasonable way to deal with the payment, and in many ways it simplified things.

Carrying the check onto the plane would be much less cumbersome than arranging for a cash amount of that size to be safely deposited.

*****

When David arrived for work the older of the two detectives he'd detailed to get the taps and surveillance set up the night before was waiting for him in the outer office of Major Crime. He waved the man toward the door to his office and led the way inside.

"We got the surveillances set up and running just after midnight"

Walker had been in the process of hanging his coat up. He sensed hesitancy in the other man, but couldn't understand what was causing it and paused to turn and face him.

"Well, what is it?"

The older detective shrugged.

"You're not going to like it, but we couldn't get authorizations for the phone wiretaps. When I called they said you'd already spoken to them and to come on over, but when I got there it was a different story. I don't know what happened between the call and my arrival sir, but they wouldn't give me the time of day. Told me to have you contact them in the morning."

David slammed the coat onto the rack.

"Shit!"

He spun around and crossed to the desk, then grabbed the phone and began to dial. The detective was still standing in the center of the office and Walker dismissed him with a wave of his free hand.

The call was answered on the second ring.

"David Walker, give me Getz."

He was put on hold for almost a minute and he felt the anger building in him as he waited. Finally he was put through and the familiar voice greeted him.

"Morning David..."

Walker cut him off, his voice twice its normal pitch.

"Why in hell weren't those taps authorized last night?"

There was a pregnant pause before the other man replied.

"I don't understand David..."

The anger was still building in him and David was losing what patience he had left very rapidly.

"What do you mean, you don't understand? We spoke yesterday and set it up, my man subsequently called you and everything was a go and then you tell him no when he arrives, what the hell is going on?"

"Easy, David. We got a visit from CSIS, an agent named Richard Hummel. He informed us that the investigation was now theirs and that they would look after authorization for the taps through other channels and that we were to forget about them. He told us you would be getting instructions regarding the matter this morning and I could expect a call from you to clear up any confusion."

David felt his anger polarizing in his hand and the fist holding the phone turned white as he unconsciously increased the pressure. Then as suddenly as it had appeared it was gone.

"I'm sorry Getz, I didn't know. I guess this thing is getting to me, I shouldn't be taking it out on you. Look, just forget this call. I'll look into this and get back to you."

As he was hanging up, Cindy poked her head through his open door.

"Detective Boyd left an envelope for you, said he would be home if you had any questions and needed to give him a call."

David was still staring blankly at the phone as he gathered his thoughts. Cindy placed the brown envelope on his desk in front of him and he picked it up, opened it and pulled out the typed report which filled two sheets of paper.

Boyd had spoken to the detectives who had investigated the original B&E involving the theft of the murder weapon and had learned that they had made an arrest in the case. The charge had been based on prints lifted at the original crime scene and the accused had given no statement other than to plead his innocence. The prints and lack of an alibi, coupled with an interesting past record for B&E would almost certainly result in a conviction and in view of that lengthy record could mean a long stay behind bars for the perpetrator once the case came to trial.

David noted that the accused had already appeared for a preliminary hearing and was currently out on bail pending a higher court trial slated for three months hence. The accused was, no doubt, back practicing his trade in the interim.

It was more than David had hoped for and it served to relieve some of the frustration and anger over the CSIS involvement in his case.

He finally had something he could sink his teeth into, something that no one could manage to interfere with.

*****

As requested, the VCR had been delivered in the morning. He pulled the curtains closed and inserted one of the unlabeled tapes into the machine then picked up the remote control and punched 'play' before settling into a chair across from the set.

The furniture in the room portrayed on the screen was immediately familiar to him. He found himself chuckling in remembrance of the many hours he had spent on that very bed sweating and grunting gloriously as he pumped in and out of Carol's oh so willing and talented body.

Surprisingly, now after she was dead, he harbored no anger at her for the blackmail she had demanded from him. After all, he had inherited the wealth of her tapes now and he could do no less than to forgive her for her foolish attempt to fleece him.

He had every intention of utilizing the tapes as she had done, more effectively of course, far more effectively.

On the screen, the black satin cover was pulled off the bed and lay in a shimmering pool at its foot. He wondered at the clarity and color perfection of the film, the quality was very good, then he mentally registered the players on the big bed, noting with satisfaction that the first of the tapes revealed George Carstairs ravenously lapping at the juncture of Carol's exquisitely formed thighs.

Impatient now to evaluate all of the tapes quickly, he pushed the fast forward and pressed on rapidly through the tape in the machine, stopping periodically to view at normal speed, the chronological visits of Carstairs to that seemingly endless flow of the fountain of youth secreted between Carol's long luscious legs.

If the remaining tapes were as good as this, the one hundred thousand dollar price tag he had paid for them would be money well spent. He found himself grinning like a fool; what one hundred thousand? The accountant would never live to cash the check and he had every intention of closing the account tomorrow and returning the funds to his own account.

It seemed ironic and very pleasing to him that the very people eagerly performing in these tapes were going to pay big money to ensure they were never viewed again.

His grin grew to laughter as he removed the first tape and inserted the second of the six.

*****

David looked up as Cindy escorted a detective into his office. He waved the man into the chair across from him and handed across the report that Boyd had earlier left for him.

"Drop in on the suspect in this B&E. Tell him I would like to see him and indicate to him that he might find the charges he is currently facing stayed if he and I can come to an arrangement. If possible I'd like to see him before a scheduled meeting that I have with the Deputy at ten o'clock."

When the detective left, David reached for the phone and dialed Wright at CLEU.

"Bob, CSIS has been meddling in my investigation. I want to talk to them about it. I could go in blind and call them up but I have a feeling it would be far quicker and more effective if I dealt with their Regional Director himself rather than work my way up through underlings. Since you two are on first name terms, could you give him a call and tell him that I am very upset and need mollifying. Suggest to him that if I hear from him before my ten o'clock meeting with my Deputy, it might serve to thwart some of the inter-agency exchanges that are sure to result if I don't get some explanations fast. You've met with this chap; you'll know how to make it sound like a reasonable request."

"Glad to help David. If you don't mind though, I'll distance myself from it. I'll tell him you just gave me a call to blow off some steam and that I thought I'd better let him know you were choked and considering stirring up as much shit as you can. I'll leave him with the impression you are a reasonable man and that he may be able to prevent any further misunderstandings over jurisdiction if sees his way clear to speaking to you before ten this morning."

* * * * *

A beaming stewardess welcomed passengers and checked boarding passes. She directed the accountant across the cabin and to the left, into the Royal Canadian and First Class sections.

Only four of the twelve seats in First Class were occupied. The accountant glanced at the boarding pass and then slid into a window seat on the right side of the plane.

As always, the treatment was the best that money could buy. It was going to be a shame to sever the current business arrangements that existed with the group of six, however necessary the need to do that had become.

Still, it wasn't as though contact wouldn't be maintained. There would, however, be a change as far as to who was in the driver's seat from this point on.

It was immensely satisfying to be shifting position and giving the orders instead of taking them for a change.

* * * * *

The detective ushered his charge into Walker's office and David nodded indicating to the policeman that he would conduct the interview on his own. The detective closed the office door on the way out and David turned to look at the prison-hardened features of the two-time loser.

"Take a seat. I'll make this fast so I don't waste your time or mine."

He picked up the B&E report and referred to it as he spoke.

"We have you dead to rights on the B&E seven months ago. When you hit Supreme Court in two months, you'll be convicted, and based on your previous record, you'll probably get from five to seven years. I'm willing to see to it that the charges are stayed, providing you can see your way clear to give me the information I want."

He let the report float down to the surface of the desk and faced the other man squarely.

"First, I want the name of the fence that handled the stuff for you and second, I want a signed statement from you naming and implicating him."

CHAPTER FIFTEEN

It was a quarter to ten and David was preparing his notes and marshalling his thoughts for the meeting with the Deputy when Cindy buzzed him to announce that a representative from CSIS would like to see him.

David smiled slightly, checked the clock and gauged if he had enough time. Foster didn't like to be kept waiting and he always had a full schedule. On the other hand, this wouldn't take long and it was important.

"Right, Cindy, ask him to come in."

Wright's assessment and description had been right on target.

Polished, assured and definitely not a field man, this guy was pure diplomat.

"Inspector Walker, I've heard some very good things about you"

David stood to shake the outstretched hand which was followed by a business card announcing that the CSIS Regional Director went by the name of Mathew Birch. He managed to return the brilliant smile that had accompanied the card with one of his own.

He didn't like this man. He wasn't used to, nor did he readily accept the feeling of helplessness he sensed in his ability to go up against the obvious power that his guest so easily wielded.

David could have vented his anger and frustration, here and now, but he knew it would accomplish nothing. He was not, at least not yet, in a position to deal, or coerce and he knew it. He would have to play the game for now.

He moved his eyes to the surface of the card and managed a more sincere smile.

"I'm afraid I have a meeting in a few minutes, so we'll

have to keep this short. I'm somewhat confused as to why such an august body as CSIS is suddenly interested in a criminal murder case in Vancouver's jurisdiction. As I am abreast of the investigation to date, I find myself wondering just what would interest CSIS in such a mundane matter, and cause them to pop up on the scene?"

The man across from him sat without invitation.

"I assure you Inspector, it is not our intention to interfere with your investigation, only, for reasons that I am not currently at liberty to reveal, to assist you in any way we can. We have our own concerns in this matter, as I'm sure you are aware. I was really hoping that we might work together here and as it is somewhat easier for us to remove certain obstacles to the investigation than it would be for you, I took what steps I could in that direction. I will of course be keeping you apprised of our progress on a regular basis and was hoping you would do the same for us."

Walker sat down and shrugged.

"It goes without saying that if I had a choice in this I would rather struggle through on my own. But in consideration of circumstances which are unclear to me and of course, that you are not at liberty to provide to me, I would be foolish not to accept whatever help that you may offer, with thanks. I do, however, want you to understand that I won't accept some kind of a cover-up here..."

His guest was about to speak when Walker cut him off with a raised hand.

"...for whatever reason and that includes what you may wish to refer to as the security of our country. I'm quite sure Canada can live through the shock of discovering that some of its most trusted and influential citizens are not what they seem. We've all been through this type of garbage before. Understand me; I will see this investigation through to its conclusion, with your help if possible, without it if necessary. My priority is the solving of murder, yours the investigation of a drug conspiracy and the pending discomfiture that our politicians may have to suffer if it should be proven that the said conspiracy has ties with those in power. I sincerely hope we can both profit from each other and further our separate goals, but do not for an instant forget that without your drug conspiracy, I wouldn't have a murderer on the loose. I believe the two things are so interwoven that the solving of the one will inevitably open the other to public scrutiny as well. If that becomes necessary I won't be put off by concerns for the security of our nation. It simply won't wash with me."

The CSIS representative smiled broadly and stood up, offering his hand again.

"I quite understand your position Inspector, and I sincerely hope we find ourselves able to meet this crisis as a team. Nothing would please me more. I appreciate your candor and you may rest assured that you can always count on mine."

Walker had trouble understanding why the other man hadn't choked on those words, but his expression revealed nothing but warmth as he shook the agent's hand.

* * * * *

David's meeting with the Deputy had not gone well. Foster was not pleased at the slow pace things were progressing.

David needed time to think and he was looking forward to lunch and a chance to discuss with Robyn what he had learned since they had last talked.

She was waiting on Cordova Street as David left the building to find himself in the midst of swirling snow. Light, dry flakes at the moment, but it had started to stick and begin to build up on the surface of the pavement.

Robyn's little Fiat Spider was coated with the remnants of the already slushy streets it had been negotiating, but David could still make out relatively unobstructed patches of grey paint here and there as he approached the car.

She pushed the passenger door open for him and he double up his bulk to get in beside her, where they exchanged smiles.

"Probably a silly question, but have you ever considered washing this thing?"

Robyn slipped the powerful little car into first gear and zipped away from the curb, tires spinning and tossing up a spray of slush across the sidewalk behind her.

"Never in the winter, the dirt protects the paint."

He laughed easily and leaned back against the bucket seat doing his best to find a comfortable position as he fought to get his seatbelt on.

* * * * *

The place was certainly nothing to look at.

People didn't come to the 'Only' for atmosphere. They came for the food. There were a few booths against one wall and a counter across from the booths. The counter was fronted by stools that offered patrons, as they were eating, the opportunity to watch the frenzied activity of the staff working in the open kitchen beyond.

The best seafood in Vancouver was served here daily and if you didn't mind waiting for a place to sit and could put up with the cramped and well-worn seating, if and when you were lucky enough to find an empty spot, it was a pure delight for the taste buds.

David and Robyn were sitting at the counter, squeezed between a uniformed beat cop and a huge Native Indian woman, who could have used a bath.

Always the gentleman, David had offered Robyn the seat beside the policeman.

The noise level in the 'Only' was always at a high pitch and there was little opportunity for conversation, but the food was excellent and neither of them minded the enforced silence between them.

All other thoughts were pushed out of their minds as they laid into the delicious chowder and contemplated the fresh fish fillets and fries that were bubbling and sizzling tantalizingly in front of them, a few feet away.

*****

The accountant left the Canadian ticket desk and glanced up at the clock.

One hour and twenty minutes until flight time. More than enough time for a relaxing lunch, if such a thing was possible at LA International.

The wait would provide a good opportunity to review and assess future possibilities.

There was much that needed to be accomplished in a very short period of time.

*****

Following David's directions, Robyn had parked the car in a vast empty lot that faced out to the water with the deteriorating and half-denuded Expo 86 site between them and the sparkling inlet.

They had both eaten more than they were used to and each had adjusted their individual bucket seats as far back as they could go so that they could stretch out in the small car and relax as they talked.

"I hope that you don't mind me using you as a sounding board, Robyn. This case has so many ins and outs and the involvement of all your sister's high-placed bosses makes it a little difficult to discuss it openly with anyone within the department."

Robyn shook her head and snuggled down into her seat a little deeper.

"If you will remember, it was me who asked you if I could use you for the same purpose first. Not only don't I mind, I welcome it. I can at least be part of the search for Carol's killer this way."

David nodded and started in.

"Okay, the first problem is the complexities of the investigation. Not from the point of view that it's an unusually difficult case as such, because I don't think that's the situation, but because of the involvement of CLEU and even more cumbersome, that of CSIS"

Robyn straightened slightly in her seat and she turned to look more directly at him.

"CSIS?"

David nodded.

Yes, the Canadian Security and Intelligence Service, Canada's CIA. They apparently got brought into it originally because of the names that popped up in the diary. If they were conducting discrete inquiries on their own I wouldn't concern myself with them, but it seems they have launched a determined effort to take over the investigation in it's entirety if they can manage it, or at least do their best to see to it that I have to come to them for anything I need. To be honest, I don't trust them.

A quizzical expression filled Robyn's face.

"Why don't you trust them David?

He frowned and shook his head slowly.

"They are too damned political. I don't mean to suggest they would intentionally try to cover anything up. It's just that while both their methods and their results may seem satisfying to them, I doubt I'll be happy with either. Unfortunately, there is very little that I can do about their involvement. I bitched to my Deputy, Foster, today and he minces around the issue as though he's walking on eggshells. No one wants to square off with CSIS. They pack too much political clout and any cop who greatly displeases them and their masters can consider any future advancement a dim possibility. I can't blame Foster for being leery of it. He knows that the Chief is going to hang on for another ten years and that means he's looking for some political position for himself within the next year or two. If he screws around with CSIS, he won't have a snowball's chance in hell of getting what he's looking for. In so many words, he told me to get along with them and I have this sinking feeling that is going to be easier said than done."

He paused to tap out his pipe, refill it and light it up, opening the passenger side-window slightly, to let the smoke out.

"What should be a relatively straight forward search for a profession hit-man is turning into a three-ring-circus, and it seems there's nothing I can do about that at the moment. I'll just have to play it by ear. So, let me tell you what I've got so far and how I think it ads up."

The radio had been playing softly and Robyn, her interest sparked and some of the feeling of fullness in her stomach gone, reached over to shut it off so she could concentrate on what he was about to say.

"Motive: obviously the CLEU drug investigation was getting too close to those at the top of the drug organization for comfort. Your sister was acting as a cutout for the guys mentioned in the diary. She took her instructions from them, and then did the entire arranging of the day to day business, banking etc. That way they kept their hands clean and nothing could be traced directly back to them. They got worried that she'd either let something slip unintentionally or that the police would pick her up and offer her a deal to reveal their involvement. Something that was pretty likely, all things considered. They couldn't take that chance, so they killed her. In so doing, they no longer had any direct link to the operation. All they had to do was replace her with some other pawn and probably make some minor changes in the organization below her to ensure the CLEU investigation came up against a brick wall. Luckily for us they either didn't know about, or couldn't find the diary and it tells us what we need to know, even though, in itself, it's really not enough to make a solid case against them. Do you follow me so far?"

Robyn was listening intently. She moved into a more upright position and nodded. David took a few puffs on his pipe before continuing.

"Opportunity: We know from the way she was dressed that it wasn't likely to have been a stranger or even a john who made the hit on Carol. Had that been the case she would have refused him entry or she would have at least been made up and more presentable. She willingly let the murderer into her penthouse. There were no signs of forced entry. He couldn't have gained access in any other way. So she knew whoever killed her. Not just knew them, but knew them well enough to feel comfortable about turning her back on them to make a phone call. I'm picking up a list today of the people who regularly attended at the penthouse from CLEU's surveillance team's coordinator. That will give me photos and whatever names they've been able to verify. I could use your help there; maybe you'll know some of these people that we haven't been able to put names to."

Robyn nodded hesitantly and glanced out through the windshield at the massing black clouds that threatened to break open any minute with the predicted downpour of mixed rain and snow.

"I really didn't meet many of her associates. She was very careful to see to it that I didn't have contact with the wrong people, whoever they were."

"But, you did meet some?"

"Yes, but only some of the girls, people who were part of her call-girl operation. That was separate from whatever else she was doing and she never discussed the rest of her life. She only let me meet people who she considered as posing no danger to me. Oh, I sometimes saw others briefly, dropping off packages and that sort of thing."

Davis considered what she had said and nodded.

"Actually, if we can nail down some of those administrative types, they might well lead us back to the big boys at the top. If you're not doing anything tonight, how about we make an evening of it, we could have dinner and then mug-shots for dessert."

She looked away from the window and smiled at him.

"That sounds good to me. Want to come to my place? Believe it or not, I can cook."

David shrugged and exhaled a final puff from his pipe before resting it on the dash in front of him.

"I was going to suggest my place, that is, if you feel adventurous and aren't frightened by boat trips in the dark."

Obviously intrigued, she flashed him a questioning look.

"Boat rides in the dark, sounds awfully mysterious or else very romantic."

David laughed.

"I suppose it could be either, depending upon your frame of mind. Anyway, it's up to you. Your place or mine?"

Robyn was very curious by this point and couldn't refuse the invitation.

"Who could resist a boat ride in the dark?"

He reached across to the ignition, checked to see that the car was in neutral, and then cranked it into life.

"Okay, it's a date. I'll pick you up about five-thirty and we can finish going over the case while we're looking at the photographs tonight. I've got to run now; couple of things to look into this afternoon."

Robyn found herself a little disappointed at the realization that his lunch break was over. She had been enjoying spending time with him and wasn't anxious for it to end, but she slipped the car into reverse and turned to look over her shoulder as she backed up to turn around.

"This morning, I had a chance to go over the envelopes that Carol left for me. One of them is a special release form for her safety deposit box. With the key and a signed release form, I can empty the box without all the hassle of death certificates and that sort of thing and I thought that I might as well plan on doing that this afternoon. If you have time, maybe you'd like to come along to get a first-hand look at what's inside."

Walker glanced at his watch and did some quick calculating.

"When were you planning to go and where is the bank?"

"It's the Royal at Granville and Robson; I've made an appointment for three o'clock."

"How about I meet you there?"

"Okay, I'll be there at about ten to three."

David shook his head and made a mad grab for his pipe as she shifted the spirited little car into second gear and slewed around a corner.

"No, that doesn't make sense. In that area of town, parking is going to be at a premium at that time of the day. I won't have any problem finding parking for a police car. Why don't I pick you up at your apartment at about a quarter to three and then we can go to the bank and then directly out to my place from there."

CHAPTER SIXTEEN

Walker parked his unmarked unit in a loading zone and made his way through the drunks and hypes to the pawn shop beyond.

The smell of must and accumulated filth assailed his nostrils as he stepped inside to be greeted by the jingling of the bell attached to the top of the dingy door.

The proprietor pushed aside a greasy curtain that divided the store from what served as living quarters at the back of the building and began waddling toward the front as David moved up to the counter.

The two men were not strangers.

They had met fairly regularly when David, as a detective, had put in his six months with the stolen property section. Part of his routine at that time had been to check with each pawn shop on a regular basis to keep them up to date on what stolen property was likely to show up and at the same time check to ensure that no stolen merchandise had somehow appeared on the shelves and in the windows of the different premises.

Recognition registered in the fat man's face as he wedged his bulk up behind the counter with some difficulty.

"Yes officer, and what can I do for you today?"

Walker didn't reply immediately. He wanted a second to assess the other man anew and mentally structure the approach he was going to use on him. He recalled that the fat man had been convicted for the possession of stolen goods previously, at least twice, but that had been a long time ago. He also remembered that the man facing him was no fool.

"Hymie, I'm Inspector Walker, you obviously remember me from years ago, when I was in the detective division. He flashed his badge at the man and continued.

"I have in my pocket a statement that implicates you in the

fencing of several articles. I also have a body to go with the statement, and that body is very willing to testify against you in a court of law. It's important for me to receive information from you on one of the articles you handled for this man; a gun, and, if, you provide me with the information I want, I'm prepared to forget the statement and the witness and leave you in peace."

The expression on the other man's face did not change. The eyes however, grew perceptively smaller, almost rat-like. He didn't speak for some time and Walker was tempted to say more, but held himself in check letting the silence work on the fat man.

Hymie finally spoke.

"You would of course be willing to supply me with some details of this serious, and I assure you, unfounded accusation. It may be that I have been used in some way, perhaps in a weak moment felt sorry for someone and didn't check well enough on the background of some goods he wished to pawn..."

Walker cut him off.

"Spare me the bullshit Hymie!"

He pulled out a copy of the statement he had taken earlier from the B&E artist and passed it across the grungy counter to the other man.

"Here, read it, take your time. Then you can decide to tell me what I want to know or I'll haul your fat ass downtown and close this place up permanently; and I'll do it today."

David turned away from the counter and busied himself looking at the menagerie of articles that hung from every available inch of the wall and ceiling.

He watched the fat man out of the corner of his eye and noted with some satisfaction the beads of perspiration breaking out on the other man's forehead despite the bitter coldness of the interior of the shop.

* * * * *

The accountant had concealed the bogus passport that had been provided and used the real one to purchase the ticket. Standing well back and observing until just prior to departure had offered reasonable assurance that no one was watching when the steward provided the necessary boarding pass.

Not travelling First Class this time, but after all, this flight wasn't a gift. Besides, the cancellation of the LA to Mexico flight had netted a reasonable return and more than covered the replacement ticket, an expensive lunch and three drinks.

All in all, one couldn't complain.

* * * * *

The sweat was running down the fat man's face in rivulets now. Pudgy fingers twisted the pages of the statement this way and that, turning it to the light as the little rat-like eyes slowly digested its contents.

David worked his way back over to the counter and was face to face with the other man when he finally looked up from the document.

"A gun you say Inspector. If memory serves, a nice little pearl-handled twenty-two automatic, give me a second, I'll just have a look at my records in the back."

This time he moved very quickly for a man of his bulk and David got the first hint that his threat was going to produce some positive results. Finally he was getting some breaks in the investigation and the overcast and snow-mixed-with-rain day had instantly become less depressing for him.

A few moments later, the fat man worked his way back to the front of the store

"A woman, maybe mid twenties to early thirties-a
looker-we've done business before."

David took out his notebook and a pen and began to make notes.

"Okay, white female, about thirty. Height?"

The fat man rubbed his two day stubble thoughtfully.

"Fairly tall, and like I said, a looker; expensive clothes and a good body."

"Color, length of hair?"

"Long, to the shoulders, dark brown or black."

"What was she wearing, did you see a car? You get a name?"

The fat man smirked.

"Said her name was Archer...Ms. Archer; for what it's worth. She was wearing a suit of some light material, very summery, with flowers."

"Would you be able to identify her if you saw her again?"

"Yes, like I said, we've done business before."

David looked up from his notes.

"What kind of business?"

Hymie shrugged.

"The same kind, a couple of times. Always twenty-twos, I think."

David took a business card out of his jacket pocket and laid it on the counter.

"You remember anything else, you give me a call."

The fat man sensed that the immediate pressure was off, and he visibly relaxed.

"This better be legit Hymie. If I find out you've been snowing me, I'll put you away for the rest of your natural life. You're not off the hook yet on this. You see what more you can dig up. You see this person again, you get all the information you can and you call me immediately."

He turned and walked out of the pawnshop.

He was about to unlock the door of the police car but changed his mind, slipped the keys back into his pocket and began to look for a pay phone.

* * * * *

Mrs. Ferguson muttered an oath under her breath and removed the binoculars from her eyes.

The ringing of the phone was normally a welcome intrusion into an otherwise uneventful day; but she'd just spotted a pod of Killer whales frolicking in the centre of the Arm, just in front of her little house, and she was loathe to leave it.

David knew her well enough to register the slight note of impatient displeasure in her voice when she answered. He knew better than to ask what particular activity he had interrupted.

"Jenny, it's David. I'm bringing a guest home for supper tonight. Do you think that you could take a couple of steaks out of the freezer for me and make sure the place is shipshape?"

Not a touch of displeasure remained in the voice now, only a recognizable edge of curiosity.

"I'd be glad too. Shipshape you say? Could this guest be a female by any chance?"

David laughed.

"Settle down Jenny. It's business. She's giving me a hand with an investigation."

It wasn't in Mrs. Fergusons nature to let the matter lie there.

"Old and ugly then, is she?"

"No, as a matter of fact she twenty-six and far from ugly, but it's still business."

There was slight pause before he received a response.

"Have you considered inviting her for the night? It's not going to be much fun making two trips in the boat in this weather"

David knew exactly what she was actually getting at, and yet, in consideration of the time of year, he had to admit that beyond the ill-concealed innuendo, the suggestion had merit. He and Robyn wouldn't likely be finished going over the material he wanted to cover till late. The thought of boating and driving her home in the late evening or early morning hours didn't particularly appeal to him, especially in consideration of the unpredictable weather. Robyn wasn't working, so it probably wouldn't make any difference to her one way or the other. The idea of her staying overnight really made a great deal of sense now that Jenny had suggested it."

"You've got a point Jenny. Just in case, maybe you could make up one of the spare rooms, and put some guest towels out while you're at it."

Another pause.

"The spare room you say?"

David laughed despite himself.

"Yes Jenny. The spare room!"

*****

In order for him to ensure that all his bases were covered, Walker spent a half hour at CLEU.

Although he had already sent a team to gather everything they could, he had arranged with Bob to personally but unofficially go over the material amassed so far in the investigation.

Wright had suggested there was a small office that might be unlocked and empty at that time of day and that possibly he might find the material he was interested in being stored there temporarily.

He wasn't sure but believed there may also be a photocopier in that particular office.

Knowing the material would probably not be available to him so readily in the future, David perused all the pertinent information the nightshift surveillance crews had put together, selected what he wanted and photo-copied it quickly

In the files there were also numerous photographs of members of both sexes entering and leaving the penthouse elevator. For the most part, the quality was good. He was sure that, providing she'd met them previously, it would provide Robyn with material of sufficient quality to allow her to provide information on any of those that had not already been positively identified.

He ran copies of everything he considered might possibly be relevant and placed the bundle into his briefcase then went down the hall to Wright's office to see if he was in. But the door, as it had been when he arrived, was closed and locked.

He then picked up the phone in Wright's outer office.

Robyn answered on the second ring.

"Hi, this isn't what it sounds like, but, how about spending the night at my place. By the time we go through this stuff, it's going to be late and running you home will be a real hassle for both of us. I've got spare bedrooms and you could come back into town with me in the morning."

Robyn's immediate response was laughter.

It served to ease the concern that he'd had that she might misunderstand the suggestion and he joined her with a chuckle of his own.

"It really would be easier, if you don't mind. You may not have to stay of course. We might get finished up early - it's hard to say. I just wanted to give you a heads up on the possibility."

"No problem. I'll pack an overnight bag just in case."

David was pleased that she seemed okay with the suggestion.

"You'll be roughing it, boat rides and all. Don't dress up, jeans and a warm coat, that kind of thing. Pick you up in about fifteen to twenty minutes."

* * * * *

The accountant added one more item to the list of things to do that day and then put away the pen and notebook.

The cabin speakers had just informed the passengers that due to a favorable tailwind, the flight to Vancouver International would be arriving approximately one half hour ahead of schedule.

The gods were smiling.

It was going to be difficult to manage what had to be accomplished in the time available as it was, and an extra half-hour was bound to come in handy.

*****

Robyn was flushed from the effort of trying on pair after pair of jeans.

Settling on the sleeveless T-shirt had been easy. She'd had many compliments from past admirers on its glove-like fit and with the soft bra it was a knockout, leaving little, if anything to the imagination.

She'd wear a sweater over it of course, but once in the house...

The jeans were something else. She'd narrowed it down to a very faded and well-worn stonewashed light blue pair of 501's and a fairly new, but almost embarrassingly tight pair of black stretch denims.

She was currently checking out the rear view of the 501's in her full length mirror. The fit was very much like that of the T-shirt that she had already selected, and they did make a nice combination.

The apartment intercom buzzed and she swore softly.

Christ, she hadn't even finished packing the overnight bag yet, and he was here!

CHAPTER SEVENTEEN

David waited for Robyn in one of the small cubicles while she and a bank employee went into the vault area with their respective keys.

When Robyn returned, he moved quickly out of the chair and crossed to help her as she and the bank employee approached.

"My God, that isn't a box, it's a suitcase!"

The container was in fact fairly large, but relatively light and Robyn laughed.

Between them they lifted it up onto the table in the centre of the cubicle where he had been waiting for her. This accomplished, the young bank clerk smiled and discreetly left the small room, leaving them alone.

Robyn inserted the separate key that Carol had left for her and opened the large container. The lid was hinged about three-quarters of the way back and it swung open easily to reveal the contents.

Robyn took the items out one at a time.

One thick manila envelope, sealed with her name on it, a similar envelope with CLEU typed on it, and six video tapes, each labeled with a man's name. They exchanged glances and Robyn used a fingernail to open the manila envelope with her name on it.

She pulled out the single typewritten sheet and began to read out loud.

'*Dear Robyn. If you are reading this then you're on your own and I hope that what I've been able to tuck away over the past couple of years will help to make the rest of your life a little easier. There is only one bank account, which I'm sure you already know about. It should contain a fairly considerable amount as I'm adding to it rapidly these days. The tapes you find in this box are some that I made of a few of my clients. The people involved have become or were already very prominent at the time and each of them has very good reason for not to wanting these tapes showing up for public viewing. I've kept them here as a form of insurance in case something went wrong, a very sensible idea, in consideration of just how deeply I'm becoming involved in other areas of my business. It was my intention to use them to apply pressure and to buy my way out of any difficulties that I might have with these men, should they arise in the future. To date, I've only had to use one tape in that way, to make sure that a police CLEU investigation into my activities was thwarted and to secure a good chunk of cash should it become necessary for any reason to drop out of sight for awhile.*

I've never been much good to the world, but I made that choice early on in my life and I don't regret it. I would like however, to do one thing right before the world forgets me though, and these tapes are my way of doing that.

Please see that they, along with the other envelope, get turned over to CLEU as quickly as you can. They'll know how to use them effectively, I'm sure.

Be careful about this sis. There is no reason to believe that any one knows about these tapes but you and me. Don't fool around with them, just deliver them right now and forget them. DO NOT open the envelope, and please don't look at the tapes themselves.

You are the only good thing that I've ever known in my life and I wish you all the happiness in the world!

FIND THAT MAN, and remember sis, I loved you very much.

XO XO XO XO

Carol'

Robyn's eyes were misty and David searched his pockets for a clean handkerchief for her. She managed tissue from her purse before he could come up with one and he picked up the tapes and gave them a cursory examination to keep occupied and to give her a chance to regain her composure.

A few seconds later she gave a good blow and smiled weakly at him. He gave her a brief hug before he spoke.

"Quite a girl, that sister of yours. I wonder what's on these tapes. Let's hope that she managed to get the six of them incriminating themselves in the drug conspiracy."

"You think she may have made these without them knowing and got them to talk about the drugs without realizing they were being recorded?"

"I've got no idea, but whatever is on them, I'm pretty sure they don't know that she was filming them at the time, and if it is that kind of thing we'd have them cold."

"What will we do with them?"

David put his briefcase on the table and opened it. He took the time to rearrange the contents, before placing the tapes and both envelopes into it and snapping the clasps into place.

"Well, we don't take them to CLEU, that's for sure. Once we know what they contain, we'll have a better idea of where they should go. Would you like to watch some movies tonight after dinner?"

* * * * *

David carried two lifejackets and his briefcase as he lead the way down the hill from where they had left the police car. He held Robyn's arm to offer support over any small patches of ice that may have formed due to the rapidly dropping temperature and was strangely pleased to find that she'd had more sense than most of his visitors and was wearing light boots, with solid ribbed soles.

At the bottom, they moved onto the ramp that led out to the government wharf and when they reached the end he put his briefcase into the boat, tossed the lifejackets into the cabin and returned to take her proffered overnight bag from her.

"Hop aboard; I'll just be a second untying her."

He held her hand to steady her as she stepped into the boat then set her overnight bag down beside her before turning to untie the boat from the dock.

It was rolling gently as result of the wake from a passing speedboat and he was careful to see that the motion of the craft didn't crush his fingers as he worked the partially frozen ropes loose.

Once the wake of the other vessel had passed, David's boat stopped its rocking. The unpredictable weather had mellowed somewhat, and it was promising to turn into a crisp, clear evening.

When he climbed aboard, he found Robyn standing in the stern. She had her arms wrapped around herself and was staring up into the sky.

"It's so beautiful and peaceful, hard to believe that we're only twenty minutes away from the centre of Vancouver."

David fired up the engine, flipped on the running lights and expertly guided the sleek craft around the flashing green beacon and out into the main channel.

Robyn made her way up to join him. The drone of the big motor made conversation impossible and Robyn turned her attention to the rapidly passing shoreline and the lighted houses and wharves that shimmered in the cold evening air.

The run up Indian Arm to David's house in North Vancouver from the government wharf was a short one. It took only four minutes to complete.

Arriving at the small, rocky peninsula upon which his home was perched, David edged into his wharf and stepped out to tie up before helping Robyn out of the boat to join him.

David then jumped back aboard and brought the briefcase and overnight case out of the boat and onto the gently rocking, floating pier. The lights for the ramp and dock, which were controlled by motion detectors, fully illuminated the area.

He had tied the boat down fore and aft, and then rejoined her. They had no difficulty in making their way up to the top. David did, however, warn her to be on the lookout for icy patches as they moved toward the attached stairs that led up to the house above.

Once they had covered the short distance to the bottom of the stairway and up to the front porch of the house, David set the bag and briefcase down on the porch.

"Stay here for a second; I just want to prepare my roommate for your arrival."

If David noticed the look of disappointment on her face he gave no indication of it as he entered the house and closed the door behind him.

Inside, he paused long enough to give an excited Cato a welcoming pat and then took him out through the kitchen and into the laundry room. He put the big dog into a down-stay and then closed the door and retraced his steps to the front door.

He opened it and waved Robyn inside as he picked up the briefcase and overnight case and followed her into the house.

He put them down just inside the door, slipped out of his coat and helped her with hers before gesturing in the general direction of the couch on the other side of the room.

"Grab a seat there and when Cato comes in, just ignore him completely. He'll probably come straight over to you and check you out, but if you ignore him, he'll come over to me after a few seconds.

David took note of the quizzical look on her face, but before she could respond he had left the room and she did as he had asked and sat down where he had indicated.

Seconds later, the big Rottweiler bounded into the room ahead of David. His head was in the air, immediately registering the scent of a stranger in the house and he moved directly across the living room toward her.

He made no sound as he sniffed her carefully, and then looked up at her.

Robyn had never been afraid of dogs. She normally got along fine with them in fact; but the massive bulk of Cato was enough to intimidate anyone and she gave an audible sigh of relief when, as David had predicted, the dog left her and crossed over to properly welcome his master home.

David smiled across at her and gave the dog a vigorous rub down, then went over to the front door and let him outside for a run. He closed the door and returned to where Robyn sat and his smile broadened.

"You did very well. He'll be fine with you now, just don't initiate any contact with him until he gets completely used to you and accepts you as belonging. Let him come to you when he wants to, but feel free to pet and speak with him if you want."

He turned back to the door and let a waiting Cato back inside.

The dog stayed with David for a few seconds, letting his master roughhouse a little with him then he returned to where Robyn was sitting and after giving her a sniff, promptly rested his big head squarely in her lap.

Robyn gave David an enquiring look and he grinned in response. She then reached out somewhat hesitantly at first and began to scratch Cato behind the ear.

In response, Cato's back end went into action as he happily wagged his little stump of a tail. Robyn relaxed and was immediately at ease with the dog and David's grin was replaced with a laugh.

"You should feel honored; he very rarely warms up to someone new that quickly. I'm going to start a fire and let you two get to know each other and then I'll show you around this disaster that he and I call home."

The house was heated electrically and it wasn't cold, but David enjoyed the sight and sound of a roaring fire when he was home in the winter months.

He crossed over to the big stone fireplace in the centre of the far living room wall and went to work. Within a few minutes flames were crackling cheerily around the kindling and working their way up to the wood above, and David stood and turned to face Robyn and the dog.

"Okay Cato, you've had her for long enough. Way you go."

The dog lifted his head from Robyn's lap and moved across the room to lie down in front of the big glass doors that filled one end of the long living room wall that fronted on the ocean, and opened onto the massive deck that ran along, and extended out over and beyond the shoreline.

David crossed to where Robyn was sitting and offered her his hand to help her up.

They began on the bottom floor: laundry room, compact but very functional kitchen, bathroom and then back into the combination living and dining room with its solid glass wall of ocean view. They ended up in front of the glass doors.

David opened them and led her outside and Cato immediately got to his feet and followed them out onto the deck.

Robyn moved with David over to the far railing and even in the darkness, she marveled at the beauty as she looked out over the water and took in the one hundred and eighty degree vista. She whistled softly.

"It's breathtaking David, I love it."

He nodded.

"Yes it really is, wait until you see it in the daylight."

They stood leaning against the railing for several minutes without speaking, then he continued.

"It's low tide right now, but at high tide, the deck extends a good ten feet out over the water. I regularly fish for Rock Cod from here at high tide."

Robyn turned her eyes upward to the sky and marveled at what she saw.

"The stars really stand out. It's like we are miles away from any civilization. It's absolutely awesome!"

David followed her gaze and smiled.

"Yes, hard to believe that we are so close to town. We came up here, Jackie and I, to look at some waterfront lots and kind of stumbled over this place. The house was for sale and although it wasn't what he were looking for, and obviously was in need of a great deal of TLC, Jackie wanted to 'just take a look'. We signed the papers that night and I've never regretted buying it."

Robyn shivered slightly and shifted a little closer to him.

He sensed that she was getting cold and he took her hand and lead her back inside the house.

Cato followed and David closed the door behind them.

"It's so remote feeling, and peaceful."

David smiled.

"The fact that it can only be reached by boat is a bit of a hassle some times, but, for the most part, I find that I enjoy even that. It seems to give me time to think things out and clear my brain. The road will be coming through in a few years, at least that's the story making the rounds. It will make getting in and out easier, deliveries and that kind of thing, but I'll miss that daily boat ride back and forth. When that happens of course the value of the property will sky-rocket and unfortunately the taxes on this place will keep in step and it will probably become too expensive for me to hang on to."

He glanced at the open stairway at the other end of the living room by the front door.

"C'mon, I'll show you the upstairs and then we'll see about rustling up some grub; you must be starved. Don't expect too much of the house by the way; it was built at the turn of the century as a summer cottage, as were most of the places on Indian Arm, and each successive owner has added on it seems. I look at it as a long-term project and do a little updating or expanding whenever I find the money and the time."

After that they toured all the upstairs rooms: the bathroom and the three bedrooms. David had added two of the bedrooms on to the original structure. The original master bedroom with its own full bathroom had been completely updated and David had put in a new bathroom at the other end of the second floor when he'd built the bedrooms.

When they had finished they returned to the living room and David added a couple of logs to the cheerily crackling flames, then led her across the room and entered the small kitchen.

"I'm afraid that I'm not much of a cook, but the place is well stocked; freezer in the laundry room is full and so is the fridge. I asked Jenny to leave a couple of steaks out to thaw. They're probably in the fridge."

Robyn gave him a quizzical look and he grinned.

"Jenny is Mrs. Ferguson, my neighbor and part time housekeeper. She's sixty-two years old, a widow and a going concern. She sort of took me under her wing after Jackie died. Seemed a little strange at first but when I look back on it now, I don't know what I would have done without her."

Robyn's features softened.

"She sounds nice."

David nodded.

"She's great. If you'd like to meet her, we could invite her over for an after dinner drink. I'm sure she's dying to meet you. I don't get many visitors and she tends to be on the curious side whenever I do, especially when they are of the female gender."

Robyn laughed.

"Yes let's do that. I'd like to meet her."

David confirmed that the steaks were indeed in the refrigerator and moved them out onto the counter and then began to wander around opening cupboards.

Robyn noted that they were crammed to overflowing with canned goods.

"My God David, you're a hoarder!"

He laughed.

"It was Jackie who got me started. She always liked to have two spares of everything. Figured we might get snowed in or something I guess. After she died, I just sort of replaced whatever I used and it's pretty well stayed the same as it was then I guess."

She shook her head slowly and then smiled across at him.

"Look, would you mind if I cooked? I love doing it and I don't get much chance, living alone as I do."

David grinned broadly.

"I thought that you'd never ask. Be my guest and make yourself at home. I prefer white wine to red if that's okay with you? I'll shove a bottle in the fridge to chill and mix us a couple of before dinner drinks while you're organizing the food. I usually make up a batch of Martini's when I get home at night. What'll you have?"

She reached for the steaks and began to open them, turning her head to look at him.

"White wine with dinner and a Martini now sounds good to me."

David slipped the bottle of wine into the freezer compartment of the fridge and then went out to the bar in the corner of the large living room to fix up a batch of Martinis.

CHAPTER EIGHTEEN

The accountant couldn't hold back a smile.

The information with regard to the specific account upon which the check had been written had been provided and it had been necessary for the issuing bank to put a hold on the funds that were now being paid out.

It had been close, just before closing time, but once the check had been presented there was the cash, just as requested by telephone from LA International earlier in the day.

An explanation as to why the accountant wanted such a large amount in cash had not been required, but it had seemed prudent to offer some reason for such a large withdrawal.

The idea that the cash was required to complete a rush house purchase had seemed a little feeble at the time but had been accepted without question by the bank employee responsible for the transaction.

The briefcase had been considered overly large when purchased at the airport after landing back in Vancouver, but once the check had been cashed, it turned out that it was no more then adequate for the job of containing the crisp stacks of banded bills as they were presented.

*****

The damn meetings had dragged on all day.

He had planned to close down the account the accountant's check had been drawn on that afternoon, but it had been impossible for him to get away. He was disturbed by this interference with his plans, but not particularly worried. After all, the accountant would be spending most of the day travelling and within a few hours would cease to be of any concern.

Closing the account first thing in the morning would have to suffice.

*****

They ate in front of the fire, Robyn, at her insistence, cross-legged on the floor, David using the front of the couch as a backrest and the coffee table between them for his plate and wine glass.

He had been joking earlier when he'd intimated that she would be ravenous as a result of the boat ride.

In consideration of how much and how well they had eaten at lunch, he found himself watching her in awe, as she dug into the simple, but more than ample meal she had prepared for them, promptly and eagerly devouring the large steak and accompanying garden fresh salad.

Robyn was clearly enjoying the meal as much as he was, and he put her surprising capacity for food down to the fact that she was highly active and probably burned off calories at double the rate he did.

Robyn's attention to her food had given him time to observe her quietly. He knew that just watching her obvious enjoyment in the simple meal was part of the reason that he was feeling so mellow and comfortable at having her with him.

In the subdued lighting in the living room the cold and now crystal clear night provided a perfect stage for the nearly full moon. The sound of the waves gently lapping at the shoreline and the heat thrown by the brightly burning fireplace combining with the flickering shadows added to the ambience. Together they managed to ensure a warm, relaxing and laidback atmosphere.

But for David, it was Robyn's presence in the room that competed, and was certainly central to the serenity of the evening.

The more he learned about her the more he liked her.

His mind drifted, recalling the women he'd been with

since Jackie. He hadn't felt this way with any of them. Robyn was special, not in exactly the same way as Jackie had been, but special none the less.

David was far too practical a man to accept anything as fact simply because it existed. He always needed to know why.

His analytical mind, occasionally picky and slow, but more often than not, faultlessly correct, came into play, turning and twisting the dilemma of Robyn and breaking it down into its basic parts. What was it that attracted him to her?

Initially, it had been personality and an outgoing, positive outlook. Then there was looks. All were attributes that she shared with Jackie.

Robyn's voice cut into his thoughts.

"You've been staring at me as if mesmerized for the last ten minutes."

David was slightly embarrassed, both at being caught watching her, and in consideration of the content of his thoughts. A slight blush warmed the tops of his cheeks.

He shrugged and took a forkful of steak and placed it into his mouth, and quickly noted that it was turning from lukewarm to cold. He chewed and swallowed before he answered her.

"Just thinking"

Robyn placed her empty plate down on the hearth beside her and lifted her wine glass, holding it in preparation to drink.

"I surmised that you were thinking, what I wondered was what it was that you were thinking about. Is it something about the case? If so, share. We are partners in this you know."

Relieved to find that she believed that his previous thoughts had related to the investigation and not centered on her, David recovered his composure and laughed.

"First it's friends, now its partners. I'll have to keep my eye on you, I can see that."

Robyn, who had been finishing her wine off in one quick swallow, almost choked on it as she joined him, their laughter filling the air and warming the cozy room even more.

Her eyes briefly rested on him in the flickering light given off by the fireplace.

In that split second Robyn realized that she was beginning to care very deeply for this complex man.

Try as she might, she could no more explain or rationalize it to herself than she could fly.

The realization struck her hard. She had imagined, she had even fantasized, but this had the potential of becoming so much more than any of that.

Oblivious to the thoughts going through Robyn's head and anxious to cover his own mental meanderings, David ploughed ahead.

"We'd better get finished up here and get to work partner, or we'll be up all night."

Robyn nodded in agreement and pivoted upward on her heels, coming to her feet in one swift motion while balancing both her empty plate and wineglass.

She did not find the thought of staying up all night the slightest bit appealing.

She couldn't remember when she had been looking forward to bed more.

"I'll wash up. Why don't you give Mrs. Ferguson a call and we can have that drink with her now. It won't take me a minute to clear up."

David finished his plate hastily, the temperature of the food now going unnoticed. His eyes had been on her as she got up and were still on her as she moved effortlessly toward the kitchen.

Robyn had no way of knowing of course, but her frenzied concern earlier in the day over what to wear had just paid off handsomely. His attention was glued to the movement of her full breasts, whose predominant dark brown nipples were clearly outlined as she walked, nor did he miss the gentle roll of her high firm ass as she left the room.

The stirring deep in his loins was strong and immediate.

He found himself momentarily immobilized as he digested

what his eyes were telling him and savored the wave of pure animal desire that swept through him. He consciously checked the sensation, stood, and crossed over to his desk and picked up the phone.

As he had expected, Jenny was waiting, none too patiently, by the phone and answered on the first ring.

And not surprisingly, she would be most pleased to drop down for a drink!

*****

He had no more than showered and changed for dinner when the phone rang. The color drained from his face when he recognized the voice on the other end of the line. It took him a second to calm himself before he answered.

"This is a surprise. You're supposed to be out on the beach enjoying the Mexican sunshine."

"I made a slight adjustment to my itinerary. You must have thought me a real fool to believe that a short stay in Mexico was going to be a satisfactory means of dealing with things. I'm a professional, remember. But we won't talk any more of that. The past is the past and we need to look to the future. In consideration of our successful previous endeavors and with a view to our future partnership, we'll simply have to let bygones be bygones, won't we? Meet me at the Rose Garden in Stanley Park in an hour; we need to talk privately."

The phone went dead in his hand. He just stood there staring at it for an eternity.

For the first time in more years than he could remember, he felt the cold chill of raw fear rippling up his spine.

*****

Mrs. Ferguson was everything Robyn had expected her to be and more. The energetic, kindly faced little lady was no doubt over sixty, but she didn't act or think it.

She and Robyn hit it off the instant she walked in the door and exchanged appraising looks.

"It's business only then, is it, David?"

Her mischievous eyes sparkled as she gave David a sharp poke to the solar plexus.

Robyn flashed him a questioning look, but the old lady's mood was catching and they were soon all laughing over the 'private joke'.

When they had finished she took Robyn's hands in hers and beamed.

"Very pleased to meet you dear, I'm sure. David is a very lucky man, if I'm any judge."

Knowing only too well that he would try to dismiss her comment with some sort of foolishness, she turned on him.

"Lord knows he has some good luck coming, even if he probably doesn't have the sense to take advantage of it when it's staring him in the face."

If Robyn had taken an instant liking to Mrs. Ferguson before, she was now moving that up a notch to a sincere hope of budding friendship. She would probably need all the help that she could muster when it came to dealing with the cementing of a long-term relationship with David, and that was something she was certainly considering at this point, and she immediately recognized an ally when she met one.

She exchanged broad smiles with Mrs. Ferguson as she spoke.

"I'll get the brandy."

* * * * *

He had dithered for a good half hour, trying to come up with a way, any way to get out of the meeting, but try as he might; he knew that it was inevitable. He forced himself to face that reality, and plan accordingly.

He did his best to put himself in the accountants' shoes.

What would he do if he were the accountant?

Obviously a continuation of the old arrangement was now impossible for several reasons. What had been implied by the suggestion of a partnership? It had to mean the tapes; it couldn't be anything else, could it? It must be the natural attraction of the possibilities of blackmail. The accountant was very much aware that he had possession of the tapes. Was it therefore likely that the accountant intended to horn in on the proceeds that they could potentially deliver?

If that was the case, then he was in the driver's seat simply because he had physical control of the tapes. Viewed in that light, it wasn't so bad. The accountant needed him alive and co-operating.

He would do as he was asked for now and use the time it bought him to come up with some method of removing the danger permanently.

Time was on his side.

*****

Neither of them had laughed much over the past few days, but it was impossible not to laugh when Jenny was in the room.

She told tall tales, risqué jokes and found the funny side of almost everything. The woman was so straightforward that she was completely incapable of guile or subterfuge.

Without actually coming out and saying so, she left no doubt in either David's or Robyn's minds that she sensed their mutual attraction and that she wholeheartedly supported it.

Although Robyn had still been somewhat unsure of her future prospects in regard to David and David was very much concerned about the complications of a serious relationship with her, Jenny's recognition, acceptance and unbounded enthusiasm for their budding mutual affection made it seem not only plausible but the only sensible outcome.

This, coupled with the warm glow left by the air of comradeship and the wonderfully relaxing sensations of general contentment spreading within their bodies in the wake of the brandies they had consumed, left them feeling very at ease and comfortable in each other's company.

An hour later, David and Robyn stood on the porch, each with an arm around the other, and watched as Jenny began to carefully, but determinedly, make her way up the stairs to her little cabin nestled snugly on the crest of the cliff above.

CHAPTER NINETEEN

Alone with Robyn again, David felt himself very relaxed and would have been content to continue enjoying the light and laid back atmosphere Jenny had left in her wake.

Such was his tranquil state that he was nowhere near as eager to get started on the contents of his briefcase as he had been before Mrs. Ferguson's visit. He was however, resigned to the task, and once they had closed the door behind Jenny he crossed over to his desk where he had left his briefcase.

As he opened it and spread the contents out, then began to organize them. Robyn scooped up the three empty brandy glasses and started in the direction of the kitchen.

"You get things ready; I'll wash these up and put them away."

David applied himself to the task; his interest spiked a little as he stacked the six tapes on the corner of the desk. He had everything ready to go when she rejoined him, bringing along a dining room chair with her so that she could sit beside him at his desk.

As she sat down, David laid the photographs and accompanying fact sheets that he'd picked up from CLEU earlier, directly in front of her.

"These are the shots taken in the apartment block entrance hall. They're pretty good considering the light in there. The reports offer what information we have on the subject of each photograph. Almost all of them have been identified, but let's take them one at a time and see what you know about each of them."

Robyn picked up the first glossy five by eight shot and leaned forward to tilt it out of the direct light to reduce the reflection.

"This is one of the girls that Carol used on an on-call basis.

There were three I believe; at least I met three of them at one time or another while visiting her. I think this girl was introduced as Candy something…Candy Apple. Not much help I'm afraid. It obviously wasn't her real name."

David looked up at her.

"According to the info I have on her, Candy Apple it is. It's a stage name. Her real name is Elizabeth Archer. She has a minor record for indecent exposure, and putting on a lewd performance. She bills herself as an exotic dancer. It indicates here that she's blonde, twenty-six years old, five foot ten, and very well proportioned. She turned up at your sister's fairly regularly while the surveillance was on. Try the next one."

Robyn put the first picture down and picked up the second.

"I only know her first name, Ursula."

"The notes have her as Ursula Kreski, brunette, five eight, good body, twenty-eight, minor record for soliciting. Next."

Robyn added Kreski's picture to the first one and selected the next. She studied it for some time before shaking her head.

"I don't know this one."

David consulted the sheet of paper in front of him.

"Her name is Melody Green. No record. Says here she went directly from high school into the military, quit after her first hitch and that she currently works as a part-time secretary-bookkeeper for a small firm. She's five eight, dark brown hair. Must have been moonlighting to make extra money"

Robyn nodded.

"Yes, I remember now, I only actually met her very briefly once but Carol told me a little about her. Apparently she did it for the kicks as much as for the money. She was the only one that considered it as almost a recreational activity."

David took a second look at the picture and shook his head as he added it to the others which were stacked at the top of the desk.

"To each his own I guess. Onward."

She reached for the next shot but he picked it up before she got to it.

"Don't worry about that one."

He placed it on top of the others she had already checked and then did the same with the next two.

"These are shots of members of the six. We know who they are, thanks to the diary, and the less you know about them, the better."

He sifted through the remaining photographs and added three more to the pile that she had begun. He then handed Robyn the next one from the original stack.

Robyn smiled and held the photograph so he could see it.

"This one's easy. That's Sheila Talbot. She and Carol knew each other from a way back. They kind of teamed up when Carol first went on the street. They've been friends for years. I think it was Sheila who first introduced Carol to the high rollers that eventually got her off the street and set her up in the apartment."

David took the photograph from her and added it to the checked pile at the top of the desk.

"That makes sense. She wasn't at the penthouse as often as the others and according to the surveillance notes, didn't seem to have visits that coincided with the arrival of the johns."

He then held up the last picture in his stack for her to see.

Robyn shook her head.

"No I've never met him.

David consulted the notes again and nodded.

"Only visited twice, and we haven't been able to put a name with the face as yet."

He put the photo to one side, gathered up the rest and put them back into his briefcase. We'll have to work on this one and find out who it is. To your knowledge, would any of these people that you met have a reason to want Carol dead?"

Robyn leaned back and shook her head.

"No, I think it has to have been the way you figured it, a professional hired by the drug people. I don't think it was any of the people in the photographs you showed me unless it was the guy in the last one."

David took a second look at the photo that she had referred to.

"Don't forget that it was someone she knew well, or she wouldn't have let him in."

Robyn shrugged.

"Then it must have been one of the six. She would have let one of them in and they were the only ones that had any reason to want her dead."

David shook his head.

"No, based on what I know of these men, I don't think any of them would have taken a chance like that. Nor would they have had the ability to do the job as professionally as it was done. I'll study these surveillance reports more carefully tomorrow and see if I can find some kind of pattern in anyone's visits that would fit in with the time of the killing. Unfortunately, we didn't have a camera working on the night of the murder itself, just an active phone tap."

David added the surveillance reports to the photographs in the briefcase and closed it then he looked across the room.

"Let's get comfortable and I'll finish bringing you up to date on the other facts I've got so far."

She followed him across to the couch and they sat down. David busied himself fixing a pipe, lit it, tossed the match into the fireplace and then leaned back and closed his eyes.

"How far did I get? Let's see, I covered motive and opportunity and we were talking about the possibility of you identifying any of the administrative types from the drug ring in the surveillance photographs. It's a little surprising that you didn't spot any of those."

"Not really. They would have probably arrived during the day when her johns were not there, and your people were taking photos of the people who came and went at night. They were concentrating on those who visited during the hours that Carol normally did her sex business weren't they? From what I now understand about the way she handled the two separate things, the johns and the drug part, it would seem to me that she basically ran one during the day and the other at night. Your people probably thought everything was done at night; that the two things were tied together and done at the same time. I don't think that she did it that way. "

David considered her words before he answered.

"Yes, that's true enough. All the shots we have were taken in the lobby and at night. We weren't concerned about what happened during the day. Not on a vice operation, which was what it started out as. I'll check tomorrow, but what you've suggested sounds reasonable in hindsight."

David opened his eyes and grinned broadly.

"You're beginning to think like a cop."

Robyn laughed.

"I certainly hope not. I'm a social worker, remember."

David chuckled.

"God, a cop and a social worker. What a partnership!"

He let his eyes close again and continued mentally marshalling the facts that he wanted to pass on to her.

He told her about the gun and the information he'd garnered from the pawn shop owner, the results from the coroner, and the lab. Robyn listened attentively, asking questions from time to time, clarifying points she didn't readily understand and questioning him as to what significance each point might hold in regard to the overall investigation.

When he had finished, he got up and crossed to the fire. He poked at the remnants of the logs and the flames perked up brightly.

Robyn was taking some time to consider the things he'd said and a final question occurred to her.

"You said the pawn shop owner identified the person who had been buying guns as Archer. Doesn't that mean that Archer is the murderer?

David glanced back at her and shook his head.

"No. Not necessarily. It's possible that whoever bought the guns was just using Archer's name. The hair color is also wrong, although that's a simple thing to change. All we know for certain from what the pawn broker told us is that the murderer was at least aware of who Archer was and that the person who picked up the guns, not necessarily the murderer by the way, was a woman. I'm not at the point of the investigation where I can say who did it yet with any certainty, but the pieces are slowly beginning to fall into place. I think this thing will make a lot more sense in few more days. In the meantime, it's going to take a good deal of basic legwork. But I'm beginning to have a good feeling about the way it's shaping up."

He stood up from the fire, stretched and yawned.

"It's getting late; we'd better run those tapes and get some shuteye."

Robyn got up and crossed to the desk to retrieve the tapes as David opened the cabinet and powered up the TV and the VCR.

*****

Despite his earlier rationalization that the accountant needed him, he was far from confident as he waited in the darkness.

The sudden sound of footsteps approaching brought the fear home. He began to sweat profusely as the figure suddenly appeared out of the night. He found himself unable to watch anything but the hands, expecting to see a flash and feel the searing heat of a bullet entering his body at any moment.

When he spoke, his voice was pitched higher than he would have liked. It exposed his fear as clearly as if he had shouted it into the darkness.

"Thank God, I was beginning to worry."

The response flowed easily, relaxed and confident.

"Afraid of the dark?"

A mirthless laugh punctuated the eerie stillness, and then the voice continued.

"If you use your head and do exactly as I ask, you've got nothing to be afraid of. Come, we'll walk as I explain it to you."

They moved off slowly, and he felt better now the initial contact was past and the fear of instant death was over. The accountant moved at a tranquil pace beside him and remained silent for a few seconds.

"You were planning on using the tapes to blackmail the others. I assume you reached that decision when you came to the conclusion that your other business dealings were about to come to an end due to the interest they've stimulated with the authorities. Blackmail was your plan to ensure you maintained your income level as best you could under those circumstances. I congratulate you on your scheme. Once I had taken the time to figure out what you had in mind, I could certainly see the potential."

They walked quietly for a few more paces before the accountant spoke again.

"There is no reason why your proposal shouldn't go ahead as planned. With one exception of course; we'll now be a team. I've thought it out carefully and I'm of the opinion that we can begin immediately. I've worked out the details and what I want from you are copies of all six tapes. We'll forward them with our demands for payment. I'm sure you've already ascertained what each is able and willing to pay. You'll receive the same demand as the others and in that way, should any of them wish to discuss the matter, you'll be able to play the part of injured party as well. In so doing, you'll be able to garner any clue that they may be considering some reaction other than the one which we desire. That will allow us to ensure we meet any such response with an effective counter measure. They'll soon learn that I have not met my demise as the six of you intended. When that happens, the blame for the blackmail will be laid directly at my feet. You'll be in a position to observe the others reactions over their dilemma and provide warning if, for example, they decide to look for me and do away with me again. It will make an unbeatable team effort, and I'm sure we'll have a long and profitable future together."

His mind had been working rapidly, assessing and weighing the words as they were spoken. His immediate concern was the protection of his own skin and he was looking for something in what the accountant was saying that would convince him that he was of more use alive than dead.

There was a hint of mutual need, but certainly no guarantee of long term security. Once he had turned over the tapes, what reason would the accountant have for letting him live? The vague inference that his presence within the group as a confidant and one who shared their plight was a reasonable enough claim on the face of it, but was it really enough to warrant keeping him alive and sharing the spoils of the endeavor?

Perhaps he was safe for the moment, but in time he was sure it would be much more convenient for the accountant to remove him than keep him around.

He sighed with resignation and nodded.

"It does appear that I have little choice but to agree."

The accountant slapped him lightly on the shoulder and smiled.

"We always have a choice; and in this case I think you've made a very sensible one. Tomorrow night, same time, same place, bring me all six tapes."

He shrugged and the question slipped out before he could stop it.

"Why did you give them to me in the first place? Why didn't you just keep them?"

"Because I wasn't sure of exactly what you'd planned for me. It wasn't until I boarded that plane this morning that I was absolutely sure of my fate. You'll never know how close I came to landing in Mexico. Lucky, wasn't I?"

High-pitched laughter floated on the air as the accountant slipped away and was lost to the darkness.

CHAPTER TWENTY

A cup of tea had appealed to both of them and David put on the kettle before they prepared to run the first tape. He brought in the steeping pot and two mugs, setting them down on the coffee table before removing the top tape from its container.

There was a label on the outside of the box. He showed it to her before taking the tape over to the machine and in inserting it.

It read 'RICHARD LONDON'.

Once he had returned to the couch and seated himself beside her, he hit the play button on the remote control.

The activity on the tape started abruptly, without preamble.

There were two naked women on a bed, which both he and Robyn immediately recognized as the king-sized one that resided in Carol's penthouse bedroom. The women were covered with perspiration and locked in a classic sixty-nine embrace. Within a few frames they had seen enough to ascertain that one of them was Carol and the other was Candy Apple.

Slightly off to the side and behind them stood a naked Richard London similarly covered in sweat and vigorously stroking his semi-erect penis with his right hand.

David reached forward and punched the 'stop' button on the remote.

"Jesus, I'm sorry Robyn. I had no idea that it was going to be this kind of movie!"

Robyn was obviously shaken by what she had seen. She still had her eyes glued to the now blank screen and was as pale as a ghost.

David swung around and inserted himself between her and the TV.

"Look, why don't you go up and take a nice hot bath. I'll skip through these quickly to make sure they're what I now think they are and then we can have a nightcap and turn in."

She nodded and stood up a little unsteadily.

"Damn, I wasn't ready for that."

David gave her a gentle push in the direction of the stairs.

"I've put your stuff in the bedroom on the right side of the hall. Jenny's laid out clean towels for you. Have a good soak. I'll give you a shout when I've finished up here."

She paused and turned back to face him.

"It's not what she was doing David, I accepted that a long time ago and I've learned to deal with it. It was just seeing her so very much alive like that."

He pointed to the stairs and she turned and began to climb them.

He stood watching until she disappeared from sight and then waited until he heard the bathwater begin to run before he hit first the 'play' button and then the 'fast forward'.

The same basic scene repeated itself several times as the tape moved rapidly to its conclusion. The girls involved changed from time to time, but the pitiful figure massaging his nearly flaccid organ never changed.

The box that held the next tape on the pile also had a label on it.

It read 'GEORGE CARSTAIRS'.

He checked the remaining boxes. Each was labeled in the same spot as the previous one. There was one tape for each of the six.

David watched a few minutes of each tape. London, a voyeur who couldn't quite get it up and reached climax only while watching two women making out, Carstairs, who seemed to have an endless craving to eat pussy, Banks who at least appeared to enjoy all the various aspects of sex with a single woman and Kincaid who favored standing above a kneeling Carol and watching with glazed eyes as she brought him to orgasm orally.

The final two tapes covered the last of them, Hampton, who liked a threesome with one partner of each sex and lastly; Bellows who just liked it with one sex, the same guy who had rounded out the threesome in the Hampton tape.

As he watched, David immediately sensed the purpose of the tapes.

The question that remained was to find out if Carol had been blackmailing all of them, some of them, or just one of them.

It occurred to him that perhaps the motive for her murder hadn't been stimulated by the drug investigation after all. How the hell did his men miss the video camera in the bedroom, or had he simply missed that in the report? Perhaps it had been removed some time before the murder took place.

Who knew about the existence of these tapes? Obviously, anyone who was being blackmailed did, and very likely the killer. Were these originals, or copies? Did the killer remove similar tapes from the apartment at the time of the killing? If not, had he been looking for them and would he now suppose that they had been passed on to Robyn?

If so, Robyn could be in serious danger.

He could hear her turn on the water again briefly and was glad that she had agreed to stay over-night. The thought of getting her home by boat and car this late certainly had no appeal for him.

He ejected the final tape from the machine and then turned both it and the TV off and closed the doors of the entertainment centre.

He re-boxed the remaining tapes in their corresponding containers and placed them in a tidy stack on his desk.

He was in the process of turning off the lamp over his desk when Robyn came down the stairs and into the room. She had her long hair pinned up and was wearing his comfortable old terry-towel robe.

Although she was lost in it, he found himself thinking that it had never looked that good on him.

She paused at the bottom of the stairs, removed the pins and shook her hair out. The robe parted slightly at the front with the movement and he caught a brief glimpse of one of her full high-set breasts before she was able to pull it closed and firmly re-belt it.

She had noted his reaction to the brief exposure and smiled.

"I hope you don't mind my using this; I didn't bring a robe."

He laughed and took his eyes from her as he turned to move across to the bar.

"Lucky robe! What will you have?"

Robyn crossed to the couch and flopped. As he turned toward her and despite the fact that the robe was firmly closed at the waist, he was treated to a second flash of flesh. This time it was a tantalizing fire lit view of legs that seemed to go on forever and ended in firm, well-formed thighs.

"Scotch with a little water please, if you have it."

He poured the drinks and carried them over to the couch, handing her hers and putting his own on the coffee table as he sat down beside her.

"There was one tape on each of the six men. I think she may have been blackmailing all or some of them. If so, that may have been the motive for killing her. It may have had absolutely nothing to do with the drug conspiracy part of her life. That possibility opens up a whole new ball game, and I'm afraid it may also mean that you might be in danger. If the killer knew about, and was looking for these tapes and wasn't able to find them, or if he did find the originals and thinks there may be copies, he might reasonably assume Carol passed them on to you for safe-keeping. That being the case, he may decide to come after you to get them. I think it would be a good idea if you dropped out of circulation for awhile."

She crossed her arms and sat erect.

"David, I'm not going to run from this. I want to play my part in helping you to find out who killed her."

He held up his hand to silence her.

"Okay, okay, but you shouldn't go back to your apartment. The killer probably knows where you live, and work. I know you don't have a lot of options when it comes to finding a place to stay; but you are more than welcome to stay here for a few days. Mrs. Ferguson could kind of keep an eye on you while I was at work, and she'd enjoy the company. No one is going to think of looking for you here and if they do I have a feeling that Cato would be a large deterrent to any attempt to approach you."

Robyn thought for a second, her eyes shifting over to look at the big dog stretched out near the fire. Then she looked back at David. The tension that had been apparent in her body seemed to fade slightly and she dropped her arms to her sides.

"Yes, I think that would work. I would enjoy Jenny's company and if I was here I would at least be able to do what I can to help you sort this whole thing out. It would mean that you and I could go over the progress of the investigation every night after you finished work. Are you sure I wouldn't be any trouble though?"

David grinned.

"Well, we are friends and partners, after all."

Robyn laughed and raised her glass in a toast. He joined her, touching his glass to hers before taking a solid swallow.

"David, in her letter to me Carol said she'd only used one of the tapes, and that was to hinder the CLEU investigation. That would mean that she had only blackmailed one of them."

David shook his head.

"Yes, I know she said that, but we don't know how long ago she wrote the letter. It wasn't dated. It might have been a year ago. She may have used one or all of the other tapes by now. It's something we should consider. But we can't take it for granted."

He held up his drink.

"We'd better get these down and call it a night. I have a hunch that I'm going to find tomorrow to be a very busy day."

He got up to tend the fire one last time and then, still standing, drained his glass and set it down on the table before walking over to the door. Cato, half asleep, didn't miss the movement and the dog was up and outside for his run before the door had been completely opened.

*****

Robyn couldn't believe it. She didn't know whether to laugh or cry.

He had brought the dog in, led her upstairs to her room, given her a kiss that couldn't be construed as anything more than sisterly, wished her a good night and then left her, closing the spare bedroom door behind him.

She'd heard him mucking around in the bathroom for a bit and then followed his footsteps past her room and the sound of him closing his bedroom door.

She rolled over restlessly and looked at the luminous dials of the clock.

That had been an hour ago. There wasn't a damn thing funny about the whole situation and it was either laugh or cry. She made her decision.

She decided to cry.

As was the case with many men, there was something about a crying woman that always got to David.

It wasn't that Robyn was crying loudly, more like semi-muffled sobs, but it was very quiet at night on the Arm and the walls of the old house allowed sound to travel easily.

He did his best to ignore it for several minutes, then sighed and got up. He slept naked, and since Robyn had appropriated his favorite robe, it took him a few seconds to locate his rarely used, velour robe from the back of his closet. He struggled into it in the dark and then opened his bedroom door and crossed the hall.

He knocked softly and heard the sobbing stop.

"Come in David."

She switched on the lamp on the bedside table as he opened the door and because she preferred to sleep in the same manner that he did, both of her well formed breasts were briefly exposed before she managed to find the top of the sheet and pull it up high enough to cover herself.

Mixed emotions: empathy for her tears, desire for her breasts. David stood like an idiot staring across at her. The last of her tears rolled down her cheek and she released the sheet as she held out her arms to him.

"Oh David, hold me, just hold me please"

He crossed to her and sat down on the edge of the bed and took her in his arms.

She hugged him to her fiercely and he found himself kissing away her tears. Then his lips found hers and her tongue found his.

Robyn freed one hand to shut off the lamp and used the other to undo the belt of his robe, then pulled back the covers and moved over to make room for him as he shrugged his robe off and let it slip to the floor beside the bed.

They locked together instantly and their lips and tongues met again. It lasted a long time and when they broke for air he moved his lips to her ear.

"You lie back and relax, I know you're hurting and feeling abandoned and alone. This is going to be just for you"

He started to pay homage to her. Not rushing, moving slowly, exploring and revealing in her sensuous beauty. First his hands moved gently over her. They missed nothing, covering, cupping and caressing, with eager determination. His lips followed starting with hers and then moving downward, deftly managing to tantalizingly skirt the now swollen and moist center of her growing need.

Robyn began to moan softly.

All the horror of the past few days melted away, obscured by her need for the touch of him. Her breath came in short, sharp gasps as she pushed the covers off them and eagerly parted her quivering legs.

His tongue was retracing its path up one long leg and then the other and it finally settle at the juncture of her thighs. Pausing there, it flickered, delved and savored the clean animal taste of her for several seconds. Then it sought out and began to work on the swollen bud at the top of her nether lips and she felt herself instantly tearing through a tremendous orgasm.

It was the first, but far from the last. His tongue continued to work on her, slowly gently at first, and then more demandingly. She was moaning deeply now, and her sporadic cries of ecstasy filled the room.

David gauged her reactions, her breathing, and the tension in her body, as he repeatedly brought her up to the edge and then back down, only to bring her up again and eventually over the top.

He measured the intensity of each rolling orgasm carefully and let her recover briefly from each before he repeated the process.

They both lost count of how many times she arched herself up to him and cried out in unabashed delight and finally she could stand it no more. At that point the thought of reaching another climax honestly frightened her. She was convinced that her body simply couldn't handle it.

David sensed that she was totally exhausted and he let his tongue gently trace the outline of her swollen lips, before he raised his head and lightly kissed her still quivering abdomen.

He moved up in the bed and stretched out beside her. Robyn was tingling from head to toe, as deliciously uncontrolled muscle spasms washed unchecked over the length of her body.

David pulled the covers up over them and melded himself against her side and wrapped her in his arms. He nuzzled her neck and whispered into her ear.

"Goodnight partner."

Through the blissful haze of wonder that filled her Robyn was aware that she had been so engrossed in what he had done for her that she hadn't managed to return the favor.

She could feel the stiff pressure of him against her hip.

The sprit was there but not the will. She was totally wiped and beyond moving.

He sensed her frustration and laughed.

"Relax and sleep; that's what you really need. I'm not going anywhere; you can return the favor in the morning, if that's what's bothering you. Just sleep now."

CHAPTER TWENTY-ONE

"It's morning!"

David groaned and managed to open one eye.

It took him a second to get his bearings and find the luminous dial of the clock in the darkness of the unfamiliar surroundings of the spare bedroom.

It read two minutes after midnight.

She was glued to his side, locking her warmth against him. He could smell her, he could still taste her. It felt good, very good.

He laughed and she growled playfully and rolled over on top of him. Her hand found him and he was instantly erect.

There were no preliminaries this time.

She straddled him and he groaned deeply as she grasped him firmly and began to slip up and down working his eager stiffness inside.

She was still wet from their earlier session, but she had been without sex for several months and he wasn't small.

It took time, but neither of them seemed to mind.

* * * * *

It was the smell of bacon that woke him.

For a few minutes he lay there, half asleep, but the smell was persistent. Robyn was lying tightly against him, spoon fashion with one arm thrown across his chest.

The afterglow of their early morning sex had not completely worn off and he luxuriated in it for a few seconds and then suddenly shot upward into a sitting position.

"Shit!"

Robyn lurched up and blinked. He looked at her, grinned, and then kissed her lightly on the cheek.

"Good morning partner, my alarm has no doubt been going off in my bedroom for the last hour and unless I miss my guess, Mrs. Ferguson is in the midst of cooking us breakfast downstairs."

Robyn flushed and literally jumped out of bed.

David's grin broadened as he enjoyed the rear view for a split second and then she was gone, robe clutched in one hand, out of the room and down the hall and into the bathroom.

He leaned back against the pillow and relaxed.

What the hell, it was only seven, and it had sure as hell been worth it!

*****

The accountant hung up the phone after letting it ring ten times. She wasn't home obviously. It was the right number, it had to be. How many Robyn Jenkins could there be?

She did work shifts, perhaps she was still at work. Wherever she was, she wasn't home and the apartment was just around the bock from the phone booth.

It was risky, but putting it off would only increase the risk, not reduce it. If it was at all possible, it was important to find out what, if anything, Carol had told or left for Robyn.

It was a short walk accomplished at a leisurely pace, ending at the bus stop just across the road from Robyn's apartment block. In less than ten minutes the opportunity presented itself.

It was a van making a delivery.

The accountant crossed the street rapidly, arriving just after the van driver, parcel in hand, had finished speaking on the intercom with the aim of gaining access to the building.

The accountant stepped up beside him and smiled.

"Here, let me hold the door for you."

The delivery man, who had been about to put the bulky

package down in order to pull the door open grinned.

"Thanks."

The accountant followed him inside and helpfully pressed the button to summon the elevator.

The delivery was on the fourth floor, the accountant continued up to the sixth.

The hallway was empty and the door was a snap, just a few seconds with a plastic strip.

* * * * *

The session was droning on, but he was only half listening. He was worried, hell he was scared stiff.

If he turned over the tapes he could be signing his death certificate, and he knew it. But what could he do, if he didn't turn up with the tapes as instructed, the accountant would only come after them.

The result would be the same, either way.

There had to be some way out of the dilemma. He certainly couldn't go on like this, his future in the hands of someone else, especially not in the hands of the likes of the accountant.

No, that was not acceptable at all.

* * * * *

Jenny began talking the instant David entered the kitchen.

"As soon as I saw the boat sitting there at the dock after six-thirty, I knew that you must have slept in. Poor Cato, he was ready for a run, I can tell you. I though I might as well get breakfast going before I woke you up. It's in the oven keeping warm; I'll just be off now. I did cook enough for two."

She winked at him.

She actually winked!

"Have a good sleep, did you dear?" David let his eyes lock with hers and grinned before he spoke.

"Yes thank you, as a matter of fact I did."

He noted the twinkle in her eye and let his grin fade as he continued.

"Jenny, I have a favor to ask. Robyn's going to be staying here for awhile. I think she may be in danger with regard to that drug investigation case that I mentioned to you last week. It was her sister who was the first victim and the killer might just be looking for Robyn now. I was wondering if you'd mind keeping an eye on her while I'm at work."

Mrs. Ferguson became all seriousness and stopped in her tracks.

"Goodness gracious, why would he want to hurt the poor girl. Is it something to do with the other murders then? The poor little thing. And her sister just being killed. Of course I don't mind. She can come up to my place when you leave if she likes, or I can come back down here. Don't you worry, and I'll keep her mind off things - we'll keep busy".

David smiled at her.

"Thanks Jenny. Oh, by the way, I don't want her answering the phone here. If I want to get hold of her, I'll call your place first. If I don't get an answer there, I'll call here, let it ring twice, hang up, and then phone back immediately. I also don't want her answering the door, though it's unlikely that necessity would arise, and make sure the two of you keep Cato with you whenever you are."

She straightened to her full height, not a large task, but an obvious gesture none the less.

"Don't you worry; I'll see to it that she comes to no harm."

Robyn entered the room, and Jenny beamed over at her.

"Well don't you look healthy this morning? Why you've simply blossomed over night!"

Robyn felt the blood rushing to her cheeks.

My god, did it show? Was it that obvious?

Mrs. Ferguson was on her way to the door as she spoke

"You and Cato come on up to my place after breakfast love, we'll have a nice cup of tea and a good old-fashioned woman to woman gossip session. Do us both a world of good!"

Once the door had closed behind her, David raised his eyebrows and Robyn laughed.

"I feel like I have a sign on my forehead flashing 'WOW, what a night'!

David laughed with her.

"Well, if you did have one, you sure as hell generated enough energy last night to power it."

Robyn flushed again.

"Where's breakfast. I could eat a horse."

*****

On the way in to work, David kept catching himself drifting off into a blissful dreamland, reliving the night in the spare bedroom.

He understood the reaction, being with Jackie had affected him in the same way. But as enjoyable as it had been, it was a little unsettling to come to the realization that his safe little life had fundamentally and irrevocably changed over the past several hours.

It had left no doubt however as to his having to come to a rational decision about whether or not he wanted to commit himself to a new relationship. That was a thing of the past.

He was hooked and he knew it.

Despite that fact, he was determined to see to it that they didn't rush into a permanent situation without thinking it out carefully. Last night was last night. They'd both been ripe for it for their own reasons. Tonight would be different; they'd talk it out and be damned sure of where they were going before they hit the bed again.

With some difficulty, he pushed the pleasing reminisces of the night of lovemaking to the back of his mind and began working on planning the day ahead.

*****

The accountant surveyed the rooms carefully, one at a time, ensuring that everything was back in place and that the apartment looked just as it had before the search.

The results of the effort had been less than satisfying to say the least.

Nothing, not a damned thing.

Her bloody sister had been dead for three days. Surely there should be something of Carol's here, papers, a will, something.

If there had been anything at all, perhaps a reasonable risk assessment could have been made. As it was, there was nothing to work from.

The main concern had been that Carol might have asked Robyn to keep copies of the tapes or some other incriminating documents for her.

Despite a thorough search, there had been nothing like that to be found. Finding absolutely nothing had to make a person wonder if there was indeed something that was being kept somewhere other than at the apartment. There was also the possibility that whatever it was had already been turned over to the police.

To spend longer in the apartment would be fruitless and foolish. The risk taken to force entry and spend a half hour in carefully searching had been high enough as it was.

Talking with Robyn seemed the only possible way to ascertain for sure if there was a problem or not. The accountant had hoped and intended to avoid such a direct contact if possible, considering it too dangerous at this point in the game. But it was obvious now that there was no other choice.

Dangerous or not, it would have to be done.

* * * * *

David spent the first half hour at work with his Staff Sergeant going over the necessary day to day administrative chores and setting up a structure to handle, on a daily basis, any exchanges of information with CLEU and CSIS.

Once that was out of the way, he started on the surveillance reports covering the six men. Vancouver was handling two personally, and the overnight report on each of these was on his desk.

David had no way of knowing for sure, but CSIS appeared to be handling the remainder, and not surprisingly, he had no report from them as yet.

There was nothing that caught his eye in the two Vancouver reports. No indication that either of the subjects had been in contact with any of the others.

He checked the clock and got up to make his way to Deputy Chief Foster's office for the scheduled morning meeting.

He was on his way out, pulling on his jacket as he crossed Cindy's office when she flagged him down.

"Call for you, line one."

David decided to take it at her phone.

"David, its Robyn. I'm sorry to bother you at work, but I have to go into town to finalize the funeral arrangements. Jenny insisted that I let you know."

He checked Cindy's clock and then got up from where he had been sitting on the edge of her desk.

"Sure, no problem, just make sure you don't go to your apartment or near work, and watch Jenny's driving, keep you seat belt on!"

"I was going to stop in at the apartment and get some more clothes and other stuff I need. I can't wear these forever, and quite frankly, your shampoo leaves a great deal to be desired."

David smiled and considered a second before he answered.

"Okay, if you have to, but take Jenny up to the apartment with you and don't stay any longer than you need to. Give me a call when you finish up there and let me know that you two are okay. My secretary, Cindy, will know where to get hold of me."

*****

Robyn found herself really quite impressed with the way Jenny handled the car and even more so with the manner in which she manhandled her small boat on the trip to the wharf.

So far, the morning's conversation, between cups of strong tea, had been light, but Robyn couldn't help but realize that she was being skillfully sounded out by the older woman.

It didn't bother her that Jenny was pumping her for information about the budding relationship between her and David. After all she clearly considered herself to be his surrogate mother and her concern for David only served to strengthen Robyn's sense that Jenny sincerely cared for him.

She could easily understand that the older woman felt it her duty to scrutinize this female newcomer into David's life and make sure she was good enough for him. Jenny's continuous stream of questions also helped Robyn to put aside thinking about the main reason for their trip into town and Robyn was grateful to her for that.

CHAPTER TWENTY-TWO

David was actually relieved to find that Foster had been called away for a last minute executive meeting and wouldn't be able to see him that morning.

He had very little new information for the Deputy in any event, and what he did have to offer wasn't likely going to make Foster particularly happy.

What the Deputy wanted was a body charged with murder and locked up. Nothing short of that was going to satisfy him.

David used the phone in the Deputy's waiting room to check in with Cindy and give her his next stop which was an interview with Candy Apple, the stripper whose real name was Elizabeth Archer.

He got his car out of the garage and started over to the address on the south east side of town. None of the three women that he had managed to set up appointments with was particularly thrilled about the thought of meeting with him, but Candy had been the most vociferous.

He hadn't expected to be welcomed by any of them. They had no desire to be involved in a murder investigation and perhaps more to the point, all three of them were unnerved by the fact that he knew they had been involved in the little sex for pay operation Carol had been running.

Of the three, he had expected Melody Green to be the most spooked by his call, but she had been businesses-like on the phone, managing to squeeze him into her lunch hour, '...and would he please not come in to the office. She would meet him out front at the appointed time'.

As he drove, he found himself wondering why Candy had been so reticent about seeing him.

Perhaps it was a harbinger of things to come; did she have something to hide?

He pulled up in front of the old house that had been broken up into apartments several years ago and parked the car.

She was in a basement suite. He knocked and stepped back to survey the neighborhood as he waited for the door to be answered. It had been a fairly good area until ten years ago, but it was now going down hill very rapidly.

The information in her file had attributed her height at five foot ten, but he was momentarily taken aback by the Amazon who answered the door.

She was wearing a thin wrap that came to mid thigh. It wasn't doing a very good job of covering its contents, if that was the purpose for which it was intended.

David found himself instantly understanding why Candy Apple could make a living stripping and he had no difficulty whatsoever in understanding why Carol had chosen her for one of her girls. He could readily see why men had been eager to take their pleasure with her in exchange for cash.

He smiled and flashed his badge.

She didn't even give it a cursory glance, simply stepped back from the door and waved him in.

"Don't need to look at that, I can smell one of you a block away."

David shrugged and moved inside. As she closed the door behind him, he surveyed what he could see of the apartment.

Small, dirty and smelling of stale tobacco and unwashed plates.

She left him standing and dropped into an overstuffed chair across from him. He looked around and selected a straight backed chair that only required the removal of what appeared to be a week's accumulation of daily newspapers and sat down.

She didn't give him a chance to speak first.

"If this is a bust, you might as well let me know right now. I'm not saying anything until I talk to my lawyer."

She was all wired up and prepared to continue and David wasn't in the mood to listen.

"Look, I told you on the phone, I'm working on the murder of Carol Jenkins. Frankly, I don't really give a shit about the little games you were playing in Carol's penthouse, unless they provide me with something that will help me find her killer. I'm here to see if you can give me any lines in that direction and that's all that I want from you."

A little of the fire left her eyes at the mention of Carol's name and that told him that there had been some feeling there.

He vaguely recalled the tape showing Candy wrapped in a sixty-nine with Carol and wondered if it had been more than just for the bucks.

Regardless, he'd found a chink in her armor and he knew it.

"You were her friend after all; and I figured you would want to help find her killer if you could."

She paused long enough to light a cigarette off the one she was about to butt out in the already overflowing ashtray and he let the silence work on her.

Finally, after a few drags, she balanced the smoke precariously on the edge of the ashtray and turned her attention back to him.

"You're on the level about not working the prostitution angle?"

He nodded.

"Nothing to do with me, I'm investigating murder. Not much sense in pursuing it now anyway, not with Carol dead. She was the brains behind it wasn't she?"

His intention was to start her talking and it worked like a charm.

"Ya, it was a good set up too. I'm going to miss it. It was real easy money and clean, no risks, no johns off the street, just the same high paying repeat customers."

"There were only the four of you girls in the operation and the one guy, right?"

Her eyes flashed again.

"Look, I'm no stoolie."

David waved his hand, dismissing the suggestion. He opened his briefcase and pulled out the photos taken by the CLEU surveillance teams and held them out to her.

She took them from him and looked at each carefully.

"Boy, you really had us didn't you?"

Walker nodded.

"Yes, we had surveillance on the building for a good month. As part of my investigation, I'm going to be meeting with each of the four of you who were involved with Carol. I have appointments with the others over the rest of the day, and I won't be asking you about anything that I won't be asking them, so answering my questions isn't going to be informing on them. I'm just giving you all the same chance to come clean with me and provide what help you can in finding her killer. I'd appreciate it if you would give me a run down on each of the others and tell me whether you think that any of them might have had a good reason to kill Carol."

She shuffled the pictures into a neat stack and looked at the first one.

"Like I told ya, it was a good setup; none of us would have hurt Carol. Christ it was a regular little gold mine for all of us."

She began to shift through each of the photos.

"Ursula, nice kid, quiet. I tried to help her get into the business, ya know, exotic dancing, but she wasn't interested. She said she could never take off her clothes in front of a whole room full of men. Didn't understand it myself, Christ, she sure as hell didn't hesitate to party at Carol's. No, she didn't have any reason to be down on Carol, and even if she did, she wouldn't have had the guts to off her."

She put that picture down and moved to the next.

"Bret, Christ, is he hung. He calls himself a model, but I've never see him in any magazines or anything. Lazy bastard, satisfied to make an easy buck any way he can. He only thinks about himself, and he's a moody asshole. He's also got a hell of a temper and capable of damn near anything. I wouldn't put anything past him; if he lost his cool about something, but I don't think he would have intentionally killed the goose that was laying the golden eggs; and that was Carol as far as he was concerned."

David interjected quickly.

"How do you spell his last name?"

He held his notebook out and studied it, as if he was reading.

She answered without thinking, which was exactly what he wanted her to do.

"H U N T E R, I guess. How else do you spell Hunter?"

David nodded and flipped his book closed.

"Just double checking, how about the rest?"

Candy looked down again.

"Melody, now there is a strange one. She could be capable of anything. She loved it, the kinkier the better. I swear that she would have done it for nothing. A real strange broad, that one, but I don't see why she would want Carol dead. It was a safe setup for her, working out her kinks at Carol's. I don't know where she going to go for her jollies now that Carol is dead."

She handed the pictures back to him and David put them away.

"Ya know, if you ask me, I'd say one of the johns did it. I could be wrong, but I think Carol coulda been doing a little blackmailing. Maybe she picked the wrong guy to try it on?"

David fixed her gaze.

"What makes you think that she might have been blackmailing anyone?"

"Because over the past coupla months she was taking pictures of us when we were doing it. You know when we were balling these guys. She showed us the camera, so we'd know where to lay on the bed so that the johns would be in the finished movies. The johns didn't know anything about it. She said that she was doin it for a joke, but I think that was a pile of bull. Once the camera was set up, she upped our cut for each session, so we didn't bitch. What the hell; it was no skin off our noses."

David nodded.

"By the way, where were you when she was killed?"

Candy's features turned cold.

"At a private party and I can give you the names of five very satisfied witnesses."

He shrugged and stood up.

"You may have to. Homicide detectives will be following up on this interview. They'll want a full statement from you."

*****

Jenny instantly sensed the fear in Robyn as she watched the girl freeze in mid-stride, just inside the door of her apartment.

There was no danger immediately apparent to Jenny, but she responded by grasping Robyn firmly by the upper arms.

"What is it child?"

Robyn took a deep breath.

"Someone has been in here. I leave my keys on top of the TV."

Jenny moved her eyes to the top of the television which was directly in front of them. There were two sets of keys lying on top of it.

With a questioning expression on her face, Jenny shifted her gaze from the keys and back to Robyn

"There are keys here, are some of them missing?"

Robyn shook her head and closed her eyes in frustration, forcing the words out.

"No…no…but they are wrong; they've been reversed. I have a real thing about it. My office keys are always on the right, and my locker keys are on the left."

Jenny wasn't sure she understood, but there was no doubting that Robyn was convinced that something was seriously amiss.

She gave Robyn's arms a little squeeze and released them, as she looked around for the phone.

"I'll call David's office; his girl, Cindy, will know how to get a hold of him."

*****

Ursula Kreski lived on the second floor of an apartment building.

Parking on the streets in the West End being pretty well impossible to find and with the knowledge that no one was going to tow a police car; David pulled into the underground parking lot of her apartment complex and parked illegally in a fire zone.

As he was in the process of locking his car, he heard the muffled tones of the radio and recognized his call sign.

He reversed the key in the door lock and pulled the door open then leaned inside to reach for the mike under the dash of his unmarked unit.

"Six"

"Six, message from Detective Boyd. He'd like to talk to you on TAC two."

David dropped down into the driver's seat.

"Ten-four, switching channels,"

He reached back down under the dash and switched to TAC two, then gave his call sign to the dispatcher.

Boyd responded on the first call.

"I guess you've been out of the car and missed it. There's been a call to the place that you went to the other day, your pawn shop guy. I'm here now, and I think that you should drop by."

"Ten-four, give me about twenty minutes."

Walker switched back to channel one and raised the dispatcher. He gave instructions to have Cindy call Kreski to reschedule the interview and then slipped the key into the ignition and started the car.

CHAPTER TWENTY-THREE

Candy wasn't receptive to Cindy's call.

"What in hell do ya think I am a bloody answering service? He left."

She hung up and Cindy simply reactivated the dial tone and called Communications. She was somewhat surprised to find that Walker had left her a message. She jotted it down quickly and then began to give the dispatcher one for David.

Jenny had said that it was urgent after all.

Cindy passed the message, along with Robyn's home number on to the Chief Dispatcher, who in turn placed the call card on the belt and watched it slip swiftly over to the area one operator.

David got the message as he was about half way to the pawn shop. He cursed softly and started looking for a phone booth. He finally spotted one, pulled up across from it, double parked, and left the car running.

Robyn had become important to him and Jenny wasn't one to cry 'Wolf'.

He was anxious as he prepared to dial.

He muffed the quarter the first time and it dropped to the floor of the booth. It pissed him off and he willed himself to relax a little as he successfully deposited a second quarter.

Despite his earlier admonition that she not answer phones, David was instantly relieved when Robyn's voice filled his ear.

He listened to her story and then considered it for a split second before commenting.

"Okay, have you finished the other stuff that you had to do in town, and got what you needed from the apartment?"

"Yes, except to get some clothes together. That shouldn't take more than a few minutes".

"Okay, pack your stuff as quickly as you can and then you

and Jenny head for my place. I'm going to send someone over from IDENT to print the place, don't handle anything that you don't need to. As soon as they get there, give them a key so they will be able to lock up and then leave. I don't want to have to worry about you two for the rest of the day. Oh, and by the way, when you're out on the last stretch of the road before the dock, you know the section that's only wide enough for a single vehicle, stop and wait for a few minutes, just to make sure you're not being followed. If another car comes along behind you, turn around and drive straight back to the Police Station and call me. If not, go on home"

He got her to repeat it back to him and then let her go.

It wasn't until he got back into the car that he realized he had left it running, something he hadn't done since his old Dog Squad days when he'd been in hot pursuit and refused to take the time to shut his car off when a stolen vehicle had been dumped and the suspects had bailed and were on the run.

He grinned to himself at the reminiscence, and then slammed the unmarked cruiser into gear, reaching for his mike to notify IDENT before pulling out into traffic.

Relieved to have his concerns about Robyn and Jenny put on the back burner, he turned his thoughts back to wondering what the hell Boyd had dug up.

As he completed a corner, he glanced at his watch. He only had one hour before his appointment with Melody Green.

One screwed up interview for the day was enough, and he was determined to make it to Melody's office on time.

There were two marked units, an inhalator rig and an ambulance parked in front of the pawn shop.

David double-parked his car on the other side of the street, directly behind Boyd's unmarked unit, locked it and headed across the road.

The ambulance and inhalator crews were pulling away as he hit the opposite sidewalk.

There was a uniform in the doorway of the shop and David flashed his badge as he passed him. He found Boyd standing at the counter, staring down at what had once been a living Hymie.

David joined him.

There was no doubt the man was dead. Half of his head was blown off.

Boyd turned toward him.

"357 Magnum, he didn't know what hit him. Base of the skull, from behind. Different caliber than the others, but considering what was in your report about the pawn shop and the fact that it was probably a weapon of opportunity…"

He pointed over to the gun display case which stood unlocked and open.

David crossed to it and noted that there were impressions in the cloth indicating that several of the guns had been removed. At a quick glance, he judged that at least four had been removed, one of which was the Magnum that now rested on the floor beside the body.

He nodded.

"It could have been random, but my first guess is that our friend has struck again all right. Who's on this with you?"

Boyd shook his head.

"Partner's off on Workman's Comp, a least until next week."

David shrugged.

"Okay, you handle it on your own. I've got interviews scheduled for the rest of the day. Keep me posted if anything worthwhile turns up, otherwise just make sure a copy of your report is on my desk in the morning."

* * * * *

Robyn would have laughed if she hadn't been scared stiff.

The very picture of Jenny taking on a murderer with a tire iron might well be something that she would laugh at later, but it wasn't one bit humorous at the moment.

Jenny was watching the rear view mirror like a hawk and

she had placed the tire iron between them on the front seat of the old station wagon.

Luckily, no car had appeared behind them when they had pulled over to wait at the spot that David had suggested earlier and after a few moments, Jenny released her hold on her makeshift weapon and put the old Chevy wagon into gear.

They both breathed a sigh of relief a few minutes later as the Government wharf came into view.

*****

Knowing what he did of Melody Green's sexual tastes, Walker was a little taken aback when she walked up to him on the sidewalk in front of the small business where she worked and identified herself.

She wore little or no makeup and the severe bun tightly pinned at the back of her head did little to accentuate the striking beauty of her long hair that had been apparent in the tapes that David had viewed the night before.

Although the baggy suit she wore couldn't completely hide her very well proportioned body, it did a pretty good job of it.

The horn-rimmed glasses completed the picture. No one would have picked her out as a high-priced hooker in a million years. It was hard for him to imagine her as the same woman who had been so profoundly enjoying the heated sessions depicted in the tapes.

In fact, it was difficult to believe she was the type that would even consider the idea of lovemaking with any real interest.

It wasn't until she spoke again that he realized he had been staring at her.

"You are Inspector Walker aren't you?"

He nodded and motioned her over to his car which was parked at the curb. The day had warmed up a little, but it was still far too cold to be holding an interview on the street.

Once they were settled inside and he had adjusted the heat to his satisfaction, he pulled out his notebook and looked across at her.

He noted that now that she was inside the restrictive interior of the car, her earlier aloof façade of cool composure had begun to collapse.

Her eyes gave her away. They had narrowed perceptibly and were darting all over the place.

He decided to let her stew for a few seconds to see if she could stand the silence, simply locking his eyes with hers as he found his pen and shifted to the next blank page in his notebook.

She didn't last long.

"I don't know why you want to talk to me, I can't help you. I shouldn't even have agreed to talk to you, do you have a warrant of whatever it is you need. Am I under arrest?"

She was ripe for the plucking.

He let out a deep sigh and set his notebook and pen on the dash of the car.

"Well, I guess that's up to you. I can arrest you if you want me to. However, if you answer the questions I'm going to put to you, honestly and to the best of your ability I don't think that will be necessary. You cooperate with me now, and you can walk away from here when we've finished, and other than having to give a follow-up statement to detectives sometime later this week, we probably won't need to speak with you again. If not, we'll go downtown now and I'll book you for prostitution."

The last of her already strained composure collapsed, and she broke completely.

"Oh my God, I just knew something like this would happen, but I couldn't help myself. You have to understand, it's like a disease with me, and I just can't seem to get enough. God what a mess!"

The tears started to roll and he gave her a few seconds to stem the flow with a tissue she had managed to fish out of the confines of her purse, before he began.

"My concern relates to the arrest of the person who killed Carol. I'm only interested in the little set up that Carol had going as it relates to the possible provision of information for me of facts that may lead to clues about the murder investigation. Answer my questions and you have nothing else to worry about. To begin with, please have a look at these pictures and tell me what you know about each of the people in them."

She wiped away the last tears from her cheeks and adjusted her glasses as he handed her the stack of still surveillance photographs.

"Candy, foul-mouthed whore! What can I add to that?"

David shifted slightly in the seat, so that he could easily watch her facial expressions and body language as he took notes.

"Well, you can give me an idea of what she was like and let me known if you think that she might have had any reason to want Carol dead, for starters."

She paused, turning her attention back to the top picture, regaining her composure almost instantly, a little too fast for David's liking, and becoming all business again.

"She'd be capable of it, I've no doubt about that, but as to what reason she would have, I have absolutely no idea. She seemed very happy with Carol's operation; it was right up her alley. We all were, for that matter, I suppose. For our own reasons of course."

David shifted in the seat again, trying to put his finger on what it was about her body language that was bothering him.

He was certain that she was playing him somehow, but he couldn't nail it down.

"I understand that she and Carol had a thing, beyond the working relationship. If that was the case, is it possible that it soured and Carol wanted to end it and maybe Candy couldn't accept the idea?"

Melody thought carefully before answering and David

knew that his hunch about Carol's sexual preference had been confirmed.

He said nothing, letting her take her time to answer him."

"Anything is possible I guess. Carol was a pretty versatile girl. I think she gave us all a tumble at one time or the other. Yes, she preferred girls to boys but I don't think she had a special thing for Candy. Besides Candy likes men, she only pulls a trick with a woman for the money."

David nodded and paused to add some comments in his notebook.

"To your knowledge, who of your group did Carol have a special thing with?"

It became apparent to him that Melody didn't like the direction that the questioning was taking and she had begun to fidget uncomfortably again. Walker sensed that he had hit a sore point and that she knew the answer to his question, but that she wasn't about to provide him with the information, for whatever reason.

He snapped his notebook closed and she jumped at the sound.

"If you'd prefer to do this downtown..."

The fidgeting stopped immediately and she paled.

"I'm not sure; at least I don't know who it was, not exactly. There was someone, but I don't think that it was one of us. She kept the business end of things very separate from her private life. It wasn't as if she took us into her confidence about her private affairs."

David was far from convinced that she was being forthright with him, but he sensed that it was as far as she was willing to go for the moment.

He took Candy's picture from her hand and pointed to the next one on the pile. She looked at it and smiled.

"Bret Hunter. Fancies himself God's gift to the world. He's in for a rude awakening when his looks start to fade. He's a real flake, up one minute and down the next, so wrapped up in himself that he isn't even aware of what's going on around him most of the time. Definitely more brawn than brain and I wouldn't trust him as far as I could throw him, but I don't think he would have hurt Carol. She was his bread and butter. He has the looks and is hung like a horse, but she could have replaced him any time she wanted to. His type are a dime a dozen and although he's not overly bright, I'm sure that, despite the fact that they had some real go-arounds over money, he recognized the fact and was pretty careful not to push her too far."

David nodded slowly and opened his notebook again to make an entry.

"Is it possible she might have decided to do just that and he flipped out and killed her? By the way, do you happen to know where he lives or what his phone number is? The one I've got is no longer in service."

"I suppose he could be capable of doing something like that. As long as everything was going well for him, he was a wimp and very subservient toward her, but as I said, he's moody and they did squabble over money and he's got a short fuse and often acts without much thought. Yes. I've got his number written down somewhere, Carol gave it to me a couple of weeks ago when she asked me to contact him for her to set up a last minute trick."

She was rummaging through her purse again. She came up with an address book and began to flip though the pages.

"879-4227, I don't have an address."

David nodded as he wrote the phone number into his book.

"Okay, let's try the next one."

He removed Bret's photo from the stack and put it away.

Melody turned her attention to the next one and pursed her lips slightly.

"Ursula. Nice girl, quiet, she did it for the money, not for the kicks, and she kept pretty much to herself. I really don't know a lot about her to tell you the truth."

Walker took the picture from her hand and closed his notebook.

"Do you have any idea as to who might have killed her?"

Melody took time to think again and then shook her head from side to side slowly.

"No, it was probably just a john like I said. Everybody who knew her well either liked her or at the very least respected her for the way she handled her business. If I had to guess I'd say it was just a spur of the moment thing with some bad john."

David straightened out in his seat and slipped the defroster switch over slightly in an attempt to reduce the condensation that was slowly covering the windows of the idling unmarked cruiser.

"Okay, where were you when she was killed?"

For the first time since the interview had started, she looked him straight in the eye.

"Home with my husband."

David's features did not give away the surprise that her answer had caused him. He noted her answer then closed his book and placed both it and his pen into the inside jacket pocket of his suit jacket.

"Be sure that you give that information to the detectives that do the follow up with you and take your statement. It may be necessary for us to confirm it with him later."

She went white.

"My God, you don't have to do that, surely."

David met her gaze and held it.

"We may have to, but don't worry we'll find a way to do it so that it doesn't relate to your… extracurricular activities."

Melody gave a soft sigh of relief and reached for the door handle. She turned to face him as the door opened.

"You don't happen to know when the funeral is going to be held, do you. I'd like to attend."

David nodded in the affirmative.

"It's a memorial service. The announcement will be in the paper tonight. It's going to be on Saturday, I believe"

She nodded and got out of the car. He was surprised to

see tears in her eyes again, but this time he sensed they were tears for Carol, not for herself.

David was also surprised to find they appeared to him to be genuine.

CHAPTER TWENTY-FOUR

David's concern about Robyn's well-being had begun to dominate his thoughts.

He had spent enough time in the office to deal with the few matters that his Staff Sergeant had left on his desk and to run Bret Hunter through CPIC, the Canadian Police databank, but he was having difficulty keeping his mind on what he was doing.

CPIC had spit out the basic information on Hunter and reflected several minor convictions involving violence, primarily common assaults. It was sufficient to allow David to make a primary evaluation of Hunter and to provide Cindy with enough information to allow her to set up an appointment for Walker to meet with him.

He had felt a little guilty about having to ask Cindy to reschedule the appointments for the interviews with the two remaining prostitution ring suspects for the next day, but knew the he wouldn't be able to fully concentrate on anything else until he'd seen Robyn face to face and satisfied himself that she was in no immediate danger.

*****

The accountant drained the remainder of the straight Scotch and stood staring blankly out at the gently bobbing freighters riding at anchor in English Bay.

Damn, that had been close.

The killing itself had been simple enough.

The stupid fat pig had actually thought he could make a deal for his silence: had had the audacity to look down his nose and demand to meet with the person who was on the receiving end of the guns that he had been providing, and if not had threatened to immediately call the police.

Later, and once Hymie had been dealt with, the accountant had found the business card there, right under the dog-eared blotter on the greasy counter.

INSPECTOR DAVID WALKER-MAJOR CRIME

The newspapers had carried Walker's name, indicating the seriousness of the crime from the police point of view. They had made a big deal of having a seasoned veteran investigator of Inspector rank personally assuming control of the murder investigations.

The presence of the business card served to indicate that the police had probably managed to find out who had been the source of the murder weapons, but there was no way of knowing exactly how much the pawnbroker may have told them before he had been silenced for good.

It couldn't have been too much, and it would probably only serve to confuse them at any rate, and he would certainly not be able to make a positive identification now, but the whole thing was unnerving none the less.

A second Scotch would have been nice, but there was the meeting at the Rose Garden tonight and that would require a clear head.

*****

Cato was spread-eagled on the linoleum in front of the door, his eyes closed and his big head in his favorite position, resting on his paws.

Jenny was doing two things at once as usual. She had a crab trap that needed repairing lying on a bunch of spread out newspapers in the center of the small kitchen floor and the room was filled with the delicious smells of fresh baking.

She had condescended to agree to allow Robyn the responsibility of steeping and pouring the tea while she fussed with patching the netting on the crab trap where it was damaged.

She tied the last knot and pushed the trap aside with a

satisfied grunt, then vaulted out of her chair and crossed and bent to peer through the glass of the oven door to check on the progress of her third batch of cookies.

"Don't know why I make so many. Don't eat many of them myself; give most of them away."

The cookies were obviously baked to her satisfaction and she opened the oven door with one hand as she slipped an oven mitt on the other before reaching inside for the tray.

The small room instantly filled with a new wave of fresh-baked fragrance and she smiled as she set the tray on a rack to cool. She turned to look at Robyn and gave her a smile of satisfaction.

"They will go nicely with a cup of tea though, won't they dear?"

Robyn returned the smile.

She had been very uptight right up until they had arrived back at Jenny's house, but the idle talk combined with the hominess of the small house and the aroma of home baking had enabled her to relax a little.

Jenny's little kitchen definitely had a safe and secure feel to it.

Jenny gingerly placed several of the hot cookies onto a plate and carried it over to the small table with its plastic flower patterned tablecloth.

As she twisted her chair back toward the table and slipped into it, Robyn finished pouring them fresh cups of tea.

"I probably shouldn't be doing this dear, and before I do, I want you to know that I'm not just being an old busy-body. What I'm going to tell you, I'm telling you for two good reasons. The first is that I care a great deal about David and think it's very important that someone shake him out of this shell he's built up around himself. The second reason is that I think you might be just what the doctor ordered."

She added sugar and cream to her cup and began to stir it slowly as she continued.

"Before I have my say though, I'd like to be sure about that last point, so I'm going to put you on the spot a little dear, and ask you to answer a few questions for me. Now, don't feel like you're obligated to satisfy an old woman; if you don't want to answer them, just tell me to mind my own business and we'll forget the whole thing."

Robyn had been answering questions all day. Where did she work? Did she have any other family? Did she want to have kids? Had she contemplated marriage, or was she a career girl?

She had lost count of the number of personal things that she had already shared with Jenny.

She had known it was all leading somewhere and had been waiting for Jenny to get up the courage to launch into the million dollar question. Now that it had arrived, she couldn't prevent herself from laughing out loud; despite the obviously serious attitude that Jenny was now presenting to her.

As soon as she did, she regretted it and immediately felt the need to apologize.

"I'm sorry, I know this is very important to you and I don't want you to think I am taking it frivolously; it's just that I have an idea what you are going to ask me, in a general sense anyway, and I'm quite nervous about the whole thing. You see David has made quite an impression on me and it's all been so sudden."

Jenny's concerned features softened and she laughed heartily.

"Well that answers the first of my questions."

They both laughed and as they did, the tension that had so suddenly filled the room dissipated just as rapidly as it had formed.

Jenny took one of the fresh cookies from the plate, tasted it delicately, then satisfied that it wasn't too hot to eat, began to nibble on it.

"Are you seriously interested in him? I may be old, but I'm not blind yet, and I can see that you're taken with each other. But are you genuinely interested in him, or is this just a short term adventure from your point o view? One thing David doesn't need is another brief affair; he needs something far more permanent than that."

Robyn finished off the cookie t she had been eating and reached for her tea. She blew gently across the top of the dainty rose-patterned cup, in an apparent attempt to cool it, but was in reality using the act more as a ploy to give her time to think of how best to answer, than because the contents of the cup actually needed it.

"I'm interested. I'm just not quite sure of exactly how much yet. I've always been attracted to older men. I've never enjoyed dates with men in my own age group; they all seem so immature and unsure of themselves for my liking. I like a man who is confident and comfortable with himself. I see that in David. I also find him very attractive physically, something that I didn't consider all that important in a man before I met David. Now that I have, I realize it is a very important factor, especially when considering a long-term relationship.

She paused to catch her breath and reached for a second cookie.

"Yes I'm interested in David as more than a one night stand, but as I said, it's all been very sudden and I find it hard to understand how I can feel so much for him already. Hard to believe and frankly, a little scary"

Jenny laughed.

"Falling in love usually is. Alright my girl, what I'm going to tell you may help you to understand David and what motivates him to act as he does. I'm sure you have been getting some conflicting signals from him and that's probably what's got you scared a little. My bet is you like what you've seen so far on the surface, and if it's real you know that something could work out for the two of you, but you're afraid of what's inside, a coldness that creeps up and exposes itself now and then."

She eased back into her chair and lifted her cup to take a sip.

"He's no doubt told you something about Jackie, I'm sure.

How much, I don't know, but probably not enough. Before he met her, he was in limbo, just going through the motions of life. His divorce hit him hard, not so much because of losing the wife but mainly over his separation from the kids. There he was at thirty-two, a bachelor again and for all intents and purposes cut off from his children as well. He didn't know how to start over, he didn't even particularly want to. Then along came Jackie. She saw all those wonderful things in him that you've now seen and she simply wouldn't take no for an answer. He didn't know how to take her at first. He wanted the happiness that he sensed she could bring him and yet he was sure she wasn't really interested in a permanent relationship with him. After all, he considered himself an old man, and her a young and very vibrant and beautiful woman. What could she possibly see in him?"

Jenny had Robyn's undivided attention. The pile of cookies was rapidly disappearing, but Robyn was hanging on to her every word.

"Jackie was a very smart girl. She didn't tell him what she wanted with him. She showed him. Every second of every minute of every day. It took him awhile to realize she was really sincere about her love for him and once he understood that, he let go completely and opened up to her. From that point on it just got better and better. The three of us were enjoying a brandy together not too long after they were married and Jackie explained the whole thing to me. David was not the least bit embarrassed about it by that time. She made him so very happy minute to minute that he found he could live with his previous hesitancy, even laugh at it. If you seriously want to catch him, you're going to have to prove to him that you really want and need him. It was a difficult thing for Jackie to do and now that he's lost her, he's simply sunk that much deeper into his old shell. It's probably going to be an uphill battle all the way: he's got a lot of hurt locked up deep inside him and he doesn't in his wildest dreams imagine he could be as lucky as he was with Jackie, a second time. But if you stick with it I think you'll find it to be a very worthwhile endeavor."

Robyn sighed and accepted a second cup as Jenny took her turn to pour.

"What you are saying is that he hasn't forgiven the world for taking Jackie away and he's convinced his one chance at real happiness is gone forever. He doesn't believe he can ever be happy like that again. He's afraid even to try?"

Jenny shook her head.

"There's more to it than that dear. I believe he actually thinks he is somehow being unfaithful to her by even considering anything but a dreary, lonely life. It's quite ridiculous of course. Jackie wouldn't have wanted him to drop out of life just because she died. Heavens, I heard her with my own ears tell him exactly that, oh so many times. Unfortunately her telling him apparently had about as much affect on him as my telling him the same thing many times since! If you decide you want a long-term relationship with him, you are going to have to prove it to him. You can only do that by showing him he doesn't have to feel guilty about loving again, and that it's not only what Jackie wanted but is also natural and right. David is a very strong and confident man in most things but he tends to think less of himself than others do and he can't understand exactly what they see in him that he can't. You show him why you want to be with him, be perfectly honest with him. He won't understand it altogether, but if you're sincere about it dear, he'll eventually accept it as a fact. Once he does that, he'll open up to you and let the hurt and the doubt out into the sunshine where it can heal once and for all."

Jenny read the lost and helpless expression in the face across from her and she paused and leaned back into her wooden chair.

"Heavens child, don't look so glum! It would appear that I've either been completely wrong about you, something I highly doubt as I'm usually pretty good at gauging these things; or that you don't have the spunk and determination I've given you credit for."

Robyn stopped toying with her tea cup and smiled.

"I'm sorry. It's just that things are happening very quickly, and you have provided me with a great deal of information in a very short time. I'm finding it just a little difficult to instantly put the right perspective on the whole thing."

The smile broadened into what became a nervous laugh.

"Don't worry; I don't think you were wrong. The feelings are there all right, stronger than I would have believed possible just days ago and I can be just as spunky and determined as necessary, when I need to be."

CHAPTER TWENTY-FIVE

Cato suddenly perked up his ears and raised his head, cocking it to one side. He had registered and recognized the sound of the boat engine long before the two women could have.

He listened for a second then stood up and moved to the kitchen door and began to wag his stump rapidly as he whined to get out. Jenny peered out the window and saw David's boat slipping into the dock.

She, Robyn and Cato waited until David had tied the boat up before going out onto Jenny's small balcony which extended out over the top of the cliff. When he began walking toward the steps, Jenny waved to him and her sharp voice, bracketed by Cato's joyful barks of welcome, boomed downward to him.

"We've decided to eat up here, c'mon up."

Robyn moved closer to the railing of the deck and Jenny placed a restraining hand on her upper arm to stop her.

"No dear, don't rely on that railing. It's unsafe. David has replaced the bottom part but the top is rotted badly and I wouldn't want you falling over. We're going to replace it this spring."

Robyn gave a little shudder and took a step back to look over from a safe distance. She took note of the 200 foot drop to the rocks below before waving. David acknowledged them with a wave of his own, and Jenny released Robyn's arm. She then opened the gate at the top of the stairs, allowing an eager Cato to race downward to meet his master.

David removed his briefcase from the boat and climbed the ramp that led to a gate at the top which opened onto the small patch of grass in front of his house. He then walked the few feet up the paving stones that led to the division of the paths, one of which led up to his front door, while the other ran diagonally across to a second gate that fronted the stairway which wound its way up to Jenny's cabin.

It was clear and cold and he was cognizant of the fact that there would likely be patches of ice in several places on the cement and stone stairway. He also knew that Cato would be coming down the stairs full tilt to meet him, and as a result he paid a good deal of attention to his footing.

Having dinner up at Jenny's would be a mixed blessing.

Although, over the past several hours he had been thinking mainly of spending time alone with Robyn, the threesome would give him a chance to be with Robyn for a couple of hours without the pressure of one-on-one closeness. It would give him a chance to gather his thoughts for the talk that he expected would take place once they were alone.

He wanted to be sure they had a chance to clear the air between them before they made love again. She needed to know that it would be unfair for her to get involved any deeper without a complete understanding of how he felt.

It would also give him an opportunity to go over the case with the two of them. Experience had taught him that he did some of his best thinking when he could bounce his ideas and theories off someone who was neither a policeman nor directly involved in the case.

In the past, he had used Jackie exclusively for this purpose, but when she had passed away, he had occasionally used Jenny to evaluate his opinions. He was inwardly pleased that Robyn had been filling that situation over the past couple of days, much in the way that Jackie had originally done.

David was already setting a long-term goal on their relationship subconsciously. He was beginning to become comfortable with that outlook.

But they both needed to take a hard and realistic look at the relationship before the night was through. He intended to be sure that she was entering into it with her eyes wide open.

* * * * *

Reaching the decision hadn't been easy. There had been options of course, but the options had crumbled one after another as he weighed them against the public exposure that was bound to be the result of each of them.

His career had started early and skyrocketed, bringing with it position and power almost immediately. As a result, it had been many years since he had actually had to deal with any serious problems on his own.

It wasn't an easy thing for him to admit to himself, but the fact was that he had managed to delegate the resolution of every serious problem he'd faced over the past thirty years.

No matter how he looked at it, this was not a problem that could be delegated. He would either have to kowtow to, or kill the accountant. There was no middle ground and no easy way out.

Once he had delivered the tapes he would be enmeshed in something that he didn't have absolute personal control over. It was a situation he had successfully avoided for the past forty years.

The instant the tapes were no longer in his hands, he would find himself a subordinate in the whole exercise. He'd be under the control of, and taking direction from the accountant.

That situation was totally unacceptable to him. The only real option was to remove the accountant permanently and that was going to take a hell of a lot of nerve.

How do you go about killing a professional killer?

Was he even capable of it?

Mentally, certainly, and even despite the age difference, he had the physical advantage.

The real question was how? He certainly wasn't a professional, but he was up against exactly that.

He had spent the day thinking it through. The hearings, boring at the best of times, had not interfered. He'd simply put on his public smile and tuned the rest of the room out. His two assistants would compile notes on whatever was necessary for him to understand in order to later make any decisions that were required from him. His presence in the actual hearings was in reality only a photo-op. It was basically a necessary evil for someone in his position as chair.

It would have to be a one-on-one situation. That was unavoidable. Too much had gone wrong in the past few weeks to even consider farming this out to a stranger. Having too many people involved was the reason that they were in this mess in the first place. There were already a number of weak links in the organization. This was certainly not the time to add a stranger to the mix.

No, this had to be finished now, swiftly and cleanly. He would have to muster the courage to do it himself.

He set his mind to analyzing what he knew about the accountant. He needed to be as prepared as possible if he expected to successfully complete the task that he had set himself.

It was true that the accountant was a professional killer.

The nickname 'accountant' had come about for that very reason. He had actually coined it himself a good eight years ago when they had first brought the accountant into the organization.

The 'accountant'. The person who takes care of the checks and balances.

The nickname had stuck and thereafter they had all referred to their new enforcer as nothing other than the 'accountant'.

He couldn't remember the last time that any of the six had used the accountant's actual name.

The original purpose of the hiring had been to find someone to look after the basic cash collections, banking and accounting. To act as an additional cutout for the group to ensure they would not have to participate in the physical movement of the large sums of cash that had to be dealt with on a regular basis.

As time had gone on, the organization had also found itself

in need of an enforcer. The accountant had been present, by way of a conference call, during a meeting when the topic had come up, more as an accidental observer, than an intended participant in that particular discussion. It had come about as an off-the-cuff response during what had been, mostly money discussions.

Up to that time, no one would had even considered that the accountant would in any way be either prepared or qualified to fill the position of 'enforcer' in the organization. In fact, it would have seemed ridiculous to have suggested anything of the sort at the time.

However, as the discussion had progressed, it was the accountant who had suggested both the solution and the best means to remove the particular individual who had been the reason for the topic coming to the table in the first place.

He, along with the others who made up the group had been skeptical at first. Yet in the end they had all been swayed by the arguments that the accountant had used to support the suggestion of branching out from current duties to fill the position of enforcer when it became necessary. By the time the meeting had finished there had been agreement among them that the accountant should be allowed to have a crack at removing the offending party, a small time pusher. The man had become turned on to the stuff himself and as a result was demanding a bigger and unacceptable cut of the action in order to support his own habit.

He had been just as surprised as the rest of the group when the accountant had not only removed the irritant, but had done it in a manner that was not only effective, but remarkably clean and smooth.

The wretched chap had simply 'succumbed to a self-inflicted overdose' according to the police report of his death.

Their gratitude had been demonstrated through financial reward and it had seemed, from that point on, a natural progression to deliver any similar problems to the accountant for perusal and eradication.

On each of these occasions, the cold efficiency had been repeated and soon the group had come to consider the accountant more as an enforcer and overall problem solver than simply a financial cutout.

It was very much the history of that cold efficiency that troubled him now.

The abilities of his adversary were not to be sold short. The accountant had proven to be a natural and was extremely good at the job of killing.

He now found himself in the position of having to turn the tables somehow.

He had to manage to do that on his own.

How in God's name was he going to go about it?

*****

Robyn was trying to explain to David how she always positioned her keys on the TV and thereby was able to know by looking at them that someone had been in her apartment and had moved them.

David was standing by the window nursing the Scotch and water that Jenny had traded him for his coat once he had made it to the top of the stairs and entered her small kitchen.

"So you're absolutely sure that the keys had been moved?"

Robyn's face began to color a little and he sensed that she had previously gone through the same kind of cross-examination with Jenny over this point. She wasn't pleased at being challenged on it again.

He held up his hands in a gesture of supplication and smiled.

"Okay, you're sure! It's just that you'd just been through a lot at the time. It's not unreasonable to think that you might have done things differently than you would have under normal circumstances."

His smile was obviously sincere and it was enough to ease the anger and frustration that had begun to be reflected in her features, and he could understand the uneasiness that now replaced it.

"I'm scared David. It was the killer, wasn't it?"

David let out a sigh and nodded his head slowly.

"Yes, more than likely I'm afraid. It means he thinks that you've got something Carol left for you or gave to you for safekeeping; something that must be pretty incriminating to him. If not, he wouldn't have risked a daylight B&E. In all probability, it's either the tapes or the diary or both that he was looking for."

The two of them sat down at the table as Jenny bustled around the tiny kitchen.

The crab trap had been relegated to the far corner of the outside balcony to make room before she began to prepare the evening meal. Cato had been smart enough to lie down under the table where he would be safe from being accidently stepped on.

Sensing Robyn's frustration Jenny looked over at her.

"Don't you worry dear…you're quite safe here."

Robyn wasn't so sure of that.

She was still much shaken by the realization that the killer had been able to enter her apartment so easily. With her doors securely locked, she had always felt safe there.

Now she recognized just how foolish she had been. She felt personally violated somehow by the fact that it had happened. She was unable to think about it without experiencing a cold shudder.

David had investigated enough break-and-enters in his time to understand how she felt. He knew it would take time for her to accept and rationalize the situation.

He was tempted to make light of it in an effort to help her to put it behind her, but this hadn't been a normal B&E, and to play down the ramifications would have been downright foolish.

Like it or not, the killer was showing interest in Robyn and it was something they had to accept and guard against. For

Robyn's own safety, she had to face the fact that she had become the quarry of a very dangerous man.

"It would appear that the killer, for whatever reason, thinks that you've got whatever it is he wants. You'll have to stay away from your apartment until we catch him and lock him up. I'll get some of our people to put one of the department's silent alarm systems in there tomorrow, although I don't think that it's likely that he'll return to your apartment again."

Robyn gave him a questioning look.

"Why not?"

"Because he's searched it once and he didn't find what he was looking for. He's either decided that you don't have it and turned his attention elsewhere, or he'll try another tack."

He met her gaze and held it.

"If he considers it important enough and thinks that you have it, he'll contact you directly and make you give him whatever it is he wants."

The color drained from her face and he continued.

"Don't worry; nobody knows where you are but the three of us. We'll have him before he finds you."

Robyn felt a chill run through her, but she did her best to put up a good front.

"I certainly hope you're right!"

Jenny interjected.

"Grub's ready!"

Although Jenny had few guests for dinner these days, she missed entertaining and she'd not forgotten how to prepare a hearty meal.

It was simple and delicious. They started with fresh Dungeness crab cocktails. That was followed by a huge helping of fresh deep-fried Rock Cod done in the delightfully light beer batter that Jenny was famous for. The fish was served with thick crisp homemade fries and a green salad.

It was a standard, live-off-the-land fare of the Arm inhabitants and it was one of David's favorite meals.

A delightful French wine, two bottles of which had been opened before the repast was finished, provided the final touch to the meal. All three of them were in a relaxed and satisfied mood by the time the last of the dishes had been removed from the table.

Jenny didn't have a dishwasher. It was something she considered to be a ridiculous luxury for a single person. They all pitched in with the washing up - Jenny with her hands buried in the sudsy water, Robyn drying and David, who was relatively familiar with Jenny's kitchen cupboards, putting them away.

Once finished with the dishes, David busied himself building up of the coals in the small living room fireplace. The addition of a couple of logs was all it took to create a roaring blaze. As he worked at it the two women made the final adjustments to the kitchen area. In a matter of minutes they had restored it to its normal sparkling condition.

The two of them then prepared a large plate of freshly baked cookies and a steaming pot of tea in preparation for the after dinner move into the living room.

As David poked at the now resurrected fire his thoughts went back to Robyn.

She reminded him of Jackie in so many ways that it was a little unnerving.

He saw Jackie's basic goodness in her, the patience, the sincere caring, humor and warmth. But Robyn wasn't Jackie. It was both foolish and unfair to Robyn for him to be making comparisons between her and Jackie and yet he also understood that it was these very similarities that had initially attracted him to her in the first place.

It was a quandary, but it was his quandary, not hers.

It wasn't going to be easy for him. It was something he would have to consciously work on. But from now on in order to be fair to Robyn, he would have to see her as an individual and not as a reflection of Jackie.

CHAPTER TWENTY-SIX

Despite the growing cold, he couldn't prevent the perspiration from forming on his brow and palms any more than he could ignore the empty feeling in the pit of his stomach.

He was very much out of his element and he knew it only too well.

He handled the gun unfamiliarly. It was a foreign implement to him and the fact that his quarry would have found it very familiar, certainly did not comfort him.

He could reasonably count on surprise, but was that going to be enough to provide the edge he needed?

There was no doubt that his life depended on it. There would be no second chance.

He did what he could to prepare himself.

He loaded, unloaded, cocked and aimed the weapon, getting familiar with the mechanics of it. It helped to build his confidence. He had never been a particularly brave man and he was struggling to convince himself that what he was going to attempt would succeed or at least was within the realm of succeeding.

For the first time in his life, he was seriously frightened. He assured himself that the feeling was a very rational one under the circumstances. He found some comfort in that.

He knew only too well that if he had any choice in the matter at all, he would be running from this whole situation. But he had no choice and the acceptance of that fact had not been easy. His whole life had been subconsciously dedicated to avoiding any type of serious confrontation and yet, because of decisions he had made, he had no one to blame for the situation that he now found himself in but himself.

His joining with the others in the creation of the drug empire had predetermined the possibility of an eventual outcome of this nature. It went with the territory and now he would pay the price for choosing that particular path.

Without further recrimination, he slipped the gun into his overcoat pocket and left the hotel room.

*****

Both of them felt a little uncomfortable at the thought of being alone together.

It was foolish of them of course. Each wanted to be alone with the other. It was just that they were a little unsure of how to proceed. Neither of them wanted to be the one responsible for causing the relationship to falter before it had been given a fair chance.

Jenny's presence over the evening had provided a buffer between them and had given each of them the opportunity to guard their thoughts. They had both unwittingly used Jenny as a barrier to frank and direct communication about their relationship.

That protection was gone now as they began the walk down the stairway toward David's house.

They walked without speaking, each sensing that what would happen between them this evening would be very important in determining their futures and in no particular hurry to rush into it.

One way or the other, it would be a turning point. If it went well tonight their lives were going to be changed dramatically.

The shared prospect of that was as daunting as it was exciting.

*****

He arrived early for the meeting, wanting to check the surroundings, to be as familiar and comfortable with them as he could.

By doing so, he hoped to make certain he had relaxed as much as possible and that he was ready both physically and mentally for what would be a very traumatic act.

The decision had been made, and he was sure it was the correct one.

There was no turning back. He was committed and as prepared as he could be under the circumstances.

* * * * *

The accountant had been stationed in a position to observe the Rose Garden parking lot two hours prior to the scheduled meeting.

It hadn't taken a great deal of imagination to recognize that there was danger in this meeting.

It had been the accountant's innate ability to assess crisis situations reliably to date that had made a dangerous lifestyle possible to maintain with relative impunity.

You did not choose this profession and be successful unless you were always prepared for and at least one step ahead of the opposition.

When had the realization come? At the last meeting probably.

The decision had been forced upon the accountant at that time by his soon-to-arrive quarry. At the end of their last meeting there had been few real options available to him.

To be honest, the accountant had probably engineered that meeting in such a way as to ensure that the frightened man would have no other choice.

He was not a man who could accept control and dominance by another, not at this point in his life. That being a fact, what real option had the accountant left him?

Yes, the outcome of this meeting had been predetermined. It was inevitable.

For the task at hand, the accountant had chosen what was considered a Saturday-night-special. It was a little unadorned gunmetal twenty-two. It was the type of gun that was used in more murders than any other.

The viewpoint the accountant had chosen had been a good one.

Under the light of the parking lot floodlights, the quarry's arrival more than an hour before the scheduled time for the meet had been immediately noted, as had the presence of the gun that the man had nervously pulled out and studied several times over the past forty-five minutes.

The accountant had no doubt as to the intention of the prey. One of them was very definitely going to be dead before the evening was over, and the accountant had no intention of being on a slab before morning.

The tapes were still important however, and to avoid the meeting entirely was not open to consideration. Possession of those tapes would ensure that future prospects remained bright.

There would be no regret after the act.

Although they had known each other for years, they could hardly be considered as friends. Business was business. One more death wouldn't affect the sequence of events as planned. In fact, if anything, this particular death would serve to enhance the end result of the blackmail angle.

After all, what would better serve to convince the others of the need to co-operate more than the death of one of their own?

*****

Cato, who had run ahead down the stairs, welcomed them at the bottom and Robyn, who had really warmed to the big dog over the day, spent time playing with him. She stood on the small patch of grass in front of David's front door, repeatedly throwing the ball that Cato had eagerly bought to them as they reached the bottom stair.

She sensed that she and David were a little uptight and she wanted to give both of them an opportunity to unwind a little before they faced the discussion that she knew was coming.

David watched the two of them for a few moments, then opened the door and flipped on the outside flood light to make it easier for Robyn keep an eye on the dog in the growing darkness. He left them and went inside to build a fire to ward off the cold snap that was obviously settling into the Arm.

He was astute enough to recognize that both he and Robyn were under pressure. Over the evening it had become obvious to him that the concern he felt over their budding relationship was a shared one. It was as much of an enigma to her as it was to him.

Seeing the whole situation as a double sided coin and sensing that she was sharing his unease served to support his resolve to clarify things and he felt the cloud of uncertainty that had been building in him throughout the day, begin to lift.

He was confident that together they would deal with it before the night was through.

*****

He'd planned it carefully.

He would hand across the briefcase holding the tapes, minus his own of course, and as the accountant reached for it he would fire through his coat pocket. After all, the fact that he had his free hand in his pocket would not seem unreasonable in view of the present weather conditions.

The best laid pans of mice and men.

The four bullets that entered his chest in perfect proximity to his heart came while he was just beginning to pass over the briefcase. He hadn't noticed the little gun that had been nestled within the accountant's right glove.

In the throws of almost instant death, his finger squeezed on the trigger of the gun in his pocket and the projectile it emitted slammed harmlessly into the pavement of the walkway at their feet.

He was dead before he hit the ground and the accountant, briefcase nestled securely in the passenger seat, was pulling out of the parking stall before the inert body had begun to lose its temperature and accept the creeping coldness of the night.

* * * * *

As David gave the flickering fire one last prod with the poker and stood up, Robyn and Cato came thundering through the door together. Robyn immediately bent to hug the big dog and settle him down from his spirited romp outside.

David smiled as he noted the obvious bond that had formed between the pair.

"Cold out there. Can I interest you in a Blueberry tea to warm you up?"

Robyn wrinkled her nose and turned her attention from the dog to David as she stood up, and began to remove her coat. Cato, tired from his ball chasing, dropped down into a lying position by the door and shifted his big head onto his paws.

"And exactly what is a Blueberry tea?"

David's smile broadened and he turned from the fire and started for the kitchen, turning his head over his shoulder to answer her.

"Ah! A Blueberry tea novice. I'll build us a couple. I think you'll enjoy it. I find them a great way to settle a meal."

Robyn hung her coat up in the closet by the door, before following him into the kitchen. She stood and watched him as he filled the kettle and plugged it in.

He ginned over at her and raised his hands to shoo her out of the room.

"No fair peeking, I want this to be a surprise. Why don't you go and have a nice hot bath and relax while I make them."

Robyn smiled impishly.

"Were you planning to bring mine up to me?"

David laughed.

"How could I refuse such an invitation, but you will have to promise to behave yourself until after we go over the case. I want to bounce a few things off you and get your perspective on them."

She raised her eyebrows a little.

"Promise, but we need to talk about us too."

*****

On winter nights, the Mounted Squad often rode marked squad cars, not their horses, when they patrolled the expanses of Stanley Park.

That was the case tonight. As the two-manned unit entered the parking area just off the Rose garden, the headlights of the cruiser caught the form of the body in their shifting beams.

At first glance, the Constable behind the wheel thought it was a couple of garbage bags that had dropped off one of the Parks Board maintenance trucks. He might have ignored it completely if he hadn't considered it a hazard to traffic.

Moments later he was standing over the inert form and was immediately cognizant of exactly what it was.

His first reaction was to search for a pulse, but the stiff coldness of the flesh he touched told him the body held no trace of life and hadn't for some time.

He immediately shouted back to his waiting partner in the patrol car to call for backup.

*****

"Ummmm, what's in it?"

David, who was standing at the edge of the tub, didn't respond immediately. He was very much lost in the appreciation of her lush body. It had a rosy pink tinge from being immersed in the steaming water and was resting just below the surface.

Robyn was a very beautiful woman and it wasn't until she had repeated her question that he pulled himself out of his reverie and answered her

"It's a secret."

She took another sip from the mug that he had presented her on entering the bathroom and she smiled over at him.

"Okay, man of mystery. Oh and by the way, you don't have to appreciate me from afar. Get your clothes off and climb in here, there's plenty of room for two."

"And what about the investigation and our little talk?"

Robyn shrugged.

"The case isn't going to go away. It can wait, and we can talk in here."

Appreciating her naked body had done nothing to strengthen his earlier resolve to talk before any further intimacy.

He grinned and shook his head slowly, then set his mug down on the floor by the tub and began to remove his clothes. Robyn's eyes stayed on him as she blatantly watched him strip. She raised her mug back to her lips and drank from it; savoring the flavor of the mellow concoction.

"It's very good. Tell me what's in it."

David had slipped off his shirt and he sat down on the john to pull off his shoes and socks.

"Well, you start with Black Currant tea, add an ounce of Grand Marnier and an ounce of Amaretto for each mug and stir with a Cinnamon stick. A couple of these and you will sleep like a baby."

Robyn laughed and watched as he stood and undid his pants, pulled them off and hung them up on one of the hooks on the back of the bathroom door.

"Who wants to sleep?"

David turned back to face her as he bent to shove his shorts off and dropped them to the floor.

In anticipation of joining her in the bath, he had become semi-erect and as he crossed to join her in the tub, she reached for him and reeled him playfully into the water with her.

She held on tight and as he sank below the surface. David reached for her wrist and squeezed gently.

"Hey, you promised to talk first!"

Robyn took the time to stroke the now fully turgid organ a few times and then reluctantly released it.

"Okay killjoy, but let's get this over with in a hurry, it's rather obvious that I'm not the only one interested in moving on to other things."

David turned on the Jacuzzi and adjusted the jets, then reached for his mug of tea and settled down further into the water.

*****

All hell broke loose when the Mounted Squad checked the body for identification.

When the older of the two men had shifted the beam from his flashlight onto the now pale features and confirmed that the information that had been gleaned from the driver's license and other papers that his partner had retrieved from the wallet, he couldn't believe his eyes.

His muttered oath filled the evening as he lurched to his feet and raced back to the radio in his cruiser.

"Son of a bitch..."

CHAPTER TWENTY-SEVEN

They had talked and it had gone well. There would be no more pressure in that area.

With the personal pressures off, they decided to soap up and rinse before they started reviewing the case.

That decision had seemed reasonable at the time, but in short order, David realized that had been the first mistake.

The second had been the unspoken agreement between them that each would wash the other. He went first and by the time he was finished, he wanted her so badly that the rhythmic pulsing of his swollen organ was almost painful.

Then it was Robyn's turn to do the washing.

She asked him to stand while she lathered him up. She did his back first and then his front, paying very special attention to what was by now her main area of interest. By the time that she got round to rinsing him, using the nozzle on the end of the five foot flex tubing, David had his eyes closed and was groaning huskily.

When she had finished rinsing him she returned the hose to its hanger.

It had become obvious to both of them that the discussion of the case was going to have to wait.

Her eyes met his briefly then she raised her hands up to cup the muscular cheeks of his ass and pulled him toward her as she shifted forward onto her knees and took him into her mouth.

David groaned deeply and his hands moved to the back of her head and cupped it gently.

*****

As they were aware of the investigation concerning the six, and knowing that he would want to be informed; the night shift detectives got hold of Boyd at home minutes after ascertaining the identity of the body that had been found in the Park.

Once contacted, Boyd relieved them of the responsibility of informing Walker. He advised them that he would look after that himself before he headed for the Rose garden.

He then gave instructions to maintain the crime scene until his arrival.

*****

The bathroom was filled with steam.

They were paying homage to each other orally, rolling on the deep pile of the bathroom rug. Their wet bodies glistened with a mixture of water and sweat and they were completely engrossed in building toward mutual satisfaction.

Their lovemaking was almost intense enough to blank out the rest of the world.

It was Robyn who finally heard the ringing phone. She reluctantly let him slip free of her mouth and managed to speak in a hoarse whisper.

"David, the phone is ringing!"

He swore softly and rolled off her onto his back. The hair on his muscular chest was matted with moisture and heaving rhythmically as he fought to regain his normal rate of breathing.

He managed to get to his feet and swore again as he looked down at her inviting form one last time before he hurried out of the room and down the hall to his bedroom. He got to the phone on the eighth ring.

He recognized Boyd's voice before the detective had fully identified himself and, despite his understandable frustration at being interrupted, David was immediately at-
tentive.

Boyd would not be calling him at home unless it was important.

He listened in silence until the detective was finished then responded.

"Okay, I'll be there as soon as I can, about an hour."

He then replaced the phone into its cradle and let out a deep sigh of disappointment.

"Shit!"

Robyn had joined him. She was wrapped in a towel. He managed a weak smile as he turned to face her.

"Banks, one of the drug barons has been killed in Stanley Park. I'm sorry, but I'm going to have to go."

Robyn nodded her understanding and managed to smile back.

She then she pulled open the two sides of the towel and flashed him briefly.

"I can't say that I'm happy with the idea, but I understand…and like the case, I'll still be here when you get back."

David laughed and moved across to her and pulled her into his arms.

The towel dropped to the floor between them as their lips met. It was a deep probing kiss of long duration. When they had finished David patted her playfully on the rump then headed for the bathroom to shower and retrieve his clothes.

"I'll be back as quickly as I can. You hop into bed and try to get some sleep."

Robyn bent to retrieve the towel and wrapped herself in it again as she followed him out of the room.

She leaned against the doorframe of the bathroom door and watched him shower rapidly and dry himself before she spoke.

"I'll sleep if you promise to wake me up when you get home."

David hung the wet towel up on its hook and smiled over at her.

"Okay, we'll pick up where we left off when I get back, providing you get some rest in the meantime."

Robyn beamed.

"It's a deal, your bed or mine?"

David laughed deeply, looking up from buttoning his shirt.

"At this point, I think we can consider mine, ours. What do you think?"

Robyn tilted her head coyly.

"Sounds reasonable to me, but I thought that we were going to discuss the case."

His laugh mellowed.

"We can do that first if you like, and if you stay on your own side of the bed until we finish. Otherwise I'm not making any promises."

Robyn crossed over to him and hugged him warmly and David reached for his robe and slipped it around her before he resumed his dressing. When he had finished, she followed him to the front door and he kissed her lightly on the cheek as he opened it and gave Cato a chance for a quick run before he left.

"Cato sleeps in my bedroom at night. He'll look after you until I get back.

Lock the door behind me when I go."

*****

Despite the early hour, traffic was royally screwed up as Walker approached the park entrance off Georgia Street.

Television, Radio and Newspaper reporters coupled with the building early morning rush hour traffic and the numerous emergency units with their lights flashing plugged the entry road to the Rose Garden area, and by extension the entry road to the Park proper.

In exasperation, David resorted to his siren and tossed his revolving blue light out his window and onto the roof of his unmarked car.

He pulled out into oncoming traffic and impatiently, but carefully forced his way into the entrance and eventually the small Rose garden parking lot.

Boyd, who had been watching for him, was at the driver's door before David had switched off his siren and retrieved the flashing light. He got out of the car, locked it, and then followed the detective toward the ambulance which had been backed up to the motionless figure stretched out under a blanket. The shapeless form was divided equally between the sidewalk and the parking lot.

The headlights of a half circle of police units, switched on to high beam, accompanied by the two powerful floods off the back of the ambulance, filled the area with bright light.

Boyd offered no comment as his boss entered the area and began to make an initial assessment.

Lifting the blanket, Walker moved slowly around the body, and then hunkered down beside it.

He examined the area where the bullets had entered, noted the ragged blackened hole in the right overcoat pocket and the palm up and splayed fingers of the right hand and looked up at Boyd.

The expression on his face was all the stimulus that was needed to bring about a response from the detective.

"Smith and Wesson .38, with a five-inch barrel. Fired once through the right pocket of his overcoat. Slug went into the pavement"

He gestured to the entry point and its identifying yellow marker.

David stood, and Boyd held out the gun, now enclosed in a plastic evidence bag with the trigger wired to prevent an accidental discharge. David examined it without physically handling the bag and then looked at Boyd.

"Standard police issue."

His eyes returned to the body for a split second.

"He obviously came here expecting trouble"

He swiveled slightly, letting his gaze take in the scene around them.

"IDENT finished with the body and photos'?"

Boyd nodded.

"Okay, tell them that they can move the body as soon as I've had a chance to examine it more closely. Give me five minutes, and in the mean time, send me over the senior uniform. I want this crowd moved to hell out of here."

He added almost as an afterthought, causing Boyd to pause in mid-turn.

"We still got a lid on this? The media don't know who he is, do they?"

Boyd shook his head.

"Not yet, but a lot of the uniforms know who he was. The Mounted guys who found the body have been talking. I don't know how long we can reasonably expect to keep the press in the dark."

Boyd left and a few seconds later a gnarled grey-haired Sergeant, who Walker knew well, crossed the lot toward him.

"You wanted me sir?"

David nodded and stood up. He touched the big man on the shoulder and led him out of the glare of the bright lights.

"Two things Bill. First, talk to all of our people here. I want Bank's identity kept from the media as long as possible. Tell your people to keep a lid on it. Second, get rid of this audience and when that ambulance pulls out send a marked unit with it to run interference. Tell them to make sure that none of those press types manage to find out where the body is being taken. They'll figure it out eventually of course, but I would like you to buy me as much time as you can."

The big Irishman nodded and turned back toward the inner circle of policeman. He moved through them swiftly, but unobtrusively, speaking to each uniformed man in turn for a few seconds before moving on to the next.

Almost immediately, the previously somewhat disorganized group of uniforms began to function again. Within fifteen minutes the only people who remained in the vicinity of the body were those required to be in the area for police purposes; and in the distance, the snarled traffic beyond the park entrance was beginning to move again.

Walker turned his attention back to the body and completed his examination of it then authorized removal before he was rejoined by Boyd as the ambulance and its escort pulled out of the lot.

They watched it leave and then the detective began to fill his boss in on what the initial examination of the crime scene had revealed.

"Thanks to the frost on the ground we've been able to put a second car in the lot at the time of the murder. It was parked three stalls away from Bank's Buick, and it came into the lot after Bank's and didn't spend as much time parked as the Buick."

They walked as they talked, Boyd leading the way to where the dark blue Buick stood, a layer of light frost glistening on the metal in the intermittent brightness given off by the flashing light of the wrecker that was patiently waiting for the go ahead to tow it.

Boyd, flashlight in hand, showed David the spot in the parking stall where the warm engine of the accountant's car had melted the frost under it, turning it into a rough oval of ice. He then guided the beam to the tire impressions left behind when the car had left the lot.

"I've had IDENT take shots of this. They tell me that the tire patterns will come up well enough for comparison tests. From measuring the area between the wheel marks left while it was briefly parked, we should be able to get an idea of size. They tell me that there is an outside chance that they might be able to ascertain the make and model."

Walker nodded and both men stepped aside as two uniformed members from IDENT began to retrieve the yellow plastic barricade tape from around the crime scene.

"What else you got?"

"No shell casings; must have used a revolver. I doubt if expelled casings would have been easy to retrieve in the light provided. We got nothing near the body; the area was pretty much chewed up by the first cars here. IDENT tried for shoe impressions in the frost, but had no luck."

Walker nodded, taking in the overall scene one more time as Boyd continued.

"Among the effects, I found a room key from the Bayshore Hotel. I figure that should be our first stop. I've arranged for an immediate autopsy and we can head to the morgue as soon as we have a look at his room."

Walker glanced around at the remaining policemen.

"Any sign of CSIS? They were supposed to have a team on Banks?"

Boyd shrugged and they turned and started back to their cars.

"That was my first thought. Nobody came forward and I didn't know if you'd want me to make contact with them now or later."

David smiled.

"Let's have a private look at Banks' room first. You know, I don't think those bastards ever intended on putting a team on him. They probably don't even know that he's been hit."

CHAPTER TWENTY-EIGHT

The accountant stood staring down at the tapes.

There were only five.

It seemed likely that the missing tape would be Banks' own and yet the remaining five would have to be checked to make sure.

There was no need to be particularly concerned over the fact that Bank's tape was probably missing. At this point, there was certainly no potential for blackmailing him anyway.

Yet having the one tape missing meant that there was still a loose thread out there somewhere. That made the accountant uneasy.

In all probability, the missing tape would eventually be found by the police. It could lead them back to Carol's death in that Carol would be identifiable in the scenes involving Banks. Having the two deaths tied together so soon was something that the accountant had been hoping to avoid, but it seemed inevitable now.

The question was, just how dangerous would that be. The police had to know of Banks' criminal involvement with Carol in any event. After all that's how the investigation had started in the first place.

The tape would add a new dimension to their investigation, but so what? If anything it might just serve to cloud the issue for them even more.

*****

It was David who noticed the VCR when they entered the hotel room. He immediately closed the door behind them and locked it.

"You search, I'll keep the notes. Keep an eye out for video

tapes."

David then drew out his notebook and pen. He wrote down the time and location and stood in the center of the room.

Following department procedure Boyd commenced the search by starting to the right of the door and moving around the room in a clockwise direction. He gave his full attention to the physical searching of the room itself and trusted Walker to keep an accurate log of the process.

Each man played his part automatically, years of experience, more than departmental procedures guiding them. Individually they had proven to themselves time after time that it was the only efficient way to conduct a proper room search.

There was nothing worse than having partners jointly search a room simultaneously.

Using that approach meant that neither man could be expected to keep track of what specific areas the other had already covered. Duplication inevitably led to confusion.

Boyd located the tape at the bottom of the larger of the two suitcases. It was stashed under soiled shirts and underwear. He marked it and initialed the case before passing it to Walker, who then crossed over to the VCR and slipped it in.

A couple of seconds of viewing told David what he wanted to know.

It was a copy of Carol's tape of Banks' sexual gymnastics. He rewound it and ejected it. After slipping it back into its case, he bagged it and initialed the bag before crossing the room and picking up the phone.

David fished out the business card that CSIS Regional Director, Matt Birch had given him when he had first visited with him in his office and then dialed.

When he had finished his call to CSIS, where an underling had assured him that 'Director Birch would be immediately advised of his call' he turned back to Boyd and nodded to indicate that the detective could now complete the search of the remainder of the room.

*****

The accountant adjusted the light over the desk before lifting the glass and draining off a good slug of the stiff Scotch.

The night had been very cold, but as the alcohol worked its way through the blood stream, warmth was finally beginning to return.

It was going to be a long night.

Making copies of the five tapes would take time, but the thought of what those copies would bring in return for the effort would make it a worthwhile and satisfying endeavor.

And in the accountant's mind that definitely justified a second, and in time a third drink.

*****

Walker dropped into the chair and stared over at the standing agent.

Undisguised anger was smoldering in his eyes and it was obviously making the other man uncomfortable.

Boyd who was on the far side of the room was obviously enjoying the scene immensely.

He, like most run of the mill cops, had no love for the, so called, elite agents of CSIS. As the tension began to build, he moved over to the bed, sat down and prepared to enjoy the exchange between his boss and Birch.

It didn't go unnoticed by the other two men that he was taking in the agent's pronounced discomfort at being reamed out by David with undisguised glee, and he didn't give a damn. David wasn't concerned about it either.

"Look Birch, if you had done what I asked - what in fact you said you were going to do - Banks would probably still be alive and I'd have my murderer behind bars."

The CSIS Regional Director had lost a good deal of the polished composure that David had faced in their earlier meeting. He paced uneasily around the room as he replied.

"You've got to understand that it isn't easy to get authorization from Ottawa for surveillance on someone like Banks, even for CSIS. My God he was the highest Law Enforcement Officer in the land after all. I did put the process into motion, but these things take time."

David cut him off.

"Horseshit. I would have been able to get the go ahead to put surveillance on him in less than an hour, which is exactly what I would have done, if you hadn't interfered.

The other man spun to face him.

"You don't understand the political ramifications. We're a relatively new agency. Christ, we have a watchdog committee man. Can you imagine what a field day the government opposition parties in Ottawa would have had if they'd twigged to the fact that we were watching Banks? My God, the man was, for all intents and purposes, both our bosses. It was a delicate issue."

Walker lifted his muscular bulk out of the chair and in one fluid motion, crossed the distance between them and squared off with the agent.

"Good God Matt, whose side are you on? What the hell is wrong with you bastards anyway? You're all ex-cops, or have you forgotten that? You've got a job to do, and no cop can do his job properly if he's worried about the political ramifications. Ask the next uniform you see on the street, and he'll remind you of that fact in case you've forgotten."

Birch let his shoulders droop for a second and then crossed to the window and gazed out at the flickering lights of the harbor below.

"I understand why you're angry, David, and I don't blame you; but please believe me - you don't have any idea of what tight scrutiny we're under. We're new at this game, and we're under a magnifying glass. If we ever want to get out from under it, we have no choice but to play the political game until they get tired of watching us."

He self-consciously reached for his tie and adjusted it in

the reflection of the window as he straightened his shoulders. David sensed some of the polish begin to return as he continued.

"No matter what you may think Inspector, I do care and the Service cares. We simply don't dare screw up politically right now. We have no option but to accept that fact. I'm the first to admit that it makes our job damn near impossible. There is a power struggle currently going on that you wouldn't believe. As a new agency we're ripe for the picking and everyone wants to be the one who pulls our strings. We have the future of the Service to consider and if we play our cards close to the vest for now, we'll eventually be able to do the job the way it should be done. In the meantime, we make allowances and we watch our asses. Christ, I don't have to tell you that this particular incident doesn't even fall within our mandate and yet politics has put it there. It isn't as if we were given the option of refusing the assignment."

Walker shrugged his frustration off, crossed over to where the other man was standing and stood beside him to join the agent in the study the lights of the harbor below them.

Neither man spoke for a few seconds. Finally they turned to face each other.

Beneath the expensive suit, David saw before him an ex-Mountie. Matt Birch was a policeman who had spent his time on the streets, who had demonstrated that he was a good cop and through his good work, and over time, had eventually made it into the R.C.M.P. elite security section. From there he had been selected for a position of power within the newly formed CSIS agency. Few members of the force possessed the abilities necessary to reach his level.

Deep inside David knew that the frustration and anger he felt over the death of Banks and the successful escape of the murderer had to be being suffered just as strongly by the man who stood beside him as it was by him.

As a policeman he could empathize with that.

"Okay Matt, let's drop this shit. I've got several dead bodies on my hands, including a few cops and I want to lock up the bastard responsible yesterday because there is a damn good probability that he's going to kill again. Let's forget how we got this far and do what needs to be done. I want everything you've got that will help me, and in exchange for that I'll do everything I can to keep a lid on this thing as far as the political side of it goes. The fact is that we've only got a short timeframe to make some sense out of this before the press realizes just who it was that just got shot. When that happens neither of us will be able to control what follows."

Birch relaxed somewhat and began to pace again.

"We really don't know any more than you do. This came at us from left field. Our political masters in Ottawa dropped it in our laps with the unofficial goal of doing our best to remove any chance that Banks might be implicated in a drug ring and to minimize the resulting damage and embarrassment to the government as a whole. His death is going to reduce the danger of that by the very fact the he no longer holds his position within the government. They will very certainly do their level best to distance themselves from him as rapidly as they can, so that if and when any successful investigation on that aspect comes to light, it will have less direct impact on them."

He paused in front of Walker.

"I'm anticipating, but I would imagine that what Ottawa will want when they find out that Banks is dead, will be for us to do our best to have his passing be of a nature that doesn't relate it back to the drug thing. If you could give me a hand with that, I think the pressure might come off CSIS, and I would be in a better position to give you any help we can. Could you see your way clear to release this as simply a robbery gone wrong, at least for now? That would in no way jeopardize your murder investigation and it would certainly be welcomed in Ottawa."

Walker let out a mirthless chuckle and shook his head slowly.

"You have a one-track mind, don't you?"

The other man shrugged.

"You have your job to do and I have mine. I'd like to see us work together on this to both of our benefits. We both know that it's not going to help your investigation to smear Banks. If anything, it will make a media circus out of it. I'm simply asking you to do both CSIS and your government a favor and let Banks' death go down as a simple robbery. You have nothing to gain by tying him to the drug ring at this point, except maybe the satisfaction at having paid me back for not providing you with what I had promised - something that I honestly tried to do but was too slow at accomplishing due to the system that I'm expected to function within. I'm not asking you to interfere with or obstruct the CLEU investigation either. That should and will eventually take its natural course. I'm simply asking you to concentrate on your murder investigations and at the same time offering you whatever help CSIS can provide you in that regard."

Walker glanced over to where Boyd was sitting.

"Release it that way. Banks was enjoying a walk in the park before bed, and was accosted by an unknown assailant, the apparent motive, robbery."

*****

It was well into the early morning hours when the accountant, wearing surgical gloves, finished preparing the last of the five packages. Each contained a copy of a tape and a simple typed letter of instructions for the delivery of the first of the monthly payments of five thousand dollars each to an offshore account. It was an amount that was significant to be sure, but something that they could all easily afford.

Each package was now wrapped in plain brown paper, addressed and marked 'personal'.

They would be delivered via courier.

*****

Boyd had just finished parking his unmarked car in the underground police garage when he spotted his boss entering through the overhead door.

He paused and waited until the vehicle pulled up abreast of him and the window slipped down.

David stifled a yawn as he slipped the car into park.

"You complete the pawn shop investigation in the morning and I'll finish interviewing the last of the participants in Carol's little prostitution ring. Then we'll get together and compare notes. The blackmail angle of this thing may well give us some leverage. I think it's time we confronted the remaining five kingpins of the drug group and apply some pressure before anyone else gets killed."

Boyd, feeling the lack of sleep, was leaning over, his arms resting against the sill of the open car window.

"You think they know who the killer is?

David nodded.

"Well, I'm sure they paid for the hit on Carol. They either know who the murderer is or else they know who knows who he is. Either way if we can get one of them to talk we'll have a good starting point. We've got to try to convince at least one of them that it's in his best interest to co-operate with us."

Boyd had his doubts about the success of pressuring such powerful men.

"Not too likely with the drug conspiracy investigation hanging over their heads. They have to know that the killer, once arrested, is likely to try for a deal in exchange for information implicating them in the drug importing ring."

Walker shrugged.

"Well they've all got to be feeling pretty vulnerable right now. They've been trying to manipulate the CLEU investigation and have been pretty successful up to this point, but now they've got the killer to consider. It may be that they believe the murderer isn't in a position to provide sufficient evidence to insure a conviction against them; after all they've been very careful up to now about distancing themselves from any of the dirty work. If that's the case they might just try to offer him up as a sacrificial lamb in an attempt to ride the whole drug conspiracy thing out. On the other hand, they have to be concerned about their personal safety by now. The killer has taken Banks out, and if they are not already aware of that, they certainly will be by the time they finish reading their morning newspapers. If they think that they can deal with the hit man by way of paying blackmail, they might go that route, at least in the short term until they can work out a method to turn the tables on him. It's a tough one to call, but the thought of paying out large sums of money can't be very appealing to them, and they have to know by his hit on Banks, that the murderer is a loose cannon and won't hesitate to kill them if they don't fall into line. No, I think that we stand a good chance of talking at least one of them into giving us what we need to get a line on our killer. If we can get one to talk, the rest may just follow like dominos in a last ditch attempt to ensure self-preservation"

David glanced at his watch.

"We both need some sleep and there isn't much more we can do tonight, not until the forensic boys have finished up. When you go up to the office to sign out, leave a note on Cindy's desk asking her to let the Deputy know that I won't be able to make the morning meeting with him. He isn't going to like it, but he'll have to live with it. See that he gets a copy of your report on Banks death and ask Cindy to see if she can set something up for a meeting with Foster tomorrow in the late afternoon. I want to have a chance to work on the five before we talk to him. Hopefully, we'll have some good info by then. That should take some of the pressure off as far as Foster is concerned. Be in the office by eleven and we'll put our heads together before we head out."

Boyd nodded and straightened up and stepped back from the car.

David closed the window, slipped the unmarked unit into gear and swung around to pull back out of the lot.

For the first time since he'd left her, he had a chance to let his thoughts drift back to Robyn. The tiredness that had begun to fill him slipped away as he formed a mental picture of her waiting for him in his bed.

It had been a long time since he'd had someone to go home to.

It was a damn good feeling.

CHAPTER TWENTY-NINE

Overtired as he was, David was definitely feeling the cold after the short boat trip home.

Cato met him at the door and David, doing his best to ensure that he was as quiet as possible, placated the dog with a head rub and then hung up his overcoat and made his way upstairs to his bedroom.

He stripped quickly and the bed felt luxuriously warm as he slipped in beside her.

He'd had the best of intentions, fully prepared to let her sleep on peacefully. But she moaned softly as he joined her in the king-sized water-bed and her arms slipped around him, pulling him tight against her.

"Wow, are you ever cold, here let me warm you up."

David laughed and twisted till he was facing her. He let his arms cradle her warmth, holding her against him. As they kissed, he felt the stiffening tips of her nipples pressing into his chest. She lifted her lips from his and reached for his hardening organ, whispering as she nuzzled his ear.

"I know just how to do that; how about we pick up where we left off on the bathroom floor?"

She didn't wait for an answer. Instead she began to leave a trail of warm damp kisses, down over his chest toward her now tantalizingly stroking fingers. David groaned.

His resolve to let her sleep until morning dissolved instantly.

He kicked off the covers and reached for her hips, pulling her over on top of him as he shifted his head down between her already parting legs.

The moonlight reflecting off the water gave the room a soft glow and he drank in the sight of her firm, willing flesh. His tongue flicked out in an exploratory caress against the silkiness of her inner thigh, then found its goal as he felt her lips close over him.

He waited until they had both had chance to enjoy the building sensations then gently rolled them over onto their sides and shifted his thigh under her slowly bobbing head as he moved her thigh into position to provide him with the same support. He then dove back between her legs and began to work on her with his tongue.

Neither was in a hurry. They lost themselves to the wonder of giving and receiving pleasure. The pace of their lovemaking was balanced and all enveloping. Tantalizingly sensuous, it was enough to ensure that when the time came, they reached the pinnacle together.

Pleasure ripped through them and they jerked in a mutual series of spasms as they drained each other of the passion that had overtaken them. They lay locked together for several frenzied minutes then he gently spun her around and pulled her up beside him. His hands found the covers and pulled them up to cover them as he nuzzled the nape of her neck and molded his body to hers.

Robyn response was a long, satisfied moan.

"Oh God, you're good!"

He laughed softly.

"Thank you, kind damsel, and I am also too damned old for you."

She pulled away from him and propped herself up on one elbow to look down at him in the moonlight.

"It so happens that I'm attracted to older men, and although you are older than I am, you are not old."

She reached down and grasped him firmly. In view of the short period of time since she had drained him, he was a little surprised to feel himself instantly responding to her touch.

Robyn laughed triumphantly.

"If you can do that, how in God's name can you consider yourself old?"

David hugged her tightly to him.

He searched for the words to express to her the intense feelings that he felt for her at that moment. The love and warmth for her that was coursing through him was all-encompassing. It was, too him, very much like being reborn and he simply couldn't put it into words, let alone communicate the intensity of it to her.

Because he was unable to tell her how he felt, his lips found hers in an attempt to convey his pleasure and appreciation. Robyn responded in kind.

He was surprised to find that he was ready for her again and he eagerly accepted the fact, shifting himself up over her warm body as she eagerly spread her legs for him. Robyn arched her back and drew him into the hot moistness of her eager body.

Her nails raked his back gently as he thrust deeply into her.

Her words were muffled as she sensuously nibbled at his neck.

"I think that I just might be falling into love with you, Inspector Walker."

* * * * *

The alarm went off at nine-thirty.

David responded automatically, switching it off and rolling over onto his back. He left his eyes closed as he stretched and it was his sense of smell that first brought him to the realization that Robyn had very much become a part of his life.

He eagerly welcomed the enduring odor of her that surrounded him. Despite the erection that he had awoken with and which was now slowly subsiding, the delicious sensation of her smell lingering in the bed was fortified by the lazy, completely relaxed, sensation in his loins.

Without opening his eyes, he tossed his left arm out to touch her and then realized that she wasn't there. He felt a flash of panic grip him briefly, but her voice short-circuited the reaction.

"Breakfast is served my lord"

The smell of bacon and eggs drifted into the room and he opened his eyes and looked up at her as she came through the door dressed in his robe and carrying a tray.

At the sight of her, his fading erection made a sudden change in direction and he reached out to grab her.

Robyn backed off playfully and smiled down at him.

"Easy tiger, breakfast first, then into the bath."

He took the tray from her outstretched hands and she gave him a small curtsy accompanied by a broad smile then turned and disappeared out the door.

* * * * *

The packages had all been delivered.

Despite an earlier agreement prohibiting such contact, phone calls between the five had been immediate and a meeting had been hastily arranged for eleven o'clock that morning.

To say that they were concerned was an understatement, given that in addition to the receipt of the individual packages, the morning paper had carried the account of Banks' death on its front page.

It was a controlled panic, but it was panic nonetheless.

It was exactly the reaction that the accountant had expected and indeed, counted on.

* * * * *

He found her in the bath waiting for him.

They made love again there in the tub, each conscious of the fact that they had limited time.

It was fast, almost frantic. They couldn't get enough of each other. It was no less satisfying because of its short duration.

*****

Walker arrived at his office at a quarter to eleven.

He had phoned Jenny before he left the house. He arranged for her to accompany Robyn into town for an appointment to see Carol's lawyer who would be handling the estate for Robyn.

He settled down into the chair at this desk and buzzed Cindy.

When she entered his office, he asked her where she had put his copy of the diary which he intended to go over before his meeting with Boyd so that he could be as prepared as possible for his anticipated meetings with the five, later in the day.

He had left the document on his desk earlier in the week, and with everything else going on, hadn't realized that it had been moved until now.

Cindy gave him a questioning look when he asked her about it.

"Oh, I gave it to that CSIS agent on Wednesday. He told me that you had left it for him to pick up."

Before he could speak, she sensed what had happened and tears began to well up in her eyes as she began to babble.

"I'm sorry Boss; he said that you had authorized it. He seemed to know all about it, he left his card, I assumed..."

David held up his hand to silence her.

"That's okay Cindy, it's not important. Would you please bring in the card he left for me?"

She stood looking at him from the doorway for a second, trying to gauge if he was as unconcerned as he now appeared, or was in reality disappointed in, or upset with her.

David knew that he was responsible for the loss, in that he shouldn't have left it on his desk. It wasn't Cindy's fault, and it wasn't that important anyway. He could make another copy from the original.

He managed a smile for Cindy and she, still not fully convinced that he wasn't displeased with her, left the room.

Walker leaned back in his chair and tried to figure out why in hell CSIS would want a second copy of the diary.

They already had the copy that he had given CLEU. Why would they want his as well?

His intercom buzzed and Cindy advised him that detective Boyd had arrived.

He put his ponderings on the copy of the diary aside and got up to meet Boyd who followed Cindy into his office and took a chair as she handed David the card that the CSIS agent had left when he picked up the copy of the diary.

David thanked her and glanced at the card quickly then put it down and turned his attention to Boyd.

* * * * *

After the battery of telephone calls from the others, a small conference room in the Hotel Vancouver had been hastily booked by Justice Richard London earlier that morning. All five members of the group, now aware that they were in all probability being watched, took pains to ensure that they were not followed to the meeting.

London was the last to arrive and he found the others drinking coffee and waiting impatiently for him. He noted the tension in the room immediately and raised his hand to thwart the explosion of questions that they were about to level at him, then he calmly removed his overcoat and hung it up before joining them at the table where they were seated.

He was pleased to note that they had left the chair at the head of the table empty for him and before he took his customary position he poured himself a coffee from the urn in the center of the table. He added cream and sugar before taking his seat and began to speak.

"Gentlemen, I know you're all concerned, but as I said to each of you earlier by phone, this is not the time for us to panic. We have faced crisis situations before and had no difficulty handling them at that time. If we keep cool heads I'm sure that we can see our way through this one too."

He looked from man to man slowly and then took a sip from his steaming cup, before he continued.

""Now, we have taken a chance by scheduling this meeting and I suggest we spend no more time together than is absolutely necessary. With that in mind, I'm going to take the liberty of outlining our present situation and open the discussion so that we may reach a consensus on how best to deal with the problems we're now facing."

He paused and glanced from man to man again and received unspoken acceptance, then leaned back in his chair.

"As I see it we have two main concerns. First, we are all being blackmailed by way of tapes that were surreptitiously made of each of us while we indulged in the delights Carol was capable of providing for us. Secondly, the accountant, whom we had expected to be dead and gone at this point in time, is very much alive and, in all probability, our blackmailer. It would appear that Arnold was either in cahoots with the accountant and that they had a falling out, or that he was the first to be blackmailed by the accountant and decided he could deal with the problem on his own without consulting us. Either way, it would appear certain that the accountant has seen fit to kill him and we are now one member short at this table…"

He paused to let his words sink in then continued speaking before he could be interrupted.

"…A member who was a very integral part of our organization and without whom we are certainly less secure. Devoid of Arnold's input we will very quickly find ourselves in the position of having little ability to keep on top of, and thereby in control of, the CLEU investigation into our business affairs. I believe that in previous discussions, Craig has already suggested that we sell our interest in the business and that he has the contacts necessary to bring that about with a satisfactory return for all of us - if, and I emphasize that if, we decided that the time is ripe for us to follow that suggestion. Now, at the time, we agreed that option was not particularly palatable but under the present circumstances, I for one believe it is a very appealing alternative to our continuing on and therefore remaining a target for the police. Jim, have your people been able to redo the diary to take all references to us out of it, and make the two replacement copies?"

Kincaid nodded and lifted his briefcase to the table and opened it then removed the three documents.

"Yes here they are, and I destroyed the originals personally."

London nodded in satisfaction.

"Good. Very good. That being the case, we only have to see to it that these replacements make their way back to the police and their case against us, as it now stands, will fall apart at the seams. If we should then decide to sell our business interests, I see no reason why we should be in any further serious danger from that point of view. I suggest we now throw that idea open for discussion and reach a determination on it before we move on to our other problem; the accountant, and the demand that we pay blackmail in exchange for preventing the tapes from reaching the public and damaging our reputations

CHAPTER THIRTY

It had warmed up a little and the forecast for snow was now being downgraded by the radio to the chance of rain squalls.

David parked the police car in the same fire zone as before. He arrived at the doorway of the second floor apartment three minutes ahead of schedule and pushed the button beside it.

He heard the buzzer ring inside, and pulled out his identification in preparation for the opening of the door.

Ursula Kreski turned out to be a stunning brunette with big brown eyes and all the right curves distributed over her five foot eight frame

Based on the knowledge that she was twenty-eight years old and had a minor record for soliciting, he was surprised to find that she appeared far more sophisticated than he had expected.

What he found facing him was a very well presented girl-next-door-type, clean, fresh, conservatively but expensively dressed, and smiling brightly.

She barely checked his ID as she waved him in with an aura of the good citizen eager to help the police with their inquiries.

There wasn't any sign of street coarseness about her as she asked him to sit in the tidy compact living room and offered him coffee, which he readily accepted.

When she returned with a mug of steaming brew for each of them and sat primly down in the chair across from him he had taken her measure and was ready for her.

"You know why I'm here?"

She took a sip from her mug and nodded.

"Yes, your secretary Cindy said you were working on Carol's murder and wanted to speak with me about it. I was very fond of Carol, and I'd like to help you in any way that I can."

David found himself accepting her sincerity at face value. He sensed she was eager to answer his questions up front without any game playing. He treated the process of the interview with that in mind.

"You've had a chance to think about it, and detectives will be around shortly to take a full statement, but for now, I'd simply like to ask you to tell me anything that you think might help me to pinpoint who might have wanted her dead."

She took another sip of the hot coffee and then set the mug down on the table between them, before meticulously crossing her legs at the ankles and settling back into the chair more comfortably.

David inwardly uttered a curse as he fell into the normal male reaction to the tantalizing brief glimpse of well formed female anatomy that was provided by that specific and practiced movement being completed within the confines of the tight and fashionably short skirt she was wearing.

That she had anticipated exactly that type of reaction from him was obvious, as was the sense that she was not only comfortable with it, but also pleased.

David conceded the fact to himself and smiled.

This was a very confident and self-assured young lady.

"First of all, I didn't kill Carol, which I'm sure is the first thing you want to know. I was at home in bed with a friend at the time poor Carol was killed and my friend will certainly confirm that fact if need be."

David took the first sip from his mug, testing it for temperature and then set it down next to hers and as he did so, she continued.

"Everyone involved with the sessions at Carol's seemed very satisfied with the arrangement. I know that I certainly was, and will personally be very hard pressed to find anything nearly as good to replace it. I can't see any reason for any of us to want her dead. You're quite right about me having a chance to think about it, and I have. I've only been able to come up with two possibilities."

David had no intention of interrupting her until she had finished speaking and he picked up the mug again and moved it to his lips as he waited for her to continue.

"I'm pretty sure that Carol was either blackmailing some of the johns or thinking about it. She was making movies of the sessions you see, and well, maybe one of them had had enough and killed her over it. Then there was her personal life. She was very much entangled with someone in a rather heated relationship. Carol swung both ways, so it could have been either a man or a woman...."

She flushed slightly; another surprise for him.

"...I mean sexually, and I got the feeling from her that it was going sour. I don't know who she was seeing. I don't believe that it was one of our little group, but I could be wrong. It seems to me that if the relationship was breaking up messily, and Carol was instigating it, that might have been upsetting enough to push whomever she was involved with over the edge. You know, 'a woman scorned' type of thing and maybe that's what got Carol killed."

*****

London drained the remaining coffee from his cup and put it down.

"It's agreed then, we will sell our operations, and Craig will oversee the details of the sale. Needless to say, it will be done as quickly as possible. Jim will see to it that the rewritten diary and the two copies are forwarded to the police. With that concern dealt with and out of the way, and cognizant of the need for us to break this meeting up as rapidly as we can manage it, let's move on to the problem that we find ourselves in with the accountant. In view of the fact that we've decided to sell to the gentlemen that Craig has already had preliminary discussions with and that these people will certainly have the means of dealing with a problem like the accountant, I suggest that we make it a requirement of our agreement for the sale that they undertake to permanently remove the accountant for us as part of the bargain. In the meantime, I think we should all bite the bullet and agree to pay the blackmail until our new associates have carried out their part of the deal as it relates to the accountant, and have seen to it that we won't be further encumbered by that particular irritant. That way, we remain at arms length and in a short period of time, we are free and clear of both problems."

* * * * *

Boyd checked in with Cindy by phone and then dialed the number that she had given him. The phone rang as Walker was in the process of weighing Ursula's words and she excused herself to get up to answer it. A second later she turned slightly to face him.

"It's for you Inspector."

David got up and crossed to take the handset from her. As soon as he had identified himself, Boyd began to speak.

"I've just been going over the record books in the pawn shop. I think I've come up with a name that may fit into the puzzle. It took some time to figure out the codes that old Hymie was using in his, under-the-counter sales records, but if I'm right, Elizabeth Archer is a name associated with the purchase of several guns over the past year or so. It would seem to support the information that he gave you when you interviewed him. I figured it was a fact that you should be made aware of as quickly as possible."

When he had hung up the phone, David turned back to face Ursula who had returned to her chair and was patiently sipping from her mug. He spoke as he crossed the room and sat back down again.

"Can you tell me how you knew that she was into a love affair and why you don't believe that it involved one of your regular crew?"

She put the mug down, considered for a second then leaned back and shrugged.

"I knew that you were going to ask me that. I don't really know how I first twigged to it; put it down to girl talk, I guess. As far as it not being one of us, I think that it was the way she talked about it early on in the relationship. You know, Carol would say things like 'god, the sex is fabulous'; stuff like that, and since she routinely partnered with all of us, I assumed that this person, whoever it was, wasn't one of the group. But as I said earlier, that was only an impression and I could certainly be wrong there. I can tell you for certain that she was not having a serious relationship with me"

Walker finished his coffee and set the empty mug on the table.

"Can you give me an idea of when you first got the impression that she was getting pretty involved with someone; how long ago was it?"

"Oh it would have been about six months ago and it was about a month ago that I first got the feeling that it wasn't going too well; although Carol didn't really ever come right out and say so. Just little things, you know, stuff that adds up over time."

*****

Still working without his partner, Boyd had called for backup when he went to pick up Archer.

He'd let the attending marked unit return to service once they had jointly ascertained that she wasn't at home.

He then used a payphone to contact Cindy and she had subsequently advised him that David had already left his first appointment and was on the way to his second.

Returning to his car, Boyd contacted Walker by radio and arranged to meet him at Hunter's apartment, which was the next name on the list of those that David was scheduled to interview and was also located in Vancouver's West End.

*****

If some of the women involved in the upscale prostitution ring that Carol had set up had proven to be a surprise when met in person, David found Hunter to be just exactly what he had expected.

He and Boyd were greeted at the apartment door by a handsome, tall, dark, well tanned and sweating body builder, clad in brief posing trunks. He didn't even bother to look at their proffered identification, simply waved them inside, and closed the door behind them.

"Give me a second, I was working out."

They followed him inside and down the hall into what had been intended to be the living room when the small apartment had been designed.

It looked more like a gym now.

Hunter scooped up a towel from the floor beside a now immobile treadmill and began to rub himself down as he waved his free hand to indicate a pair of wooden straight-backed chairs on the far side of the room near the window.

Boyd and Walker dropped into them as Hunter tossed the damp towel onto the handhold at the top of the machine and slipped into a blue silk robe, before settling down into a chair located against the wall beside a weight bench.

Walker slipped his pipe out of his pocket and held it out questioningly.

"Mind if I smoke?"

Hunter shrugged.

"Your funeral man."

As he struck a match and brought the flame to the bowl, David took the opportunity to gauge the man sitting across from them.

He had dealt with men like Hunter before, brawn, good looks and very little brain.

This interview wasn't going to be a challenge for him and he frankly doubted that it would reveal much of value.

A man like Hunter was too self-centered to pay much attention to what went on in the world around him and consequently he would, in all probability, offer little valuable insight into the case.

"As you were advised over the phone, we're investigating Carol Jenkins's death. You were one of her string, and we'd like to know what if anything you can tell us that might shed some insight into her killing. To start with, perhaps you could tell us where you were when she died?"

Boyd had pulled out his notebook and was prepared to take notes.

Hunter shrugged.

"Sure. When did she die?"

"Early Monday morning."

Walker could almost hear the gears turning and wouldn't have been surprised to see a whiff of smoke puff from Hunter's ears as he concentrated on drawing his mind back in time and searched for an answer to David's question.

He and Boyd exchanged glances and the detective gave him a knowing grin,

They said nothing and finally Hunter spoke.

When he did the words were slow and deliberate.

"I was in bed, with an old broad that I do a couple of times a month. She lives in West Van. Jeez, you're not going to have to talk to her are ya? Losing the business at Carol's has been a real drag on me, you know, money wise. I only got a few other regulars that I've built up over time. You talk to her and she probably won't have fuck-all more to do with me; and she pays well for it, man."

Walker ignored the question.

"What time did you leave her in West Van?"

Hunter paused again before answering.

"It was an all-nighter, must have been about eleven the next day that I left. Her old man was back east for some conference thing. She wanted it again in the morning, so I didn't leave until after eleven I think; ya it was after eleven."

He stood up and crossed over to face them.

"Listen man, I didn't kill Carol if that's what you're thinking. Why the hell would I do that? She found me hustling my buns on the street when I was seventeen, and brought me out of all that shit. I got regular bread every month from her and clean work with no hassles. You're nuts if you think I did it man!"

Walker raised his hand to cut him off.

"Relax Hunter; we won't need to check your alibi unless we find out that you have a pressing need for it. The problem is of course, that in view of your record for violent assaults, you look like a pretty good possibility to me. I don't have a better suspect in mind at the moment. Until I come up with one, I'm not about to ignore any possibilities; so the sooner that I come up with one the better it will be for you. Now, how about telling me what you think might have happened to Carol."

Hunter stood silently for a few seconds and then dropped back into his chair and shrugged.

"I don't know man; I mean this really screws me up. Things were going real good for me you know, and now it's all fucked up. Shit, I didn't kill her. Sure we had words now and then, but I never laid a finger on her, and I sure as fuck don't know who the hell offed her."

Walker looked over at Boyd and raised his eyebrows, then stood up.

"Alright, but you think some more about it, and if you come up with any new ideas, give me a call."

He held out a card and Hunter got up to take it. Boyd tucked his notebook into his inside jacket pocket and stood up and moved toward the door. David dropped in behind him.

As the detective opened it, Walker turned back to facer Hunter.

"Detectives will be dropping in on you later in the week to take a complete statement from you. They'll call first. Don't screw them around, just give them what they need, or I assure you, they'll haul your ass down town."

Walker and Boyd remained silent until they were inside the elevator and it had begun to move. He glanced at his watch before looking across to Boyd.

"I want to call our boy at CSIS and check some things out. You call the office and get someone to drop in on Archer's booking agent to see if he knows where she is, or knows where we can get hold of her. Once that's out of the way, individually confirm the meetings scheduled with the five for this afternoon. We might as well put a little more pressure on them. We'll meet a block away fifteen minutes before the first of them and touch base again. Were you able to set them up for every one and a half hours as I suggested?

Boyd nodded.

"Ya, pretty well. I had to do some juggling around, but the first is at two o'clock with his Lordship Justice Richard London at the Courthouse. He says he can only give us a half hour. I didn't argue; I figure that will give us long enough. The second interview is at three and then every hour and a half after that. It's going to be a long day, but with any luck, we should be through them by eight or eight-thirty."

CHAPTER THIRTY-ONE

Walker used a pay phone to call the CSIS number listed on the card that had been provided to him earlier by the Regional Director.

He had a short wait and then Birch came on the line.

Matt, David Walker. I have a couple of questions for you and I'd like some up-front answers."

The response came without hesitation.

"Fire away."

"Who is Agent Richard Hummel and why did he pick up my copy of the diary?"

There was a pause and David wondered if he was about to be snowed again. He said nothing, and Birch cleared his throat before speaking.

"Hummel is our appointed CSIS liaison man with the R.C.M.P. He is, in reality, an R.C.M.P. member who has been assigned to us as a CSIS Agent with the sole purpose of liaising with the Federal Police Agency and more to the point, to ensure that we are kept under the magnifying glass as far as the Mounties are concerned He also happens to be the son-in-law of the Commissioner. I have no idea why he picked up the copy of the diary, but I can tell you that our instructions from our boss with regard to our take over of the investigation from CLEU came through Hummel and that, despite my position here in B.C.; I have little or no real control over his actions. Does that answer your questions?"

David took a few seconds to digest the information then he responded.

"Yes and now a few things are finally beginning to make some sense to me. Let me make sure that I'm reading this correctly; basically this guy is an R.C.M.P. plant whose job is mainly to keep his boss apprised as to what your agency is involved in; that right?"

There was no hesitation this time.

"I couldn't have put it into simpler terms myself. As I said, I have little real control over this asshole, but I can haul him in here and ask him a few questions if you like."

David thought for a second.

"No, not just yet; there's something else that I need to check, and if it pans out, I think that I might just be able to provide us with a little control over him that will surprise the shit out of him. If my suspicions are correct, I may be in a position to charge him with criminal obstruction of a murder investigation and that should sure as hell give him pause and perhaps make him a little more prepared to provide us with some answers. Just keep this to yourself for now and I'll get back to you on it shortly."

*****

Boyd got into the driver's seat of his unmarked unit and slipped the keys into the ignition. He didn't start the car, but pulled out his pack of smokes and lit one then took a deep drag before leaning back into the seat.

Archer's booking agent had been uncooperative initially but Ted had applied some pressure and although it was like pulling teeth, he had managed to get a little information out of the slime-ball.

He reached for his mike and tried to raise David on the radio through the Chief Dispatcher, but got no answer. He then fired the car up and began to cruise as he looked for a pay phone, with the intention of calling Walker's pager and leaving him a message to contact him when he was back in his car and on the air.

*****

David's second call was to the property office.

The phone was answered on the second ring, by the old Sergeant who ran that office, which also housed the evidence lockers.

It only took him a few minutes to confirm that the diary had indeed been picked up two days previously by a CSIS agent by the name of Richard Hummel. The man had produced a warrant ordering the turn over of the evidence to CSIS. All the paperwork had been in order and the agent had signed for the diary as required.

David had hung up the phone but was still standing in the phone booth mentally evaluating the information when his pager went off.

He reached for it, read the brief message and left the booth to return to his car and the radio.

* * * * *

Elizabeth Archer pulled the curtain aside to assure herself that the person who had rung the doorbell next to the front door of the run down motel unit was who she expected, then she let it drop back into place and moved across to the door to open it.

She quickly waved him inside and closed the door behind him, locking it firmly.

"Christ, you took long enough!"

Bret Hunter shrugged.

"Shit Candy, it takes time to get cash ya know. It's not like I keep that much bread around my place."

She let out a sigh of relief and sat down on the bed that dominated the room.

"You got it then. Thank God! I've got to get the hell out of town for awhile. Our plans to set up are going to have to go on hold until the heat comes off and things settle down, and if I were you, I'd fucking well do the same."

His gaze rested on her for a few seconds as he was making up his mind.

"Ya well, here it is."

He handed her an envelope and she took it from him eagerly and ripped it open to satisfy herself that it contained what she had asked for.

He watched her count it then continued.

"Look, you'd better tell me where you are going to lay low so that I can get in touch with you when all this shit blows over."

As always, and knowing only too well what he was capable of, she felt uneasy around him. She had no intention whatsoever of displeasing him.

"Ya, sure, no problem."

She quickly wrote out an address and phone number on the back of the ripped envelope that had contained the cash and passed it to him.

She then slipped the money into her purse and turned back to face him, managing a weak smile.

Hunter studied the address and phone number for a few seconds, and then turned back and just stared at her for what seemed to her, a very long time.

She felt beads of sweat beginning to form on her forehead and between her full breasts. She did her best to maintain the smile and eventually he shrugged and slipped the envelope into his pocket.

*****

David met Boyd as arranged and before they went to the first of their scheduled afternoon appointments Boyd brought him up to date on what he had found out about Elizabeth Archer. In turn Walker brought the detective up to speed on what CSIS Agent Richard Hummel had been up to with regard to the diary and copies.

They were seated in David's car, sheltering from the heavy rain as they awaited the arrival of the appointed time of the first interview.

David had adjusted the defroster but had shut the wipers

down.

"So, from the looks of it, Archer is on the run, but who the hell is she running from? It would appear that she's might be the one who's been getting the guns for the murderer from the pawn shop according to what you found in the records of sale. Question is: is she running from the murderer or us?"

Boyd shrugged.

"We won't know the answer to that until we find her."

David let out a sigh and checked his watch.

"Okay, as soon as you get a chance, I want you to put out a Canada-wide warrant for her arrest; material witness is good enough for the time being. Now let's get on with our interviews, it's going to be a bloody long night."

*****

They were still sitting in the judge's waiting room of the courthouse under the watchful eyes of the elderly secretary a full fifteen minutes after the scheduled interview time.

Justice Richard London had every intention of demonstrating to them that this was his domain and that he was fully in control of what went on in this building.

The point wasn't lost on Walker and he recognized it for what it was and played the game without comment, biding his time by reviewing his notes on the case.

Boyd sat next to him paging through magazines to pass the time.

It was two-sixteen when the muted buzzer sounded on the secretary's desk and she picked up the phone, listened briefly and replaced it into its cradle before looking across at David.

"Justice London will see you now, through that door and then take the second door on your left."

Richard London had been idly passing the time in his chambers since leaving his courtroom at one-fifteen.

He'd had plenty of time to change out of his robes for the upcoming interview, but as part of his intention to drive home to these policemen just who they were dealing with; he had chosen to remain in his formal court attire.

The meeting of the five earlier had gone as well as could be expected and he was satisfied with the decisions that had been reached before it ended.

His only concern now was whether or not the four other members of the soon to be dissolved group would be able to ride out the inevitable tension that would be presented to them over the next few weeks. They would be under considerable pressure while awaiting the accountant's removal and all ties to their former business enterprise had been severed.

He had stressed to them that they had nothing to fear, and had only to continue to live their lives as upstanding citizens. As long as they did that and provided the police with no evidence to the contrary, all would be well in about a month's time.

The question remained. Were they individually capable of handling the stress of an interview with the police?

He would have a better idea of that once he had dealt with this Walker and gotten a feel for how sure of his case the Inspector was. It was for that reason that he had seen to it that he would be the first of the five to meet with the policeman.

He had the advantage over Walker in that he knew precisely what evidence the Inspector had, or thought he had. He knew exactly how to handle him, and once he had done so, he would contact each of the others and tell them exactly how to deal with the policeman during their interviews.

Hopefully that would be enough to ensure that they all got through their meeting with the Inspector unscathed. If they managed to do that, he doubted that they would hear from the police again before the accountant was removed.

Once the accountant was dead, London knew that the entire situation would be sanitized to the point that, despite suspicion which would have no supporting evidence, they would all be in the clear as far as any chance of them actually being charged criminally.

The door to his chambers opened and Walker and Boyd walked in.

He stood and smiled.

"Sit please gentlemen. Sorry to have kept you waiting, but the demands of our justice system must take precedent I'm afraid."

Walker and Boyd presented their identification and took the two padded armchairs that sat across the big desk from London who had already reseated himself.

"And how may I be of service Inspector Walker"

David took the time to bring out his notebook and pen before he spoke.

"Well my Lord..."

London cut him off with a wave of his hand.

"We are not in my courtroom now, and since you are here in an official capacity, please drop the formalities. You have a job to do, and if I can be of assistance to you, rest assured that I will not hesitate to do so."

The smile broadened and David knew that he was being played.

"Fair enough. I'm investigating a series of murders, starting with that of Carol Anne Jenkins and including those of three policemen and a shop owner as well as the killing last night of the Solicitor General. It has come to my attention that you may have been acquainted with the Jenkins woman and that you were a friend, and have possibly had some business dealings with Arnold Banks."

London leaned forward and rested his arms on his desk. His expression was one of thoughtfulness and the smile had faded.

"Yes, I knew Arnold well. I read about it in the morning paper. Horrible thing that. Robbery the article said. Our streets have certainly become more dangerous in recent years, but then you know that as well as I do. Carol Jenkins you say, no I don't believe that I know the name. Did she appear in my court? I do have a heavy load and may well have forgotten."

David shook his head.

"No, I don't believe so. This would have been a contact of a more personal nature."

London smiled and sat back from the desk.

"Ah, I see. Well Inspector, I really don't think that it would be in my own best interest to discuss my personal life. However it would seem prudent for me to endeavor to ease your mind as best I can. I assume that what you are primarily concerned with is whether or not I might be able to remove myself from your list of possible suspects in these crimes. That being the case, perhaps you would be kind enough to tell me exactly when the murder of this Carol Jenkins person took place."

David saw clearly that London was confident that he could hold his own in what was obviously a carefully scripted response to an anticipated line of questioning.

The fact that London was being openly ambiguous about knowing Jenkins told him that the man was probably aware that David had access to the sex tapes and could thereby easily prove that London not only knew her, but knew her intimately.

London was not denying knowing her, simply exercising his right to refuse to discuss it further, and David had no doubt that his Lordship's position on that point was not about to change.

Walker had expected that other factors would have come in to play by this point. He had anticipated that London would be concerned as to the CLEU investigation, the possibility of blackmail and certainly about the fact that the hit man was on a murder rampage that, with the death of Banks, must have come very close to home for him.

Yet, there was no apparent outward sign of stress in the man sitting across from him.

The question was, why not? There certainly should have been.

London was affecting a confidence that he simply should not have had, and that told David two more things.

The first was that he was not going to be able to pressure London for information. Any attempt to do so would fail dismally. He would be dismissed sharply if he tried any such thing and he knew it.

For whatever reason it was obvious to David that London very confidently believed that he had nothing to fear from Inspector David Walker. That fact made a second point very clear to David. The murderer and the group of men heading the drug operation were definitely no longer in bed together. They were now at odds, and London was quite confident, for whatever reason, that the murderer was not going to come out on top after the confrontation.

That meant that the murders were not over, and that if he wanted to catch the murderer and be of any help to CLEU in their investigation, he was rapidly running out of time.

To date, each dead body had cut off a dangling loose end in the investigation and there weren't that many of them left.

He was wasting his time with London and he knew it.

He looked up from his notebook, and gave the man with the confident smile across the desk from him the approximate date and time of Carol's murder. London reached for his calendar and flipped through the pages before he settled on a page and spoke.

"Ah yes. I was at a meeting at home that night and it ran quite late I believe. I'll give you a list of the names of the gentlemen who attended that meeting with me. I'm sure that they will be pleased to confirm the date and time for you."

He quickly wrote down the names on a pad and ripped off the top page and handed it to Walker.

David glanced at it briefly, but he already had a good idea of what names the list would contain and after quickly confirming his assumption, he folded it up and placed it into his notebook, then closed it and stood up.

CHAPTER THIRTY-TWO

They were back in David's unmarked unit at two-thirty. He started the engine and adjusted the heat and defroster controls on the dash to deal with the fogging of the windows brought about by the dampness of their outer clothing and then he swiveled slightly in his seat to face Boyd.

"When you set up the interviews, you mentioned that you had to do some juggling; was London the one that you called first?"

Boyd thought for a second, and then shook his head.

"No, I figured Banks would be the hardest one for us to see, he spent most of his time in Ottawa…"

David nodded and cut him off.

"I thought as much. And when you called them, you got the 'I'll have to check my schedule and call you back' from each of them, right?"

Boyd nodded in agreement.

"Ya, but I expected that. These guys are all pretty busy types."

Walker chuckled mirthlessly.

"Oh yes, and in the end, when they called back, it was London who was the first person available for us to see, right?"

Boyd gave him a quizzical look, and David continued.

"You didn't structure the order of the meetings - they did, or more specifically I'll bet that London did. And, unless I miss my guess, within a few minutes each one of the remaining men we have appointments to see today will have been individually prepped as to how to deal with us. They will, without doubt, have agreed upon their stories and all we will get from them is a similar rendition of the same scenario. Each will alibi the others for the time that Jenkins was killed."

He opened his notebook, unfolded the list that London had

written out for him and handed it to the detective.

"Familiar group of people eh?"

Boyd shook his head and leaned back into his seat as he refolded the slip of paper and handed it back to David.

David shoved it back into his notebook and dropped it into his jacket pocket.

"Although we can't cancel the remaining appointments at this point, and you might even, by some miracle, be able to pull something of interest out of one of them, I have no doubt that the rest of these interviews are going to be a charade. You can handle them on your own; there's no point in both of us being there. I can find better ways to spend my time."

He glanced at his watch.

"You've got enough time to put out that Canada-wide pickup for Archer before you have to see the next of them. Do that and I'll follow up with CSIS on the missing diary and copies. Give me a call on the TAC channel if you mange to get anything important out of them, but barring that, just call me when you've finished and we'll touch base before you call it a day. What days off you got this week?"

"Monday and Tuesday, I'm duty for the weekend."

Walker nodded.

"Good, you clear your desk of anything else you've got going and ride shotgun on this investigation over the weekend. I have a feeling we're running out of time on this, and that it's going to heat up again very soon. We've to get on top of it as quickly as we can, or I'm afraid we're going to end up with a nice neat package being delivered to us that will look very good, but stink to high heaven in reality. We'll find ourselves facing nothing but closed and locked doors when it comes to the truth. I have a sense that our murderer has turned on his old bosses and that they're going to be hiring a hit man to take him out. It's the only concept that fits the amount of confidence that is leaking out of that pompous asshole London. We can't lose site of the fact that these bastards know more about our bloody investigation than we do, simply because they have access to information from three separate investigations, being run by three different agencies. We know what we are doing and some of what the others are doing, but they have lines to not only our investigation, but CLEU's and, I now have little doubt, CSIS's as well. That gives them the edge on us and we have very little time left to reach the murderer before they do. Once they do that, we not only get a body instead of a murderer, but they ensure that we can't get him to turn for a deal with us and send them all away for a very long time"

David paused for a breath and to clear his mind a little.

"I'm going to take everything we've got so far home with me tonight and go over it from start to finish to see if there is anything we've missed. I'll call you if I need to bounce anything off you. I want you to cover the Jenkins's Memorial with me tomorrow, but other than that you just spend your time working this file, and call me if you spot anything worthwhile or there are any new developments."

* * * * *

The accountant waited patiently, concentrating on what had just transpired and what it meant. It required the periodic use of a cloth to wipe away just enough of the condensation on the inside of the windshield of the LaBaron convertible to ensure that there was enough of it cleared to provide an unobstructed view of the front of the seedy motel.

It would have been far more comfortable to start the car's engine and use the heater and defroster. But that might have been enough to make the vehicle stand out among the other vehicles that were parked in the dark, litter-filled lot.

The set of peering eyes that randomly appeared from behind the nervously shifted curtain that covered the inside of the single, small and filthy window that fronted the unit in question were wary, and the accountant had no wish to be spotted.

It seemed to take forever, but the drug deal that had been

going down in the dimly lit alcove next to Candy's unit was finally wrapping up and the two shadowy figures who had been involved, had parted and moved off in separate directions into the pelting rain.

Candy's name had been used at the pawn shop.

One more loose end was about to be removed.

* * * * *

David watched Boyd climb into his unmarked cruiser and pull away then got out of his own car and reentered the courthouse.

He found a payphone in the foyer and called Matt Birch at CSIS, told him about the diary that had also been picked up from the VPF Property Office by Agent Hummel and requested that an interview with the man be set up as soon as possible. He also asked that he be present for it.

Birch agreed without hesitation and it was arranged for four o'clock that day.

David then checked the time and on the off chance that she and Robyn would be back from the appointment with the lawyer, he placed a call to Jenny's cabin.

He let the phone ring eight times before he returned the handset to its cradle.

He wanted to get together with Birch and discuss the way to deal with Hummel before they interrogated him and that meant he had to head over there now.

David knew that he would continue to worry about Robyn and Jenny until he was certain they were safely back up the Arm, and wanted to put his mind at ease about that before the interview took place. In that way he wouldn't be unduly distracted by his concern for them and thereby unable to give his undivided attention to the interrogation of the CSIS agent.

He'd try calling Jenny again before the interview itself.

There was a good chance they would be home by then.

*****

Boyd managed to get the cross-Canada warrant out on Archer before he headed for the next interview on his list.

He didn't doubt for a moment that Walker's assessment of the value of the remaining interviews was very likely correct. However he was hoping that he just might be able to get something out of the remaining men that would be of value, and in so doing, impress his boss.

It was an outside chance of course, but it was worth a try and he wasn't about to accept the fact that the entire enterprise was doomed to be a futile waste of time.

He was going to give it his best shot.

*****

Jenny hadn't hauled out the tire iron on the trip back, but she did keep a wary eye on the rearview mirror as they drove the lonely gravel road back toward the government dock, and she did pull off where the road narrowed and slip the station wagon into park.

Robyn's mind was elsewhere, still marveling at the value of the estate that Carol had left for her. In addition to the cash were bonds and investments and the lawyer had roughly estimated the overall value at somewhere close to one million dollars.

Robyn had been flabbergasted and still found it difficult to believe.

Jenny's act of pulling off to the side of the road and stopping the vehicle had brought her out of her thought process and as she looked over at the older woman there was a trace of anxiety in her voice.

"It anything wrong - did you see something?"

Jenny, eyes glued to the mirror shook her head slowly.

"No dear, but David did say that we should be mindful when on this road."

Robyn visibly relaxed and leaned back in her seat. A few moments later, Jenny apparently satisfied that they were not being followed, pulled back onto the road and accelerated.

*****

Boyd was not in the best of moods when he left Bill Hampton's office.

If the rest of his remaining interviews went as well as this one had he would surely be wasting his time.

Hampton had been sweating, there was no doubt about that, but he had stuck to the basic story that London had fronted earlier in the day. Try as he might, Boyd had been unable to shake him.

As he climbed into his unmarked unit and started it up, Boyd was definitely not looking forward to the rest of his day.

Three more to go and he was soaking wet and tired.

His frame of mind was beginning to match the weather.

*****

The accountant stepped out of the shower and luxuriated in the heat of the steam filled bathroom for a few moments, toweling down at a leisurely pace.

God it felt good to get warm.

Fucking weather was a downer, but at least there would be time to rest up and relax now.

There was nothing pressing on the agenda for the moment. The memorial service wasn't scheduled until one o'clock tomorrow.

A few drinks and maybe some mind-numbing television, and then bed and good nights sleep for a change.

*****

Wet and chilled from the boat ride, Jenny and Robyn, let

by a bounding Cato, began the climb up the stairway to Jenny's little cabin.

Cato managed to make the trip up and back down to them three times before the two women reached the small deck overhanging the cliff that fronted Jenny's cabin.

Jenny, who had been leading the way when they reached the gate, opened it and the dog shot through, followed by Jenny who held it open for Robyn.

Both of them were, unlike Cato, a little winded from the climb and Robyn, her breathing somewhat labored reached out for the top railing for support as she went to catch her breath. Jenny, not unkindly, immediately admonished her.

"Careful dear, remember that railing isn't trustworthy."

Robyn nodded and withdrew her outstretched hand. Jenny unlocked the door and the three of them went inside to be greeted by the welcoming warmth of the small kitchen.

Jenny immediately began 'mother-henning'.

"Come now child, goodness you'll catch your death. I'll get you a towel and you sit down by the stove there and warm yourself up"

*****

It was ten to four when David asked to use a phone and Matt directed him to the boardroom next to his office.

"Use the one in here. That's where we'll interview Hummel."

David closed the door behind him and crossed the room to the credenza against the wall at the other end and picked up the phone to call Jenny.

She answered it on the second ring and he was immediately relieved to hear her voice.

"Hi Jenny, it's me, you two made it back safe and sound I see."

Jenny laughed.

"Don't you worry; we're just drying out and warming up. I

managed to talk Robyn into taking a hot shower, poor dear, she was soaking wet and chilled to the bone. I've put her clothes in the dryer, she will want to talk to you I'm sure..."

David cut her off.

"I'm just about to go into a meeting, and I don't have time to talk right now, but if you could let her know that I should be home in a couple of hours, I'd appreciate it."

CHAPTER THIRTY-THREE

When David left the boardroom and returned to Birch's office he found another man seated in the chair across the desk from Matt's. The man, David took to be Agent Richard Hummel stood and extended his hand.

"Inspector Walker, I'm agent Hummel and I understand from Matt that you have some questions for me."

David took the hand in his and shook it firmly, all the while gauging the agent.

Young, late twenties, short for a Mountie, but had the haircut, carriage and demeanor nonetheless. Well cut suit and supremely confident. At first glance, at least, a man who was at peace with himself and the world around him.

David took an immediate dislike to him.

He took pains not to demonstrate that assessment in either his handshake or his facial expressions.

Birch stood up and led them out of the office into the boardroom and closed the door behind them. As soon as they were seated David spoke.

"I understand you have the diary that I placed in a VPF evidence locker, and some copies I made of it. I was wondering exactly why that would be? I asked your Regional Director here and he didn't seem to be aware of it. I think he's as curious about your actions as I am."

Both David and Birch were starring at Hummel by this point.

Hummel's expression didn't change but he shifted his gaze toward Birch.

"Matt, I'm not sure that I am at liberty to provide the Inspector with the information he's interested in."

Birch, who strongly disliked being addressed by his first name by a subordinate in the presence of another officer, was in no mood for bullshit and was having none of it.

"Listen Hummel, I've put up with a lot of crap from you in the past, but the Inspector here is hunting for a cop killer and tells me that he's actively considering charging you with criminal obstruction in a murder investigation if he doesn't get some satisfactory answers from you post haste. I for one am not going to interfere with him if he does. I suggest you tell him what he wants to know and make sure that he's absolutely satisfied with your answers and that you do it immediately because I can assure you this is not a man you want to piss off."

The color drained out of Hummel's face.

Birch had never spoken to him in that tone before.

Since his arrival at the Vancouver office, Birch had avoided him as much as possible, preferring to have as little to do with him as he could. The Regional Director had clearly disliked the whole situation of Hummel's posting as R.C.M.P. liaison to CSIS, but had outwardly accepted it as something that he was obligated to live with.

It was clear to the agent now that Birch was no longer prepared to live with the posting as a necessary evil, but was perhaps going to use the present set of circumstances to shed himself of the problem permanently.

The safe little cocoon of protected influence that Hummel had been comfortably resting in over the past few months was suddenly in danger of being shattered and he knew it.

He looked from Birch to Walker, and sensed immediately that the VPF Inspector was seriously prepared to do what had been threatened.

He needed to think, and he needed to do it very quickly. He felt an urgent need for a smoke. He reached into his pocket and pulled out his cigarettes and lighter.

He noticed that his hand was shaking slightly as he used the lighter and he instantly rested it on the edge of the table.

His mind was working furiously as he took a deep drag and then set the cigarette down into the ashtray in front of him. He was suddenly feeling very vulnerable and was desperately searching for the best way out of the untenable situation that he suddenly found himself in.

He realized that both men were watching him carefully and that neither of them had any intention of speaking until he responded.

There was not going to be any give and take here.

Birch had delivered him an ultimatum.

He reached for the cigarette and took another deep drag and as he exhaled David, who had been watching the body language, carefully noted that the agent's shoulders had dropped slightly. He felt the little adrenalin rush that always came when he knew a quarry had been broken.

Hummel cleared his throat and took a deep breath and let his eyes lock with the Director's before he spoke.

"Look, I was just following orders. I need to make a phone call before I'm at liberty to say any more about this."

Birch looked over at David.

"Well at this point, you are not dealing with me; I suggest that you ask the Inspector if that's okay with him."

*****

Robyn, wrapped in one of her benefactor's fluffy robes, which reached only about mid thigh on her, gratefully accepted the dry clothes that Jenny pulled from the dryer and clutched them tightly to herself.

"Thank you so much, they feel absolutely wonderfully warm!"

Jenny laughed and Robyn headed toward the bathroom to change.

Jenny returned to the kitchen where the kettle was boiling cheerfully and filled the teapot before arranging a selection of cookies on a plate and setting it in the center of the small table.

Cato, who had up to this point been in his favorite position when in Jenny's place, immediately recognized that the preparations going on about him would mean that the two women would be sitting at the table shortly, and that the space under the table he was currently occupying would soon be at a premium.

He got up and moved across to the mat in front of the door and circled on it a couple of times before flopping down again.

*****

David and Birch had allowed the agent to make the requested call in privacy.

The two of them had returned to the Directors office, leaving Hummel alone in the boardroom.

The conversation had lasted a good ten minutes and the previous outward signs of confidence and superiority that had been part of the agent's demeanor at the time of his arrival for the meeting had completely disappeared by the time he reentered the Director's office.

Both David and Birch had no doubt that the call had not gone well for the agent.

The man who dropped back down into the chair that he had initially used, bore little resemblance to the cocky self-assured one who had originally arrived for the meeting.

Birch tried very hard, but he just couldn't resist.

"I hope you found the Commissioner well."

David resisted the urge to laugh, and Hummel felt his face flush, and then began to speak.

"My instructions came directly to me from an assistant to the Solicitor General. In view of the fact that Arnold Banks has been killed and that this whole situation has become far more complex than was originally indicated, I've been ordered to co-operate fully with the Inspector."

David took out his notebook and pen and waited for Hummel to continue.

"We were asked to collect the diary and the copies because they were deemed to contain information that could affect the security of the country. It would now appear that this wasn't the case and that it's possible I may have been being used by Banks for his own purposes. I've been directed to return the documents to the Inspector and to give him any further assistance I can. I have the materials you are looking for locked up in the safe in my office, I'll get them for you immediately."

He got up and neither Birch nor Walker commented as he left the office.

*****

Jenny slipped the last bite of her cookie into her mouth and stood up to take the now empty plate over to the sink. As she did Cato got up and stretched then followed her across the room. She set the plate down and smiled over at him.

"You'd like a treat too wouldn't you big boy?"

She reached up and opened the cupboard door directly above the sink and took out a box of dog treats and selected three of the bone shaped biscuits from it before returning it to the cupboard and closing the door.

Cato promptly sat and remained absolutely motionless as Jenny balanced one of the treats on the big dog's nose and stepped back.

The huge Rotti's eyes were almost crossed at he concentrated on the treat, and his ears lifted slightly in anticipation of Jenny's command.

Jenny stood a few steps away from him and admonished playfully.

"You wait now, be a good boy."

Drool began to form at the corners of Cato's mouth, but he waited.

Jenny laughed at the sight and gave the much awaited command.

"Okay!"

Instantly the dog flipped his head back and opened his mouth. The treat arced slightly upward and was immediately snapped out of the air before being victoriously chewed and swallowed.

Robyn, who had been watching the whole enterprise with great interest burst into surprised laughter and began to clap.

"Very impressive indeed, my goodness he's well trained."

Jenny laughed.

"He never misses."

She repeated the trick with the other two treats and Cato nailed each the instant that he received the command authorizing him to do so. When the last trace of crunched treat had been lapped up off the floor, Jenny crossed to the delighted dog and gave him a pat on the head, as she spoke to Robyn.

"You have no idea how well trained he is. Early in his career David did a stint as a Police Dogmaster and he has trained Cato up to police standards. Because I have to look after him a lot of the time, and he is fully protection trained, David has shown me exactly what he is capable of and what the necessary control commands are. It's absolutely astonishing dear; to watch him when he is given the command to attack, and of course one must be very careful around him, because he has also been Master-Protection trained."

Robyn gave her a questioning look and Jenny explained.

"That means that he has been conditioned to make the decision to attack on his own without command if he deems it necessary. It's the only time he is allowed to do anything without receiving a direct command from his handler. You have to always take care not to create a situation that could trigger that response in him. I know he can look very harmless, but I also know what he is capable of. I can tell you, it gives me pause every time I'm with him. He's so loveable and affectionate, you'd never think it of him; but if at any time Cato considers his master or any one he loves is in imminent danger, he will instantly launch into a full scaled attack upon that threat, whatever it may be."

*****

Hummel, as good as his word, returned five minutes later with the diary and the two copies.

David saw little point in drawing out the meeting. He slipped the documents into his briefcase and stood up.

He had what he had come for and he had better ways of spending his time than watching Hummel squirm.

He would leave that pleasure to Birch.

*****

David was back at his office by five and found a message on his desk that had been left by Cindy before she had gone for the day. It was a request to get hold of Carl Higgins in the Identification Squad and was time-stamped at 16:30 hours.

David glanced at the clock on the wall across from his desk and thought it was worth a try. He picked up his phone and dialed the IDENT local.

Higgins picked up the phone on the second ring, and David grinned to himself.

"It's past quitting time Carl."

The response was instant.

"Yes, and I was on my way out the door, when some idiot Inspector, who should be well on his way home by this time of day, was dumb enough to call me. You in your office?"

"Yes, just got in the door."

"Right, I got some info for you on the vehicle involved in Bank's murder. I'll drop by on the way out."

The phone went dead in David's hand.

Things were definitely looking up.

CHAPTER THIRTY-FOUR

The thundering rain that had overshadowed most of the day had begun to let up as David reached the government wharf and parked his unmarked unit.

By the time that he was pulling his boat into his own dock the precipitation was down to a light drizzle.

A cheery ribbon of smoke drifted upward from the chimney and the bank of windows that formed most of the front wall of his house that faced the water had all the curtains open and the interior was brightly lit.

As he was tying up the boat, he could make out Jenny and Robyn looking out at him with Cato, hind end swaying between them. He smiled up at them and waved.

* * * **

Justice Richard London was sitting at the big desk in his den.

He had just put the phone down and was lighting up a celebratory cigar.

Each of the others had now made contact with him after their interviews.

In consideration of the need to be careful when speaking to each other over the phone, they had set up a simple code system at their last face-to-face meeting that allowed them to talk to each other by phone without making any direct reference to their business activities. While it didn't allow them to discuss everything in the detail he would have preferred, it did allow them to communicate without risking the provision of evidence by way of any wiretaps that may have by this point been placed on their personal phone lines.

With this restriction in place, the general tone of the conversations told him more than the actual content itself. He was relatively sure that each of the others had been able to maintain their outward reflection of the unified front that they had agreed on at the last meeting. It appeared that they had all managed to keep their cool and that the police had been unable to rupture the solidarity provided by their combined defensive armor.

He had been concerned that, in consideration of the strain that they were now all under, one or more of them might panic and come apart at the seams, but it seemed that they had all weathered the storm.

In addition, Bellows, in his call, had indicated that the discussions that they had agreed should take place with the crime organization to buy them out were progressing very well and that in fact a deal in principle could well be completed before the coming weekend was over.

Things had gone better than he had expected and now that he had taken the last of the calls, he felt some of the tenseness that had built up over the day melting away.

He got up to pour himself a brandy

It would go well with the cigar.

*****

Boyd parked the unmarked pool car that he had been using over the day in the main police lot, returned the keys and mileage slip, then headed for the Major Crime office.

He was tired, hungry, still wet, and felt that he had wasted most of his day.

Walker had been right, the bastard's had one story and they were all sticking to it like glue.

When he entered the outer office, he found it empty. He glanced up at the situation board and noted that the afternoon shift team of detectives had chalked themselves out on a homicide call in the east end of Vancouver.

He hung up his overcoat and then crossed over to the

cubicle he and his partner shared and dropped into his chair, before firing up a smoke and reaching for the phone.

* * * * *

They were all in the kitchen cleaning up after dinner when the phone rang.

Jenny was washing, Robyn was drying and David was putting things away.

David's glanced at his watch, and noted the time. He placed the dish he had been holding on the kitchen counter and turned to go and answer the phone.

"That's probably Boyd, I asked him to call me when he was through with his interviews."

He left the kitchen, entered the living room and crossed to his desk to pick it up.

Boyd identified himself and moved directly into the results of the interviews.

"Well you had it pegged all right. They all had the same story and they had it down pat. Each of them alibis the others and confirms that they were meeting at London's place on the night that Carol was killed. They all say the meeting ran long into the morning. They breakfasted before calling it a day apparently. A couple of them were obviously under strain, but they wouldn't change their stories one iota."

David dropped down into his chair and shifted the phone to his other hand as he reached for the notebook in his pocket and pulled it out.

"I thought as much. It's obvious that they must be working on some way to deal with the CLEU investigation. Whatever they have planned, they expect it will take them off the hook. They also have some strategy to deal with the murderer, who is more than likely blackmailing all of them. These guys have a lot of connections and I don't think they'll want to let things go on much longer the way they are. They aren't about to just sit back and suffer. They've got something in the works."

"Ya, that's the general impression that I got today all right."

"Okay, not much we can do about it for now. I'll give Wright a call at CLEU on Monday and give him our take on it. I do have something that you can work on over the weekend though. Carl Higgins got back to me this afternoon with some info on the Banks' killing. Based on the tire tread impressions that were left at the parking lot at the Rose Garden, the car that the murderer used that night was either a Chrysler New Yorker or a LaBaron. I'd like you to run all the names of our perspective suspects through the Motor Vehicle Branch and see what you come up with for personal vehicles. I can't help but think that the drug group and the sex group are too intertwined to mean that the killer isn't a member of one of them. Start with the people who were directly involved with Carol in the sex thing. If you get nothing there, include London and the others. As much as I can't see one of them being directly involved in the killings, I'm convinced that our man is a member of one of the two groups, or at least interrelated in some way."

Boyd interjected.

"Ya, makes sense, the murders relate to both groups. I figure it's likely that he is somehow tied in with each of them. I'm bushed, and about to call it a day. Okay if I start running the check with Motor Vehicles in the morning?"

"Did you manage to get the pickup out for Archer?"

"Yep, a couple of hours ago. Nothing yet."

"Okay, call it a day. I want you fresh tomorrow for the memorial. I have a feeling that our killer will want to attend and I want you to document which of our suspects turn up. Reschedule your hours - work a ten-to-six shift."

"Will do."

* * * * *

The uniform blocking the doorway to the run down motel was a veteran who immediately recognized the two Major Crime Detectives when they climbed out of their unmarked unit after pulling into the parking spot in front of him.

He had recorded their names in his notebook before they reached him and he slipped the book back into his pocket and stepped to one side as he spoke.

"Thought you should know, the victim is that Archer broad that was put out by Detective Boyd for a Canada-wide pickup earlier today."

* * * * *

Jenny stayed for one of David's special after dinner Blueberry teas, but could not be persuaded to stay any longer, despite Robyn's suggestion, and David's immediate agreement that she was more than welcome to.

Jenny had simply smiled and given Robyn a knowing look.

"Nonsense dear, you two have things to do I'm sure, and you certainly don't need me around for that. Besides the fire must be down to coals up at my place by now; and it isn't going to be a warm night. I'll have to make sure that I get a roaring blaze going before I crawl into my little bed."

* * * * *

Boyd had just left the office and climbed into his car when his pager went off. He swore softly to himself as he reached inside his coat to pull it off his belt and read the message.

He sat their for a few seconds digesting it then sighed deeply, opened the door, and got out of the car to head back to his office.

Moments later he was speaking by phone with the senior of the two duty Major Crime Detectives who were on the murder in the east end.

"Sorry to call you man, but I'm afraid you're going to want

to know that the Archer broad that you put the Canada-wide out on this afternoon has just been whacked."

The exhaustion that had been settling into Boyd's body was immediately replaced by a shot of adrenalin and he checked his watch quickly.

It read nine-fifteen.

*****

David was bringing Robyn up to date on the meeting with the CSIS Agent and the resulting recovery of the diary and the two copies.

He had just opened his briefcase to take them out to show her, when the phone rang.

David set the documents down on the corner of his desk and picked up the phone. He was surprised to hear Boyd on the other end.

"I thought you were headed home."

"I was, until Anderson paged me. He and Gillespie are out at a homicide call in east Van, and the victim is Elizabeth Archer. Twenty-two in the back of the head. Looks like you were right, this isn't over. IDENT is headed out for forensics. I know that you wanted me around for the memorial tomorrow, and I've got the Motor Vehicle Branch stuff to run in the morning, but I should go out on this to make sure that we don't miss anything. Being that they aren't up to speed on this particular investigation, Anderson and Gillespie might not know exactly what to look for."

David considered the situation briefly before answering.

"Well one of us should be there for sure. Look, you'll get there a lot faster than I could. You take it and give me a call if you get anything that can't wait until the morning. Forget the running of the vehicles. I'll come in early in the morning before the service and do that. You concentrate on covering Archer's murder. Just leave your report on my desk when you wind it up and I'll go over it in the morning while I'm in the office. If you can manage to get a decent sleep once you're through, you could still be able to make it for the memorial. You know all the suspects well enough to pick them out and I'd certainly like to have you there. If you are up by noon and can make it, great. If not I'll have you use the duty detectives and give them photos to work from."

"Don't worry about that Boss; I'll make the memorial service."

*****

David hung up the phone and stood staring at it for a few seconds, then when Robyn, who had been washing up the tea cups and putting them away, came back into the room he looked over at her.

"That was Boyd. Archer has just been killed."

Robyn froze in mid stride and the color drained from her face.

"My god, is it ever going to end?

David shook his head slowly.

"No, not until we catch him I'm afraid."

He glanced back at the phone briefly and then over to her, weighing his words carefully before he continued.

"Look I don't want to alarm you unnecessarily, but this means that we have to be really careful about insuring that the murderer doesn't find out where you are staying. This guy has already tried for you once. He wasn't just visiting your apartment for the fun of it."

Robyn nodded slowly and absently reached down to pat Cato who had picked up on her unease by smell and had immediately crossed over to stand by her.

"Well I do feel safe here."

David nodded.

"Yes, but there is the service tomorrow to consider. I don't suppose that I could convince you not to attend?"

The color returned to her face and she shook her head

firmly.

"No. I couldn't do that."

She let her eyes meet his.

"You will be with me won't you, tomorrow I mean."

David moved across to her and took her gently into his arms.

"I have no intention of letting you out of my sight until this bastard is locked up."

Robyn slipped her arms around him. He felt her shiver slightly and he kissed the top of her head.

"How about another Blueberry tea?"

Robyn broke the embrace and looked up at him. She managed a smile.

"Sounds good to me. Let me make them; I need something to do."

David nodded and his eyes stayed on her until she had left the room. He wondered if he would ever get tired of enjoying watching the motion of her ass under tight jeans.

He decided that it was highly unlikely. As she disappeared into the kitchen he returned to his desk and picked up the diary, and flipped it open.

He began to page though it absently as he planned how he would handle the memorial the next day.

He was going to have to split his time between keeping an eye on Robyn and working the crowd.

Robyn, who was in the kitchen plugging in the kettle, heard him utter the oath."

"Son of a Bitch!"

She turned and went back into the living room. David looked over to her and held the diary out in front of him.

"It's been doctored. I haven't checked it all, but unless I miss my guess, everything that relates to the drug ring is gone, names, dates, everything."

He dropped the book onto the desk and picked up one of the copies and flipped through it randomly.

"Redid the copies too, no wonder those bastards were so

confident during their interviews, they already knew all about this."

CHAPTER THIRTY-FIVE

Emergency vehicles with their lights still flashing had completely blocked the front of the motel unit where the killing had taken place. When Boyd arrived at the scene of Archer's murder he had to settle for a parking spot at the far end of the motel lot.

As he locked his car and started toward the unit in question his eyes passed over the inevitable crowd of looky-loos that had formed just to the side of the motel office. He paused in mid-step, then changed direction and headed directly toward the group.

He was focused on one particular member of that crowd, a young man wearing jeans and a dark hoody. It was someone he knew very well.

The guy that Boyd had in his sights looked briefly away from the activity in front of the motel unit and spotted Boyd coming toward him. The detective noted the fear that instantly registered in the other man's eyes.

Anticipating that the man would attempt to flee, Boyd closed the remaining distance between them at a run and had the man firmly by the arm before he'd managed to get more than a couple of steps away from the small crowd.

"Hang on Billy. How abut you and I have a little talk."

Intense fear now filled the small time drug pusher's eyes and he looked quickly around at the others who had been standing in the group watching the police activity.

"Not here man."

Boyd nodded and turned his head to indicate his car at the other end of the lot.

"Okay. Let's have a talk in my car."

He led the now resigned and submissive figure back over to his unmarked pool car, then put him into the back seat, briefly checking first to see if the car that he'd drawn from the motor pool was one that had the locking plungers removed from the back doors and couldn't be opened from the inside.

Satisfied that it did, he closed the door and moved around to the driver's side of the unmarked cruiser and got into the driver's seat.

He hauled out his cigarettes and shifted in the seat to face a now somewhat more relaxed Billy and offered him one then lit them both up and exhaled.

"Okay son, what have you got?"

Billy glanced out of the tinted rear window at the crowd. Satisfied that the attention of the group was still locked onto the police activity, he took a deep drag and turned back to face Boyd.

"Look man, I had nothing to do with it"

Boyd cut him off.

"You've got something for me Billy, now cut the shit and tell me what it is or I'll haul your ass to jail just on principle."

Billy sucked in another deep lungful of smoke and nodded.

"Okay look, I was here for the last few hours, ya know - doing my thing, and I noticed this car. It was sitting way over at the end of the lot. I thought it might be the drug squad, ya know - setting up on me, so I worked my way around the back and came up behind it and well I could see right away that there was only one person in it. You guys always work in twos, and it was a convertible ya know, fancy one, not like the shit that you guys drive."

Boyd pulled out his notebook and pen.

"What make was it? You get a plate?"

Billy shook his head.

"No make or plate man, but it was red and a convertible like I said; and it was all fogged up inside. I couldn't see much but it just seemed to me that whoever was in it seemed to be watching the room over there. The one where the cops are now. No other reason for it to be there man, ya know what I mean.

*****

David checked every page when Robyn returned to the kitchen to prepare the teas.

There was no doubt about it; they had done a thorough job on the diary. It had been completely sanitized. Anything that had to do with the drug activity had been removed.

He swore to himself and tossed it back onto his desk.

Robyn, by this time standing at the bar, looked over toward him and raised the two steaming mugs.

"Let's finish these by the fire, and you can bring me up to date on the rest of the investigation"

David crossed the room to join her and she placed the mugs on the coffee table near the fire and David added some wood to it before he joined her on the couch.

*****

Boyd left Billy in the back of his car and walked across to the motel room. He flashed his badge to the uniform who he recognized and entered the door to the room.

Anderson spotted him and crossed to meet him just inside the doorway.

IDENT was in the process of photographing the room and the two of them took pains to stay out of the way as they talked.

Gillespie who was acting as evidence officer was standing off to the right, just inside the doorway observing what was taking place and making notes.

Boyd got the gist of the crime scene from Anderson and then led him out of the dingy room and over to his car, where the waiting Billy provided the investigating detective with a full statement of what he had observed

By the time that they had finished with Billy, the coroner's unmarked station wagon had arrived. They turned Billy loose and he and Anderson returned to the crime scene.

* * * * *

David brought Robyn up to date on the dismal results of the interviews that had been held with the drug syndicate members. He told her about the forensic results on the tire impression found at the scene of Bank's murder.

They had finished the Blueberry teas and David, who had been very angry about the sanitized diary, had mellowed out slightly.

Robyn was digesting what he had told her. She stretched slightly and put her feet up onto the coffee table.

"You said you think that the murderer has to be tied in with either the drug part of it or with Carol's sex set up, or both, It just occurred to me that I might be able to help there."

David, who had just gotten up to poke the fire, paused and turned to look at her.

"What do you mean?"

Robyn shook her head.

"Well, I don't know if it's important, but I remember Carol telling me that one of her group was having some kind of domestic breakup. Whoever it was, was going to have to move out of wherever they were living and needed to earn some extra money in order to afford to set up in someplace new. This was quite a while back. She didn't tell me who it was, but she did mention to me that she had set that person up with the drug guys in some kind of working capacity. Record keeping and banking stuff I think, in order for them to earn some extra cash. I don't know if it means anything, but whoever that person was, they would have then become a member of both groups."

David put the poker back into its rack by the fire and turn to face her.

"Carol didn't say which one of them it was. She didn't say anything else that might give us any idea of which one she was helping?"

Robyn shook hear head.

"No it was just a brief comment in passing when I was visiting with her one day."

David nodded.

"Well it could be very important, let me know if you remember any more about it."

The phone rang and David crossed the room to his desk and picked it up. It was Boyd

"Sorry to bother you at home Boss. I happened to spot Billy Simpson when I arrived at the Archer murder scene. He was part of the usual crowd of onlookers who were watching our guys at work. Anyway, I know that he works that area on a regular basis, so I grabbed him and he tells me that he spotted a car, at the murder scene earlier and that it seemed out of place. It was a red convertible. Anderson and Gillespie are handling the murder, and I've seen enough to tell me that it's our boy who did the job on her. I was thinking that maybe the idea of running the suspect vehicles might be more urgent than we thought. We've got two bits of info on a vehicle that may be being used by the murderer now. It could be the best lead that we've got to date. I thought that I might head back into the office right now and see what the Motor Vehicle Branch has to offer, if that's okay with you?"

David glanced at his watch.

"Yes, go ahead, but make sure that you get enough sleep at some point to be able to make it to the service tomorrow afternoon. I want you there even more now. I got the bloody diary and copies back from CSIS all right, but they aren't the originals. They've been sanitized. Nothing about the drug group's activities is left. It's no wonder that you got nowhere with the interviews; those bastards must be bloody confident that they can beat this thing, but we can worry about that later. I'm pretty well convinced that Robyn Jenkins is on this guy's hit list. For the time being we've got to concentrate on our killer and make sure that we get him before he kills again."

*****

Boyd touched base with the investigating detective team and arranged for them to drop off a copy of their initial report for his attention. He then headed back to his car to return to the office.

He finally had something that appeared to be a worthwhile lead. He also hadn't missed the trace of concern in his boss's words when David had referred to the Jenkins woman.

Obviously she had become more than just a party of interest in the investigation as far as Walker was concerned. With that realization, a new dimension had been added to the pressure for them to solve the case quickly.

A hit with the vehicle could be all it took to zero in on the prime suspect, and Boyd was eager to return to his desk and see if he could make that happen.

* * * * *

Immediately after speaking with Boyd, David got out his notebook and flipped to the back page. He found the number he wanted on his phone list and called it.

It rang four times before it was picked up by Carl Higgins.

"Carl, David Walker. I have a favor to ask."

There was a pause before Higgins responded.

"And what might that be Inspector?"

"Would it be possible for you to go into the lab tomorrow and finalize the tests on the material that we recovered from the hospital murders? I wouldn't ask normally, but we've just had another killing and it's the same suspect. This thing is getting out of hand and I'm getting pretty desperate here. I know…"

Higgins interrupted.

"You want me to pull one of my little miracles out of a hat and save your ass, is that it?"

Walker laughed.

"Something like that Carl. I really wouldn't be asking if I

didn't think it was important. I know that you have staff in on the weekend that you could put on this, but we both know that there is no one who can do this kind of stuff better or faster than you can. I'd take it as a personal favor if you would go in and handle it yourself."

There was a pregnant pause but David said nothing further.

Finally Higgins spoke.

"Flattery will get you everywhere, but you definitely owe me one Inspector Walker."

The line went dead and David was smiling to himself as he hung up the phone.

* * * * *

Boyd leaned forward and let his elbows rest on his desk, then lifted his hands to his eyes and rubbed them gently.

It had taken him almost two hours, but he had managed to complete the running of his two lists of suspect's names through the Motor Vehicle Branch He now knew what vehicle or vehicles each of them owned.

He had also learned that the LaBaron was the only model that was offered as a convertible. The New Yorker was offered as a sedan only.

That aside, none of names that he had checked owned either a New Yorker or a LaBaron.

He'd had high hopes for a hit. To say that he was unhappy with the results would have been a gross understatement. He was getting ridiculously tired and the disappointing results hadn't helped with his mood.

He reached for the switch of the lamp on his desk and shut it off.

Well, experience had taught him that most murder investigations went this way. If they couldn't be solved in the first couple of days, they could drag on forever. Nothing but dead ends and lots of legwork and then that one little break that blew the whole thing wide open.

Unfortunately, experience also told him that that little piece of evidence that would provide the break was more than likely some thing, or a group of things that were already tucked away somewhere in the massive stack of information that made up the file that had been created over the term of the investigation. It was likely to be something that just hadn't been picked up on yet.

It was a frustrating process but, what the hell, tomorrow was another day.

He got up, grabbed his overcoat and headed for the door.

*****

David propped himself up on a couple of pillows and began the process of lighting his pipe. Robyn, stretched out on the bed beside him, had her eyes closed and he was enjoying watching the gentle rise and fall of her sweat covered breasts as she worked at regaining her normal breathing pattern.

"You know, it seems unlikely to me that any of the people involved in the sex thing with Carol would have been in a relationship that would bring a great deal of financial hardship when it ended."

Robyn opened one eye.

"Boy, you switch gears quickly don't you? I'm afraid my mind was elsewhere. You might want to give a girl a few seconds to forget that she just made love before you expect her mind to function normally."

David laughed.

"Sorry. I was just thinking about what you said earlier. About one of them also going to work for the drug cartel to make extra money because they were facing a domestic breakup. It doesn't seem very likely to me that any of them would be involved in a relationship permanent enough to mean that a breakup would leave them that short of ready cash."

Robyn shifted to a sitting position and shoved a couple of

pillows behind her then leaned back against the headboard beside him.

"That's true enough; perhaps we need to dig more into their personal lives."

David nodded and exhaled a cloud of smoke then turned to rest his pipe in the ashtray on the bedside table beside him.

"Yes, I'll make sure that the detectives who take the follow-up statements from them do that. But I think maybe we should review the information that I've already gotten from them in the initial statements. Maybe we can narrow it down a little. There are only the four of them. I can't think of anything off the top of my head, but I'll go over my notes on the interviews in the morning, with the idea of assessing personal relationships to see if I can spot anything that stands out."

CHAPTER THIRTY-SIX

In the morning over breakfast, David had tried one last time to convince Robyn not to attend the memorial service for her sister, but she would have no part of the idea.

A cold front from the north-east had moved in overnight and the temperature had dropped to well below freezing.

Weather reports indicated that the front would remain over the area for several days, bringing with it predictions of the last heavy snowfall of the winter season. It was to be compounded by a severe wind chill factor and whiteouts caused by snow drifting at the mercy of heavily gusting winds.

It took David twenty minutes to chip the ice that had already formed away from the ropes and windows of the boat and he started it up and left it running as he went back into the house to get Robyn for the trip to the government wharf.

Despite his urgings to dress warmly she was determined to wear a dress to the service and he shook his head in exasperation as he took in the expanse of pantyhose covered legs that would be exposed to the weather once they left the warmth of the house.

Robyn, anticipating his reaction, had taken the precaution of placing her heels in a bag to take with her. She was wearing boots and heavy socks in view of his earlier admonishment about the icy conditions they would be facing before they got to the car.

She gave him a challenging look and placed her hands on her hips.

"I know, I know, but I can bundle up in one of your winter coats and I'll stay inside the cabin when we get to the boat, and it's only a short trip to the dock."

David raised his hands in acceptance.

"Okay, I'm not saying another word, but we'd better get

going. I'll probably have to spend another twenty minuets chipping the ice off the car once we get to the dock."

*****

Boyd had only been able to get five hours of sleep in before he'd found himself wide awake. It had been enough, and he found himself charged and eager for the day to begin.

Walker had a gut feeling that the murderer would be attending the memorial service and the detective had worked for his boss long enough to have learned that that type of comment coming from David usually had merit.

The fact that none of the suspects owned a red LaBaron convertible had been disappointing, but it was the vehicle that Boyd was sure the murderer was using. If he was right and Walker's gut feeling was on the mark, that LaBaron was going to be parked at the funeral home where the memorial service was being held.

Boyd managed a quick breakfast of poached eggs on toast and then made a call to David's home on the off chance that he might catch him before he left for the office.

When he got no answer he grabbed his coat and headed out the door.

*****

The accountant had been up early, and was now in the process of eating a drive through breakfast in the parking lot of a MacDonald's that was located in Burnaby. It was ideally situated only two blocks from the funeral home.

The recon had including a visit to the funeral home on the pretense of arranging for an anticipated upcoming service for a seriously ill father. It had been necessary to ensure familiarity with the surrounding area. It had provided a full awareness of all escape routes available, as well as a good idea of the general layout of the funeral home itself. The accountant now had a good impression of the access and egress points to the building

The exercise had provided the necessary sense of well being that had always been an important part of any project that the accountant undertook.

There had been no difficulty in locating the electrical panel for the home, when the necessity for the use of the facilities had come up during a tour of the building. There had been lots of time to wander about without raising any suspicion from the few staff members who had been encountered in the hallways.

Always be prepared for emergencies. Always anticipate the unexpected. Always be comfortable in your surroundings. Always keep one step ahead of your adversaries.

The clock in the dash of the LaBaron read 11:45.

An early morning check of the offshore account had indicated that all the blackmail payments had been made within the time specified on the notes that had gone along with the packages containing the tapes.

All of them had fallen into line as meekly as had been expected.

There had also been time to pick up the airline tickets before the service was scheduled to begin.

The accountant was pleased with how the whole thing was going. If everything went this smoothly over the next couple of days that last little loose end would be successfully snipped off. The whole mess would be over and it would be nothing but sun and sand by Monday afternoon.

Maui was absolutely gorgeous at this time of year, and this would be a very long overdue vacation. After that and with the help of the beautifully forged passport that had been kindly provided for the trip to Mexico - a new Identity and a whole, brand new lifestyle!

* * * * *

David re-read his notes on the interviews he had conducted with Carol's four sex ring associates. He was unable to pick up on anything specific that he might have missed. But by the time he had finished the last of them he had a nagging feeling that what he was looking for was there somewhere.

He would have liked to go over them one more time, but that would have to wait. It was nearly noon and he and Robyn would have to leave his office now if they wanted to make the service on time.

*****

Boyd was at the funeral home by 12:15.

He spent a few minutes checking the parking lot that, at this juncture, contained only a few cars.

He then made a circular sweep through the residential area around the home, checking the side streets. There was no sign of a red LaBaron convertible.

It was early yet, and he hadn't really expected to find the car. He'd wanted to be sure that he was familiar with the area and would know exactly where to search for it once the service had begun.

By 12:25 he was back at the home. He parked his unmarked pool car near the parking lot exit and got his camera equipment out of the back seat.

He would be discretely photographing everyone who attended the service for later evaluation. He didn't anticipate that the actual photography would take very long, in that he doubted that the turnout would be very large.

*****

The accountant returned to the LaBaron and dropped into the driver's seat, then opened the briefcase and slipped the tickets into one of the inside compartments before removing the little twenty-two and placing it in the right front pocket of the heavy winter coat.

Hopefully the coat would suffice to keep the chilling cold

at bay on the two-block walk to the funeral home.

A few moments later the LaBaron swept back into the MacDonald's lot and into a parking space located next to one of the exits and some distance from the main building of the red and yellow fast food outlet.

It took a few seconds to place the briefcase out of sight under a blanket in the back seat and with that done, the accountant got out of the vehicle, took a quick look around, left the lot and began to walk briskly toward the funeral home.

* * * * *

David spotted Boyd's unmarked unit in the funeral home lot and pulled his own car into the parking spot beside it.

He exited the car and moved around to the passenger side to open the door for Robyn and helped her out, steadying her as she searched for her footing on the treacherous ice.

She was wearing heels and David shook his head in disbelief, but said nothing.

The wind was beginning to pick up as they moved across the lot toward the building.

The few inches of snow that had fallen overnight hadn't been of the wet variety. It was being easily moved about by the wind and banking against any obstacle in its path. The temperature had been dropping by the hour.

David did his best to shield Robyn from the worst of it with his bulk, but they were both covered by a light dusting of snow by the time they reached the door and entered the building.

He helped Robyn locate the funeral director and left her with him while he went back to speak with Boyd who had unobtrusively positioned himself in a small hallway next to the cloakroom just inside the main door.

The two of them entered the small room and after David had hung up his and Robyn's coats, he pulled the door closed.

Boyd, camera slung around his neck was the first to speak.

"I've checked the lot and the streets within a two block area, no sign of the LaBaron, but it's early yet. Once I've got the pictures and the service has started I'll go back out and do it again."

David nodded his agreement, and handed him one of the portable radios that he had picked up earlier from headquarters.

"Good. Use TAC channel one so we can keep in touch. I don't expect anything to happen while the service is on; too many witnesses, but I'll stay with Robyn anyway. If our boy turns up he'll probably try to get a positive ID on Robyn and then follow her after the service is over. He's going to want to be one of the first people to leave because he will have to get back to his vehicle and be prepared to follow Robyn when she leaves. You stay by the door and watch for anyone leaving early."

* * * * *

Weather such as it was, the accountant had been somewhat concerned about the probability of being the only person attending the service to arrive on foot. That concern dissolved rapidly upon entering the parking lot.

Several vehicles had just arrived and melting into the crowd of people headed for the main door had been a simple task.

Spotting a couple of familiar faces the accountant smiled and exchanged greetings as they made their way inside the building and out of the blowing snow.

* * * * *

Boyd waited until the service had begun, then slipped out the door and went back to his car.

He placed the camera in the back seat of the somewhat battered unmarked unit and then fired it up, switched on his heater and defroster and turned on the windshield wipers to remove the accumulated snow. While he was waiting for the engine to warm up he ran a test on the portable radio that David had given him. Walker, who was using an earpiece, responded immediately.

It took a few minutes for the high mileage Chevy's heating system to clear the mess away adequately enough for Boyd to safely shove it into reverse and begin his foray out through the lot and then onto the streets. He carefully searched for the LaBaron; his eyes straining to see though the now driving snow.

* * * * *

David had positioned himself to the rear of the small seating area of the chapel.

He had been surprised to note that approximately fifty people had turned up for the service. He had expected a smaller turnout but it appeared that Carol had had more friends than he'd supposed.

Just prior to the service commencing the majority of those in attendance had approached Robyn, assumedly to express their sympathy at her loss and he had Identified Bret Hunter, Melody Green and Ursula Kreski among them.

The service was supposed to be relatively short, running no more than a half hour.

At approximately twenty minutes into it the accountant reached into the left pocket of the heavy coat, used a thumb to flip off the cover on the small remote unit and then pushed the button that was thereby exposed.

The entire funeral home plunged into darkness

The sound of the explosion at the far end of the building didn't reach the room where the service itself was being conducted. A power failure during this kind of a weather system, while not expected, was certainly not particularly surprising. At least it wasn't to the others in attendance.

David, on the other hand, was immediately alarmed and leapt to his feet.

He tried to make out shapes and forms in the darkness of the large room as he struggled though the standing crowd and shoved his way unceremoniously toward where he had last seen Robyn.

* * * * *

Boyd had covered the area that he had considered a reasonable distance from the funeral home and had not spotted the car.

He was about to abandon the search and return to the parking lot when he saw the MacDonald's and decided to whip in and pick up a much needed coffee from the drive-through.

He couldn't believe his eyes at first. He slammed on his brakes the instant he recognized it.

It was a red LaBaron convertible. It had been there for awhile. There was a skiff of drifting snow covering it.

The plate was partially obstructed by snow; and he could make out only three of the numbers.

The portable on the seat beside him crackled and he recognized David's voice. There was no preamble.

"Boyd, Walker, get back here as fast as you can."

Boyd was torn. He wanted to get the full plate number and examine the car, but the tone of his boss's anxious call won out.

He reached for his blue light, opened his window and tossed it onto the roof of the unmarked unit, then hit the siren and tore out of the lot, ass-end slewing as the tires bit for purchase on the slippery snow-covered surface of the road.

As he rounded the first corner he reached down to grab the mike under the dash and keyed it. He gave the dispatcher a description of the car and it's location in Burnaby and asked for the closest Vancouver unit to attend and stay with the LaBaron until he gave further instructions.

* * * * *

There was only one person on foot to be seen in the entire block.

Struggling against the strong gusting wind, the well bundled figure paused to take note of the unmarked police unit with full emergency equipment operating as it slid dangerously around the corner and nearly mounted the sidewalk before racing away in the general direction of the funeral home.

Despite the miserable weather conditions and unsure footing, the accountant picked up the pace the instant the vehicle had swept by.

*****

David managed to locate Robyn in the confusion and haul her into a corner.

It was a good ten minutes before the funeral director managed to turn on the small battery powered emergency light system that provided enough illumination for David to guide her out to the main door and into the swirling snow.

In his rush to get out, Robyn had broken a heel and it took all his willpower to keep his mouth shut as he helped her limp across to his car and got her safely inside.

Boyd's unmarked unit, emergency equipment still operating, slid sideways into the parking lot behind them just as David slammed the passenger door of his own car.

CHAPTER THIRTY-SEVEN

David asked Boyd to stay with Robyn as he moved to a position where he could observe the group of people who had now left the building and were making their way back to their vehicles.

They were all well covered against the winter storm and it was impossible for him to clearly make out specific individuals in the blowing snow that was now swirling though the lot.

He gave it up as a lost cause and moved back to his car were Boyd was waiting with Robyn.

*****

The accountant didn't wait for the windshield to completely clear.

Within seconds the red LaBaron was out of the lot and moving carefully up the small hill that overlooked the parking lot of the funeral home.

The vehicle reached the top and pulled in to park.

The slight elevation was enough to make the activity below relatively clear despite the blowing snow and the accountant's attention focused on the unmarked police unit with the flashing blue light, and the other vehicle beside it.

*****

As David opened the driver's door of his car, Boyd was returning the mike to it's holder beneath the dash.

"I found a red LaBaron convertible in the MacDonald's lot a couple of blocks away. I was about to check it out when you called me back here. I arranged for one of our units to come over and sit on it when I left it, and the unit just got back to me.

The car wasn't there when they arrived. I've got a partial plate, and they are running it for me now."

David nodded and looked across at Robyn.

"I'm going to be busy following up on this car and I don't want to have to be worrying about you. I'm going to arrange to have a marked unit take you back out to the government wharf and get Jenny to meet you there. She can take you back to my place where you'll be safe until I get finished up here. I'm pretty sure that the LaBaron is going to lead us to our murderer, and I want this bastard locked up before the day is out."

Robyn opened her mouth to speak but David had already turned to Boyd.

"Get dispatch to send that unit that checked on the car over here. He must still be close by. I want Robyn safely out of harm's way while we do our follow up, and he can get her the hell out of here."

*****

The funeral home lot had emptied of vehicles with the exception of what appeared to be two unmarked police cars.

Now a marked police car had joined them and the uniformed driver was talking with the other two men.

Yes and there was a woman getting out of one of the unmarked cars to join them. It was Carol's sister. Imagine the stupidity of wearing a short dress like that in this weather; and she was getting into the marked police car.

This was going to be risky, but the accountant had no choice.

The LaBaron pulled out from its parking spot and moved slowly down the hill as the marked police cruiser made its way out of the lot and slowly moved off.

*****

David was back in his office.

He had his notebook out and was painstakingly going over the interview notes yet again.

Boyd had gone off to get the results from the partial plate number that he'd managed to get from the LaBaron.

The phone rang and David picked it. It was Carl Higgins.

"Ah Inspector Walker, now why would I expect to find you in your office on a Saturday, could it be the same reason that I find myself here as well?"

David chuckled.

"Afternoon Carl."

There was a crackling sound and the next words sounded tinny and hollow. David took from it that Carl had put him on speaker while he read from his notes.

"David I'm getting some interesting results from the hair that was snagged inside the wig, and I've got a partial print off the stethoscope. Not much to help you Identify your shooter I'm afraid, but it may be enough to confirm Identity once you make an arrest. I've still got a couple more tests to do, but I wanted to let you know that I'll be finished today and I'll call you when I'm done."

Boyd came in through his open office door. There was a piece of paper in his hand and he wore a dejected expression on his face.

David took note of it and was about to end the conversation with Carl and inquire as to what was wrong, when he realized that the phone in his hand had already gone dead.

He hung it up and looked up at Boyd.

"What is it?"

Boyd shook his head.

"I'm beginning to think that I should consider returning to uniform. The car is registered to Allan Joseph Olson. What are the odds that there would be more that one red LaBaron convertible running around the lower mainland?

David's brow furrowed.

"Within a few blocks of the funeral home, pretty bloody slim I would say. What address do you have for him?"

Boyd raised the sheet of paper and read it off.

"The car is a lease and it was leased here in Vancouver just over a year ago."

"Give the leasing company a call and find out what you can about this guy, and run his name through CPIC. Let's see what you come up with there."

Boyd nodded and left the office.

*****

The weather being as bad as it was, the traffic was light.

The accountant was having no difficulty in keeping the marked police car in sight.

They went directly east on Hastings Street and the accountant looked down at the gas gauge as they began the turn onto the bridge leading into North Vancouver.

God, just over a quarter of a tank!

Why were they leaving Vancouver, and where the hell where they going?

This would not be a good time to run out of gas, and the option of filling the tank was no option at all.

The words echoed in the interior of the LaBaron.

"Stupid…Stupid…Stupid"

*****

Jenny, bundled up against the blowing snow and gusting wind, and looking twice her normal girth, used a old axe handle that she kept in the cabin of her little boat for that very purpose, to smash the ice from the ropes tying her craft to the far side of David's floating wharf.

With some difficulty, she managed to toss the stiff lines aboard. She held her breath as she turned the key and pressed the starter.

The old engine had rarely let her down, but the conditions were certainly not the best; and she refused to exhale until it caught and began to rumble, if not happily, at least with a reasonable trace of determination.

Jenny exhaled and sucked in a fresh breath of air, thanked God, and moved slowly out into the channel.

*****

David was still going over the interviews, and getting pretty damn frustrated, when he heard Boyd came back into his office.

He tossed the notebook onto his desk and looked up at the detective who was standing in the doorway and was, thank Heavens, at least smiling.

"He's with Foreign Affairs, travels internationally a lot and has an Ottawa address at the moment. I've got the local Foreign Affairs Office here trying to track him down so I can speak to him by phone. CPIC has nothing on him. Foreign Affairs say that he is not out of the country at the moment and that they should have no difficulty in getting a phone number where he can be reached from the Ottawa office. They'll call back as soon as they have it."

*****

The marked cruiser had pulled onto some god-awful back road and although they were moving slowly now, it was taking all of the accountant's concentration to keep the unit in sight through the blowing snow while struggling to keep the car on the road.

To have a set of snow tires would have helped considerably, but who could have known that the simple task of following the stupid woman would end up on a bloody jungle trail.

The gas gauge wasn't helping.

The accountant couldn't stop checking it over and over and now looked away from the road briefly to check it yet again. It was still showing a quarter of a tank but it was bound to start to drop soon.

Looking away from and then back to the road, the account swore and slammed on the brakes.

Not a good thing in consideration of the icy roadway.

The accountant gripped the wheel, frantically willing the car to follow the sudden curve, but it was fruitless. The LaBaron drifted slowly but surely sideways until the passenger door came to a rest against a tree. The car was barely moving when it impacted.

The accountant was badly shaken by the whole incident, and spent several minutes regaining composure before taking the vehicle out of park and putting it back into drive.

Miraculously the summer tires caught and the convertible slowly moved back out onto the road and into the tire tracks of the police cruiser which by this time was long gone from view.

* * * * *

Following David's instructions to the letter the uniformed Constable had slowed to a stop at the point in the roadway that Robyn had indicated. They sat there with the engine idling for several minutes before they began to move again.

Moments later they were at the dock.

Under normal conditions the parking along the cliff side of the road that ended at the government dock was at a premium. It was especially bad under the present weather conditions.

Robyn could see the running lights of Jenny's little boat approaching. Confident that the craft was Jenny's, she suggested that the Constable not bother to park, but instead showed him where he could turn the cruiser around, thanked him and got out of the car.

The wind was gusting more heavily now and she clutched her coat tightly around herself and lowered her head as she started for the stairway that led down to the floating wharf.

*****

The accountant had not met a single vehicle since leaving the paved roadway and was shaken as headlights appeared from around the corner ahead. The LaBaron immediately slowed and pulled as far as possible over to the right side of the narrow road.

The cruiser slowed too as it swung wide to come around the LaBaron. The Constable was concentrating carefully on managing to keep his vehicle moving in the deep, drifting snow.

It never occurred to him to look at the vehicle he was passing and even if he had, he wouldn't have recognized it as a specific make or model. Not in the growing darkness and near whiteout.

But the accountant had been studying the marked cruiser very carefully and had noted that the vehicle contained only the driver.

The police car's tire prints were still clearly outlined on the roadway and the woman would be found at the end of those tire prints.

The accountant sat parked for several seconds, fighting a rapid heart rate and with eyes glued to the rearview mirror until the cruiser had disappeared from sight.

Only then did the LaBaron begin to pull out into the centre of the roadway again and start to move along the tracks that had been left in the snow by the police car.

Moments later the red convertible rounded a corner and stopped abruptly.

The accountant couldn't believe it. After all this, the road had come to a dead end at some god-forsaken government marina. There was a brightly lit boat pulling away and heading out into the channel. It passed directly under one of the large spotlights that festooned the dock and the accountant could clearly make out its bright yellow paintwork.

Frustration and disappointment intermingled for an instant and then turned to full blown anger as the LaBaron was jammed into park.

The accountant's forehead rested again the top of the steering wheel and the gloved hands pounded the sides of the instrument for several seconds.

Damn the luck!

The head eventually lifted and the flickering anger in the eyes began to fade as the accountant read the large sign that stood just to one side of the single phone booth at the end of the road.

It read 'WATER TAXI' and it gave a phone number

*****

Jenny had demanded that Robyn stay in the cabin while she tied the boat up to the far side of David's floating dock. That done, she returned to help her out.

They huddled closely together against the blowing snow as they made their way up to David's house and slipped quickly inside.

Cato greeted them with delighted pleasure and Jenny suggested to Robyn that she stand by the fire and warm herself up and then get changed into more practical clothing before they went up to her small cabin. While she was waiting she would give the big dog a chance to do his business outside.

*****

The accountant's ungloved hand, which had been feeding a quarter into the coin slot of the payphone, was damn near frozen.

But after a drawn out sob story about having arrived late for an important meeting and missing the person who was supposed to be waiting at the dock, and more importantly, offering to pay five times the normal fee, the water taxi operator had agreed to make a pick up at the dock.

Even better, he readily recognized the bright yellow boat that the accountant had described to him, and knew precisely where on the Arm the owner resided.

Things were looking up, at last!

After hanging up the phone and quickly pulling the glove back onto a cold hand, the accountant returned to the LaBaron and, with some difficulty, managed to get it parked somewhat off the main roadway, leaving the car amid the clutter of the other snow-covered vehicles that crowded the edge of the road and parked against the almost vertical rock face that bracketed the road on the side across from the water.

CHAPTER THIRTY-EIGHT

Jenny and Robyn, who was now dressed in jeans and a warm sweater and one of David's heavy coats, slowly made their way with Cato up to the cheerily lit little cabin at the top of the bluff.

The steps were treacherous. There were many frozen patches. The ever shifting and drifting snow was being driven by unpredictable and violent gusts of wind.

By the time they reached the gate that led to the deck that extended out over the rock face from the small frame structure they were shrouded in a thin film of snow. Jenny opened it and they quickly made their way across to the doorway of the cabin.

Robyn, who had lost her footing on a couple of occasions during the climb, but recovered before she went down, lost it on a bad patch of ice a few feet past the small gate.

Luckily Jenny was aware of the treacherousness of that particular spot and, anticipating the danger, was in a position to quickly reach out to steady the younger woman.

The welcoming blast of heat that flowed from within the cabin as Jenny opened the door and waved Robyn inside was a much appreciated treat for all three of them.

Cato waited patiently for his invitation to enter and shot through the door the instant it was received. Jenny quickly followed the dog inside and closed the door firmly behind her, talking more to herself than Robyn.

"I've got to spread some salt on that spot of ice before someone kills themselves. But first I'm going to stoke the fires; what a night!"

* * * * *

The only occupant on board the taxi was the man behind

the wheel of the small but sturdy little craft.

It was a lucky break. It meant that there would be only the one person to deal with later.

They exchanged money and pleasantries briefly, and then the boat began to move and the operator turned his concentration to the task at hand.

The accountant was paying special attention to the specific actions of the water-taxi operator as they pulled away from the dock.

He was a diminutive creature, probably in his early seventies.

But it wasn't the man himself that the accountant was interested in; it was exactly what was involved in operating the boat itself that was of paramount concern.

It seemed relatively simple, but the accountant would have to be the one behind the dimly lit gauges and throttle controls on the trip back and a good grasp of just what expertise was required to manage that was absolutely imperative.

*****

They were in David's office, waiting impatiently for the call and were on their second cup of stale coffee.

David was sitting at his desk close to the phone and Boyd was on his feet moving about the office restlessly as they talked.

"So what position will CLEU be in as far as their investigation goes now that the diary had been sanitized?"

David leaned forward to rest his elbows on his desk and kept one eye on the phone as he answered the detective.

"Well the job done on the diary was a good one, but it's a long document and an expert will be able to determine that it's been tampered with I'm sure. In any event, several people have seen the original in addition to me. Wright has read it for sure and so has Robyn. And we can all testify both to the fact that those at the top of the drug conspiracy were named in the original text and that the book that we now have is not the real thing. It will be enough to justify a continuation of the investigation. Whether or not the investigation will be successful in the end will depend upon how much effort is put into it, but I think we can be pretty certain their nice little set up won't last much longer. If they get out now and can cover their tracks they may escape prosecution, but their little empire is finished, and I've a feeling that those tapes that Carol made are going to surface and destroy their shiny reputations and their tidy little lives are going to crumble around them. That fact alone will be a sort of justice I…"

The phone rang

Boyd, who was now perched on the corner of David's desk, picked it up immediately.

David could only hear one side of the conversation. He was pleased to note that the detective was making notes on the pad beside the phone.

The call was short and sweet and when Boyd hung up he passed the pad to Walker.

"That's his number Boss. He's there now and awaiting your call."

David placed the call.

*****

The number of houses lit up on the shoreline diminished as the water-taxi moved eastward away from the bay containing the government wharf. It was running a parallel course with the shoreline.

In a few minutes the operator of the craft was pulling into David's floating dock and the old man at the wheel gestured upward at the small brightly lit cabin on the bluff above David's waterfront house.

"That's it, Jenny Ferguson's place."

He shoved the transmission into neutral and was about to say something else when the accountant put a slug into the back of his head.

The idling craft gently nudged the dock and the accountant, completely ignoring the twitching form lying on the floor of the cabin, moved quickly out of the cabin and onto the main deck and found a partially frozen line in the stern, grabbed the stiff coil, and stepped out onto the dock.

It took a few seconds with the stiffness of the rope and having to use gloves, but a single line tying the stern to the floating wharf was finally managed.

The bow drifted a short distance from the dock but there didn't seem to be a great deal of strain on the stern line that was in place and the accountant was satisfied that it would be enough to keep the craft in place until the job was done.

*****

After building up the fires in both the living room and small kitchen stove, Jenny began to bundle up into warm clothing again.

"I just want to put some salt on the worst patches of ice that have formed on the deck. Why don't you put on the kettle, dear, and we'll have a nice cup of tea to warm us up when I come back inside."

Cato, spotting her putting on outdoor attire and in anticipation of a run, eagerly got up from his usual position under the table and moved toward the door.

Jenny shook her head.

"No boy. You stay in where it's warm. I'll only be a minute."

The dog, obviously disappointed but obedient to the command, dropped into a sit by the door.

Now bundled up against the storm outside, Jenny reached for the bucket of rock salt that she kept near the door throughout the winter season, and picked it up.

*****

David held the phone closer to his ear as he carefully listened to what Olson was saying and then asked him to please repeat it.

Then he slammed the hand unit into its cradle and bolted upright out of his chair.

"Son of a Bitch! Of course, it all fits now!"

Boyd, who had been standing just to the side of the office door leaned forward slightly and raised his hands quizzically as David grabbed his overcoat off the coat rack and began to struggle into it while moving towards him across the office. He shoved the detective none to gently out of the doorway and pulled the door closed behind them.

"What?"

David was already halfway to the elevator.

"We'll take my car; I'll tell you on the way."

* * * * *

The accountant was being careful to approach the top of the stairway as quietly as possible. With the near deafening sound of the roaring wind it probably wasn't necessary, but the footing was unsure and it wouldn't do to alarm those inside the small frame building.

The gate hadn't been completely latched when it was last closed and it opened easily allowing access to the small deck area.

The account pulled the gun out and had taken only a single step toward the door when the outside flood light over the doorway blazed into life and the door suddenly opened.

The light from the interior of the kitchen now combined with that of the powerful porch lamp, suddenly pierced the darkness and the waves of blowing snow sweeping across the deck.

The accountant was momentarily blinded by it, and Jenny, who was only six feet away from the shadowy figure couldn't believe her eyes. She immediately saw the gun glinting in the bright light

"What on earth!"

Her instantaneous and unconscious reaction at the sight of the gun was to lift the bucket in her hands and throw it.

The accountant, still half blinded and caught completely off-guard, had only a split second to react, and did so by attempting to dodge to the side in an attempt avoid the incoming missile.

It was a successful move from the point of view of the bucket of salt, which simply grazed the accountant's right arm, but, unluckily for the accountant, it also led directly to the accomplishment of two other things.

In jumping sideways, the accountant had unfortunately landed on the large patch of ice that Jenny had specifically targeted for salting and as a result, went down on one knee; and the finger on the trigger of the gun had involuntarily clenched during the abrupt change of direction, causing the weapon to discharge.

Jenny was subconsciously aware of a moving blur out of the right side of her peripheral vision. She then felt an impact on that side of her body and she too went down into the snow.

The accountant, struggling to regain balance and raise the gun to fire again saw only a huge dark shadow and a flash of white teeth as the big Rottweiler, now completely airborne, went for the gun arm as trained. Cato snapped his powerful jaws shut just above the wrist, instantly delivering 2800 pounds per square inch of jaw pressure to the tip of each tooth in his mouth.

Robyn had raced to the doorway as soon she heard the sound of the shot and saw Cato spring through the opening from his sitting position by the door.

She reached the doorway in time to see the dog, who had still been airborne at impact, lock onto the arm and drop immediately to the deck to spread-eagle himself and dig in his claws to gain purchase and therein provide himself the with best possible position for traction. She heard the resulting sickening sound of crushing bone and the high pitched scream emitted from the accountant's mouth as the first searing stab of pain reached the brain.

The dog, who outweighed his adversary by a good 80 pounds, then threw his head and shoulders from left to right in rapid succession, shaking the accountant like a rag doll.

As the Rotti's powerful upper body swung to the left, the gun dropped from the accountant's limp and useless hand. When it swung back around to the right; the accountant was literally jolted upward into the air and completely off the surface of the deck.

Jenny, her legs tangled, was still lying on the deck but she had reached out and picked up the gun and then managed to get the command out.

"Out Cato!"

The dog responded instantly, opening his mouth and releasing his grip. The result of that action was that the accountant's unencumbered body, which at this point had been lifted completely off the surface of the deck, flew sideways toward the far railing.

Cato moved to follow but Jenny gave him another command.

"Down Cato…DOWN!"

The dog dropped immediately but his forward motion caused him to slide on the slippery surface and when he finally came to a halt he was barely inches from the edge.

The top railing shuddered momentarily as the accountant's flailing form impacted with it. Then it splintered and broke free to topple over the side and downward over the edge of the bluff.

The accountant's shrieking body seemed to poise in mid air briefly, the arms frantically flailing for something to grab on to, and then Robyn, her face frozen in terror, watched it drop over the edge.

She bent down to help Jenny, and was spared the horror of witnessing the accountant's pain-wracked body follow the remnants of the shattered railing on the long spiral plunge downward, through the darkness and swirling snow, to impact against the rugged, craggy expanse of the rocks two hundred feet below.

* * * * *

David, Jenny and Robyn were in the house huddled on the couch near the fire warming up and Cato was lying on the carpet directly in front of Robyn.

She had not allowed the dog to move more than a few inches from her since the traumatic incident that had taken place up on Jenny's deck, and Cato seemed to understand and accept that she needed him to be with her.

Boyd was still outside under the floodlights on David's dock speaking with the four members of the R.C.M.P who had arrived a half hour earlier in a forty foot marked patrol motor launch. They would be responsible for handling the accountant's death as it had occurred within the limits of the District of North Vancouver and was therefore within their jurisdiction.

David got up and moved over to the window as the group of men below, flashlights in hand and carrying a body bag, moved down along the beach and then out of sight around the corner toward the back of his house.

He thought to himself that what was left out there on the rocks behind his house wouldn't be easy to put into that bag.

The snow was still falling steadily, but it wasn't drifting as much by this point, the gusting wind having died down considerably. Conditions had definitely improved but moving safely about on the rocks near the shoreline was no simple task and David was glad to be able to watch the activity from the warm comfort of his living room.

He turned back to face Jenny and Robyn, and picked up where he had left off.

"So as soon as Olson told me that his wife had reverted

back to her maiden name, Melody Green, once the divorce had become final and that as part of the settlement got the use of the LaBaron until the lease ran out, all the pieces of the puzzle immediately fit together and I knew instantly who our murderer was."

It was much later that night by the time they felt like eating, but simultaneously the three of them realized that they were famished and after a brief discussion they decided on salads and T-bone steaks.

Everyone had one steak - except Cato.

He got three, and they were personally deboned and served to the big Rottweiler by Robyn before anyone else was allowed to eat.

It seemed fitting to all concerned.

There were no complaints heard from either Jenny or David.

Other books by Patrick Laughy

Alumni

The 4th Reich: Book 1 Parts 1 and 2

Coming soon

More titles in The 4th Reich Series

Atlantis: A Fantasy Series

29021960R00185

Made in the USA
Charleston, SC
29 April 2014